T0197006

THE ARCHIVIST

THE ARCHIVIST

A THRILLER

ALAN REFKIN

THE ARCHIVIST
A THRILLER

This is a work of fiction. All the characters, names, incidents, organizations, and dialogue in this novel are either the products of the author's imagination or are used fictitiously.

iUniverse books may be ordered through booksellers or by contacting:

iUniverse
1663 Liberty Drive
Bloomington, IN 47403
www.iuniverse.com
1-800-Authors (1-800-288-4677)

ISBN: 978-1-5320-4714-5 (sc)
ISBN: 978-1-5320-4716-9 (hc)
ISBN: 978-1-5320-4715-2 (e)

Library of Congress Control Number: 2018904525

Print information available on the last page.

iUniverse rev. date: 05/22/2018

Previous Books by Alan Refkin

The Wild Wild East: Lessons for Success in Business in Contemporary Capitalist China
Alan Refkin and Daniel Borgia, PhD

Doing the China Tango: How to Dance around Common Pitfalls in Chinese Business Relationships
Alan Refkin and Scott Cray

Conducting Business in the Land of the Dragon: What Every Businessperson Needs to Know about China
Alan Refkin and Scott Cray

Piercing the Great Wall of Corporate China: How to Perform Forensic Due Diligence on Chinese Companies
Alan Refkin and David Dodge

To my wife, Kerry, whose warmth and depth
of kindness always envelop me.
To Ted and Iona Schumacher.

CHAPTER

1

THE FOOTSTEPS WERE GETTING CLOSER. They weren't the fast-paced tempo of someone running. Instead the pursuer had a methodical pace, which echoed down the moist cobblestone streets. Yesterday she wouldn't have given these footsteps a second thought. Yesterday her life had been different. She stopped and listened. A moment later, there was only silence. Then it dawned on her. If she could hear him, then the reverse was also true. She silently cursed herself for not realizing it sooner. How else would he have been able to follow her through the maze of narrow streets she'd been traversing? She slipped off her shoes and put them in her backpack. When the footsteps started again, they were no longer behind her. Instead they headed off in another direction and soon faded into the distance. Even so, she realized she was far from safe. Daybreak was five hours away, and no one was likely to come into this area until then. Of equal concern was the fact that she was lost. The erratic path she'd taken in trying to evade her pursuer had brought her into the city's business district. But exactly where she was within that area she had no idea. She thought about breaking into one of the surrounding shops and hiding until daylight. But every store had steel shutters that protected both the doorway and display windows, leaving her no option but to remain in the open.

She continued running, hoping to eventually recognize a landmark that would allow her to pinpoint her location. When that happened, she'd know how to get to her destination, where she'd leave the package she had in her backpack. Ten minutes after taking off her shoes, she again stopped and listened for her pursuer. Absolute silence permeated the area. She decided to crank up the pace, and even though she didn't know exactly what was ahead of her, she wanted to get as far away from her pursuer as possible. But on her second stride, something sharp sliced deep into the sole of her left foot. She stumbled and fell on her right side, the backpack cushioning most of the fall. Her foot felt as if it were on fire. She wanted to cry out in pain, but instead she bit her lip, knowing that any sound might give away her position. Looking behind her in the dimly lit street, she saw a long piece of jagged metal jutting from between two cobblestones. Her foot was sliced from end to end, and blood was seeping out of the gash with abandon. Trying to stem the flow, she removed the shoes from her backpack and put them back on. Hopefully the tight fit would compress the slice enough to slow the bleeding. She'd try to compensate for the sound of her shoes on the cobblestones by walking slower. Hopefully her pursuer wasn't close enough to hear it. But the first time she put weight on her foot, she collapsed in excruciating pain. She clenched her teeth to keep from screaming as tears of pain streamed from her eyes. Using the shoe to compress the wound was a bad idea. If she had any chance of continuing, she'd have to go barefoot.

She was angry for not taking her cell phone, which she'd left charging in the bedroom. But everything had happened so quickly. There wasn't time to grab it then. She barely had an opportunity to write down the recipient's address, stuff everything into her backpack, and escape into the alleyway behind her residence. If she hadn't been working on her computer at one in the morning, she was sure she'd be dead. Her pursuer would apparently do anything to get the package she was carrying. She understood why, as its contents were critically important to at least a few countries and possibly more. But she wasn't even certain what she was carrying wasn't just an elaborate hoax. That was why earlier that day she had tried to send it by special courier to someone she knew could verify its authenticity.

The problem was that the transportation company she regularly used was on strike. It seemed there was always a labor disruption of some kind going on in Italy. In a strange way, the workers' demand for higher wages had saved her life. If the courier had taken it, she wouldn't have been up late getting the recipient's address off her computer. Nor would she then have heard the approaching footsteps or seen—against the courtyard wall of her residence—the shadow of a man carrying a gun.

As she continued walking, every step was agony. Her pace was now so slow that she'd all but given up hope of finding a landmark and escaping her pursuer, resigning herself to the fact that he'd eventually find her if by no other means than from the blood trail she was leaving. She was looking for a place to sit down and let fate take its course when she recognized the name of the business directly across the street from where she was standing. She'd been there a couple of times but only during the daytime. It looked different under the dim streetlight. Nevertheless, she had her landmark, and it was less than a block from where she needed to deliver the package. Adrenaline and hope coursed through her body. She decided to drag her injured foot across the moist cobblestones and limit the weight she was putting on it. She wasn't going anywhere fast, but there was no question in her mind that she'd at least get to her destination.

The piazza was deserted when she entered. She decided to put on her shoes to try to keep the blood trail from leading her pursuer to the package. She knew the pain would almost incapacitate her, but she felt there was little choice.

Stepping with one foot and dragging the other, she eventually reached the destination. As she turned and looked behind her, she was pleased to see that there was no trail of blood exposing the path she'd taken. She immediately felt as if a burden had been lifted from her. The package was safe. Now it was time for her to escape. She began dragging herself back through the piazza, hoping to get to one of the side streets and then a nearby residential area where she could summon help. She'd gotten nearly two-thirds of the way there when

ALAN REFKIN

she thought she heard something to her left and turned slightly. That was when something slammed into her back with such force that the air rushed from her lungs and she was hurled to the ground. She couldn't breathe. It felt as if someone were sitting on her chest. With some effort, she turned over on her back. Looking up, she saw a tall, well-dressed Asian man standing over her. He held his shoes in his left hand and a gun with a suppressor in his right.

The stranger squatted next to her. "Where are they?" he asked in a voice that was not much above a whisper.

She had no breath. Gasping for air, she saw that her white knit top had a red spot and that it was growing.

"Where are they?" he repeated in almost perfect English.

She was starting to get cold, and her eyesight was becoming unfocused. She didn't want to die, but she knew that was the only possible outcome.

"Where you'll never find them," she said, her voice barely audible.

"Pity," the man replied just before her head snapped back and her empty gaze fixed on the stranger.

CHAPTER

2

THE TALL DARK-HAIRED ASIAN WOMAN watched the man look nervously about as he unsteadily crossed the street. He was middle-aged, and he wore a cream-colored three-piece suit, white shirt, and solid brown tie. He carried a black ballistic nylon travel bag over his shoulder, which she guessed contained his personal items. The man kept his head down and held his left hand to the side of his face as he walked, probably hoping to avoid being noticed or giving away his facial features. If she had a sense of humor, she would have laughed. Being Asian, carrying what amounted to a suitcase, and wearing a suit in the Caribbean was anything but inconspicuous.

Dusk was gradually turning into night, and the man had difficulty navigating the uneven and cracked sidewalk, stumbling and falling several times as he tried to stay on the three-foot-wide path. She wasn't surprised. Through the window of the restaurant he'd just left, she'd watched him consume three martinis and a bottle of wine in the space of a little more than three hours. She thought he was probably celebrating his committing the perfect crime. He'd soon learn it wasn't all that perfect.

She'd been told by the old man that most of the people who hid their money on this island came only once. That was because the government required anyone establishing a bank account to sign the required documentation in person. After that, all transactions could be done over the internet. In coming here, most ignored the island's only airline, preferring to use their own aircraft instead. There was a number of those parked at the airport, one of which was hers. The man she was following had arrived on the airline. Therefore, she knew there was no way he could leave until the following day. The island's only airport was closed at night because the surrounding mountains and short runway made nighttime flights too dangerous.

The woman understood why the man chose this island. If she'd embezzled half a billion dollars, she'd also choose a country where no amount of coercion by a foreign government could force it to reveal the names of its depositors. The high fees their banks charged guaranteed their clients' anonymity.

She'd hunted many men like the one staggering before her, each believing he was too smart to be caught. They all thought they could hide forever and live well off the money they'd stolen. The man she was watching undoubtedly believed his crime would go undetected for another week until he failed to return to Beijing from his supposed vacation. But the truth was the old man suspected what he'd done as soon as he left for the Caribbean, and he was never wrong. The person she was looking at was only one of many embezzlers that he'd sent her to kill.

The man eventually made his way into the hotel at the end of the street, a one-story white clapboard structure whose paint had long ago cracked like alligator scales under the hot tropical sun. It was built in the 1960s, but the constant humidity, storms, and ravages of the sun made its exterior appear to be a half century older. The hotel's twenty guest rooms were lined up in a single row at the edge of the beach, affording each guest an unobstructed view of the ocean. Each room had a small wood-decked patio, and in the center of each one there was a white plastic table and four matching chairs. Three wooden steps provided access to the strip of sand separating the hotel from the ocean.

When the dark-haired woman entered the lobby, her prey was walking away from the check-in desk and toward the guest rooms. Following at a cautious distance, she saw him enter the sixth room down the hall, after which she turned, hurried out of the hotel, and ran to the beach. When she stopped in front of the man's patio, she saw that his drapes were open and the lights were on. She didn't see him inside the one-room accommodation, which meant that he was probably in the bathroom. Going onto the raised wooden deck, she looked at the aged sliding glass door. Grabbing the back end, she gently jiggled it up and down while at the same time pulling it toward her. Soon the hooked bolt worked itself free. Sliding it open, she entered.

The room was approximately five hundred square feet, decorated in 1960s retro modern, with white ceramic floor tile laid in a diagonal pattern throughout. The king-size bed was centered on the wall to the right as one entered the room. On the opposite wall, a black leather-faced bar extended from end to end with six bottles of unopened liquor resting on top. In front of it were two white vinyl and chrome backless swivel barstools. A white Petrie sofa occupied the center of the room and offered a view of the ocean. In front of it was a driftwood coffee table with a smoked-gray glass top. The bathroom was beside the sliding glass door. The man was wiping his mouth with a washcloth when he walked into the bedroom. In one quick motion, the dark-haired woman encircled his neck with her left arm and placed crushing pressure on his trachea while at the same time pressing on the back of his neck with her right hand. The man blacked out before he understood what was happening.

She lowered the embezzler to the floor, turned him over on his back, and took off his clothes, leaving on only his tighty-whities. She then bound and gagged him with bathroom towels, being careful not to make the bindings so tight that they would leave marks on his skin. Once the man was secure, she searched his pants and jacket pockets until she found the small piece of paper that experience told her would most likely be there. If it wasn't, the gloves would come off and she'd have to torture him until she got what she needed. Fortunately that wasn't necessary, and she placed the paper on the coffee table behind her. Removing a cell phone from her pocket, it took less than five minutes to repatriate the stolen money. The woman walked to the bar, grabbed a bottle of vodka, and opened it on her way back to the unconscious man. Kneeling beside him, she gently slapped the side of his face.

The woman watched as the man's eyes opened and went wide as he saw her looking down at him. She studied his face, and from those she'd caught in the past, she knew what would come next—an attempt to communicate and convince her that it wasn't him. And when he found out he was bound and gagged, he'd make a brief attempt to break free, and when he realized the futility of his situation, he'd express self-serving remorse. Looking into his eyes, she again saw this sequence unfold. Now that he'd been caught, he wanted forgiveness and a reset so that he could return to his life the way it was. No harm, no foul. That wasn't going to happen. It was time. The dark-haired woman straddled his body and sat on his chest, pinning his head between both her knees. With his hands tied behind his back, there was little he could do to resist. The woman reached down and squeezed his nose between her thumb and forefinger until he was just about to pass out from a lack of oxygen. Releasing her grip, she removed his gag and allowed him to take in a mouthful of air before squeezing his nose and pouring vodka down his throat as he gasped for air. Before he choked, she allowed him to breathe and become oxygenated, and then she repeated the process. This continued until the man had consumed enough vodka to put his blood-alcohol level off the chart, after which she wiped her prints off the bottle. Then she pressed his hand firmly on it before letting it roll onto the floor. The embezzler was still breathing but not moving when she got up and opened the patio door. She wiped her prints off whatever she'd touched and then hoisted the unconscious man onto her shoulders in a fireman's carry. The man was heavy but not unbearably so. She walked across the patio and down to the water until she was knee-deep. Then she slid the man off her shoulders and held his head several inches below the surface.

When the man's body hit the water, he awakened, struggling with whatever remaining strength and consciousness he had to try to get to the surface. But with his legs and feet still bound, it was futile. He eventually stopped moving, but the woman continued to hold him under water for another minute before removing the towels that bound him. The incoming tide would eventually carry him back onto the beach and erase her footprints. He'd become another drunken businessman who had drowned while going for a swim. The old man would be satisfied with her performance.

CHAPTER

3

LI FANG—OR ANNIE, AS SHE was called by her friends—was locking up her office at the National Library of China in Beijing. As usual, she was late. For the past half hour her boss had again tried to convince her to spend the weekend with him in Shanghai, telling her that they were soul mates and belonged together. The fact that he was married didn't seem to enter the equation, at least not on his side. He finally left, but he promised to continue his efforts of winning her over. She couldn't wait.

As she passed through the lobby, she noticed two young men in casual dress and an older man wearing a dark business suit and standing near the three glass exit doors. The older person looked to be in his early sixties, with jet-black hair cut so near the scalp that it looked like stubble. Getting closer, she noticed that his neck was so wide that his head gave the appearance of connecting directly to his thick torso. At six feet and with a ramrod straight posture, he exuded an air of authority. In his hand was a photo, and he quickly put it inside his jacket pocket as she approached the exit.

"Li Fang?" he asked.

"Yes."

"We're with the government. Come with us," he said brusquely, briefly showing her his credentials and offering no other explanation.

This sent a sharp chill down her spine. She knew the government could do virtually anything they wanted. China was not America.

They could put her in jail for up to two years and then let her go without so much as an apology.

"Why? What have I done?" she asked, the tone in her voice betraying that she was confused and scared.

The man in the suit ignored her question and took the backpack off her shoulder, while the two men with him each grabbed an arm and escorted her into the waiting black Audi that was parked outside. Once the car pulled into traffic, the man in the suit, who was in the front passenger seat, looked inside the backpack. Examining its contents, he extracted the Lenovo laptop and turned it on.

"Your password?"

Annie didn't say a word. She was more scared than she'd ever been in her life. She'd never been picked up by the government; however, she'd heard stories of those who had, and they all ended badly. She decided to say nothing. The man on her right slapped her hard across the face after a nod from the person in front. She quickly blurted out the password as the man next to her was preparing to hit her again.

The older man logged into her computer and found what he was looking for in a desktop file. "So it's true," he remarked, more to himself than to the others.

"Miss Li, I only have a few questions," he said as he turned his head toward the rear of the car. "If you answer me honestly, we'll take you to our office so you can make a written statement. Then we'll drive you home. If you don't—and believe me, I'll know if you're telling the truth—you'll go to jail, and we'll ask you the same questions there. Only we won't be as nice."

"I'll answer any question you ask."

"Then let's begin. I know that you received an email from a friend of yours living in Venice, Italy. Her name was Gina Moretti."

Was?

"You translated some documents for her."

Annie wanted to scream. When she saw the credentials of the man in the suit, she thought this might have something to do with what she'd seen. Now he all but confirmed it. How could she be so stupid? It was well known throughout China that the government, especially the People's Liberation Army, monitored all domestic and international internet traffic. This was done by Byzantine Candor, a name that no Chinese citizen mentioned openly yet was infamous throughout the country for having the best computer hackers in the world. If an email was sent into China, they were reading it.

"Do you have any copies, electronic or paper, of what you received from Gina Moretti and the translation you sent to her? An electronic backup perhaps?"

"There are no copies or backups," she responded, her voice quivering with fear. "I translated everything on my laptop and then emailed it."

"Second, has anyone else seen what was sent to you? Anyone besides Ms. Moretti, that is?"

"No."

"Let me off here," the man in the suit said to the driver, pointing to an area just ahead.

When the car came to a stop, the person seated to Annie's right got out of the Audi and opened the passenger door for the older man.

"Verify what she's told us is true. I need to be sure," Annie heard the man in the suit say. The younger man bowed in acknowledgment, closed the front passenger door, and got back into the car. A moment later they reentered Beijing traffic.

The man in the suit caught a passing taxi and took it to the Ministry of National Defense compound. No ID was necessary as he bypassed perimeter checkpoints. His face guaranteed access, and he continued into the August 1st Building. No one approached or stopped him as he walked briskly through the lobby, past the metal detectors and the guards standing at attention. Only eleven people could circumvent the building's tight security, and he was one of those. On the far side of the lobby, a private elevator that had no visible access panel opened automatically when it detected the RFID security card in his jacket pocket. Moments later he got off on the top floor. He said nothing to the military guard who came to attention when he exited, and he continued toward a large reddish-tan oak door at the opposite end of the floor. Imprinted in gold letters on it was *General Lin Bogang, Chief of the General Staff of the People's Liberation Army.* When he entered, everyone who was working at their desks stood at rigid attention until he went into his office and shut the door behind him. They wondered why he wasn't wearing his uniform and why he was carrying a civilian backpack in his left hand. But they knew that question would forever go unanswered.

General Lin set the backpack on his desk, removed the laptop, and pushed the power button. As the computer was booting up, he eased himself into the deeply padded black leather chair, unlocked the top drawer of his desk, and removed a small stack of papers. When the log-on appeared, he leaned forward, typed in the password, and opened the desktop file he'd looked at in the car. Scrolling through the scanned pages on the screen, he carefully compared them to a copy of the documents that he'd received several days ago from Major Cai Fu, an attaché and intelligence officer assigned to the consulate at Florence, Italy. His attached report detailed a call he'd received from a local who was requesting a translation. He knew this wasn't unusual, as the Chinese government long ago instituted a policy of providing this service at a very low rate because of the gold mine of information it often produced. Therefore, the procedure was that anything to be translated was first given to one of the intelligence officers assigned to the consulate, who would then read it over for proprietary or useful information.

The report from Cai Fu explained that the person who scanned and sent him the pages to be translated also stated that one of his staff had emailed them to a friend of theirs in China. He went on to say that the reason he needed the consulate's translation was that he didn't believe that a version produced by someone's friend would be academically recognized. Therefore, he decided to use the Chinese consulate to get a more defensible translation that would withstand scrutiny by the academic world. Fortunately, the major asked and was given the name of that staff member, but the person he was speaking with didn't know the identity of the translator in China.

Cai Fu initially believed that what he received was a hoax because it severely contradicted Communist Party teachings. He put in his report that he was leery of even providing a translation because of the falsehoods these documents contained. That decision, he wrote, needed to be made by the highest possible authority, which is why he sent it to the ranking military officer in China and ignored his chain of command. He also put in his report that in the unlikely event they were accurate, the secrets could be better contained with only one person in authority knowing of their existence. General Lin knew Cai Fu's actions were wholly self-serving because whatever happened, his discretion and deference would be appreciated and rewarded.

When he received Cai Fu's email and read the attached documents, he knew they were authentic. In fact, because of a past encounter, he'd been quietly searching for these same papers for many years. However, even with the resources at his disposal, he couldn't find even a single clue about where they might be hidden. Until now.

He considered himself adept at politics. One had to be in order to rise to the highest military position in a country ruled by a body as bureaucratic as the Chinese Communist Party. Therefore, he understood that the party's influence was largely based on the people's acceptance of communist ideals that were long ago established and handed down by their beloved founder, Mao Zedong. He also knew that these documents would destroy the people's belief in the party. This gave whoever possessed them control over the country's leadership. But to make that happen, he needed the originals. Anything digital, such as the scanned copies in his possession, could be forged. He subsequently ordered Cai Fu to find the documents and bring them to him, using any means he felt appropriate. Once they were in his hands, everyone who'd seen them needed to be eliminated—if the plan he was formulating was to be successful.

He reached across his desk to the small stack of papers he'd set next to the computer, selected the top document, and began to read.

It is December 1935, and I feel safe and at home in Shaanxi. My comrades and I control this area and take pleasure in the fact that our enemy is some distance away. I have just been through one of the darkest moments of my life. I started this journey with eighty-seven thousand of my comrades, and after more than a year of unimaginable hardship, I finished with less than ten thousand.

When we arrived in Shaanxi, we were starving and exhausted, and our clothes were in tatters. We resembled a group of peasants and vagrants rather than an army. But I was still exhilarated. After surviving a journey of nine thousand kilometers, I know that nothing can defeat us.

I received word from my friends in Moscow that Comrade Stalin has proclaimed me the leader of my country. In doing this, I'm sure he has his own agenda, but that's of less concern than the survival of my army. Without Comrade Stalin's assistance, we will all perish. He told me that my adversary, Chiang Kai-shek, has asked him for a secret treaty, seeking to unite both their forces against our mutual enemy, Japan. While I am not opposed to my country signing such an agreement with the Soviet Union and have myself many times entreated Comrade Stalin to help me keep Japan from gaining control of my provinces in the north, I have in the same breath told him that I alone can speak for the Chinese people. He agrees and said he told Chiang that he must make his peace with me and that both our armies need to be united if we are to effectively engage our mutual enemy in concert. I know Comrade Stalin does this because he doesn't believe the Japanese can successfully attack the combined land masses of both the Soviet Union and China. Having our combined armies engage the Japanese, within our borders, is therefore critical to his wartime strategy of keeping them out of his country.

Comrade Stalin has a great deal of influence over Chiang because he's held his son, Chiang Ching-kuo, captive for the past ten years. During this time, he's adopted the ways of the Soviets, married a native Belarusian, and had a child. Chiang has never seen his grandchild—an agony that must haunt him.

I firmly believe Comrade Stalin is naïve with respect to Chiang. He will never understand that Chiang is more interested in killing communists than he is in killing Japanese. His hate for Chinese communists consumes him and blinds him to all else.

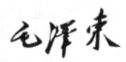

CHAPTER

4

THE MARCIANA LIBRARY IS ONE of the architectural gems of Venice, Italy. Located at the end of Saint Mark's Square in front of the Doge's Palace, the two-story building has Doric columns on the ground floor with Ionic ones above. Adding to its visual elegance, the entire structure is crowned by a balustrade containing corner obelisks and twenty-five statues of classical deities and heroes. Entering the Marciana, an ornate two-flight staircase leads to the vestibule, above which is Titian's La Sapienza. From here one enters either the library room, which contains many great works of art, or the administrative wing.

The library's curator, Pietro Luca, had just returned from identifying the body of Gina Moretti. Her death had been a tragic blow. Although he was nearly a decade and a half older, he was in love with her. This didn't manifest itself instantaneously. At first, there was an infatuation with this new intern from the United States, who came from a bilingual family and spoke passable Italian. She'd applied for an opening at the Marciana soon after she received her master's degree, which was unusual since most employees had a bachelor's degree at best. Therefore, he expected her to last only a year. Two at the most. Most Americans fall in love with Venice upon seeing it, but very few choose to work and live there for an extended period, especially since the city is one of the most expensive in Europe. It gradually became apparent to him that her love for Venice and the Marciana would never wane. One year became two, and two became three and eventually nine. He liked her American attitudes. It was refreshing to experience an uncensored enthusiasm and love of life. He knew most single Italian women her age wanted to find a husband, settle down, have children, and not work. She was different. She loved her job, didn't want a serious relationship, and traveled around Europe whenever she had holiday or vacation time. Perhaps it was an older man's fantasy, but he wanted to be more than just a friend. He wanted to be her companion. They were both single, and in Italy, romance was a part of life.

When she failed to come to work for two days, he immediately began to worry. He suspected something was wrong. That wasn't the case with any of his other employees. They were Italian, and punctuality was a variable in their lives. But even after working at the library for nearly a decade, she still retained the American traits of punctuality and reliability. If she was sick or going to be late for work, she'd always call or ask someone to pass a message along to him. The fact that she hadn't now worried him.

The following day he phoned her apartment. There was no answer. He then called her friends, at least the ones he knew, but they hadn't heard from her either. He even walked to her apartment and knocked on the door. There was no response. Perhaps she was too sick to answer the phone or the door. He didn't have a key, but with the help of a small bribe, he was able to get the landlady to open her apartment for him. He was surprised to find that her bed had not been slept in and that her cell phone and purse were in the bedroom. He became alarmed. He phoned the local police and asked if he could file a missing person report. The officer on duty asked several questions and then told him to come to the station and fill out the required paperwork.

When Luca entered the police station, he was escorted to a small conference room just off the lobby. A few minutes later, Chief Inspector Mauro Bruno entered, introduced himself, and took a seat next to him. Bruno was in his late forties. He was of medium height, and he had the weary look of someone who had seen too much of the dark side of life. He had salt-and-pepper hair combed straight back, a neatly trimmed black moustache with flecks of gray, and piercing brown eyes. His dark blue suit was neatly pressed, although Luca could see that it was worn and shiny from age. Bruno carried a cup of espresso in each hand and placed one in front of Luca as he sat.

Bruno asked the curator if he had a picture of the woman he believed was missing. Luca reached into his inside jacket pocket, removed an employee photo, and handed it to Bruno. The chief inspector intently focused on it for some time, after which he slowly placed it on the conference room table.

"I believe this is the woman who was murdered two days ago in the Campo Santo Stefano," he said in a gentle voice that expressed compassion for the person seated beside him. "Since we found no identification on the body, we were in the process of running her fingerprints through various databases to try to determine her name."

"Murdered? Are you certain that this is your victim?" Luca asked, seeming to dispute what he'd been told. Picking up the photo of Gina Moretti, he handed it to Bruno so the chief inspector could have another look. "Because my Gina wasn't into drugs or anything else that could get her killed."

"Now that we have her name, I can get her fingerprints from Rome before the end of the day to determine if she's the victim," he said, putting his hand on Luca's shoulder. "But I'm sure you'd like to know before then. If you want to accompany me to the morgue, you can visually confirm whether we have the body of Gina Moretti."

Luca felt light-headed at the thought of seeing the woman he loved lifeless on a cold steel table. But not knowing would be an even greater torment. "I'll go," he said, his voice choked with emotion. As he stood to leave, he turned to Bruno. "Why wasn't this in the newspaper or on the radio? If the killer is still out there, other lives could be at risk."

"The mayor wanted to keep this quiet. It's the height of tourist season, and he didn't want to start a panic where they might decide to leave early or bypass our city entirely because they felt unsafe.

Instead he ordered us to intensify our investigation and increase our night patrols," Bruno said with a sigh.

Luca knew the mayor was afraid about bad publicity and would go to almost any lengths to keep bad news out of the press. "Do you have any clues?" he asked as they left the room.

"None."

The following day Luca went to the library earlier than usual. He'd been awoken out of a sound sleep by a call from Cai Fu, whose boss apparently wanted to buy the papers he'd sent for translation. Luca wasn't in the mood. The Marciana didn't sell items from its collection. He was about to hang up when he heard the sum that the man was willing to pay. It was beyond imagination. This would allow him to retire in comfort for the rest of his life. He'd no longer be a civil servant but a man of means. He'd never been tempted to break the law, at least not to this extent. But an opportunity like this only came along once in a lifetime. With Gina dead and advancing in age, he decided to take it.

It was eight in the morning, and most employees were enjoying the calm before the doors opened to the public at ten. Cups of latte, cappuccino, and espresso along with plates of biscotti littered the information desk in the vestibule. When Luca entered a full two hours before his normal arrival time, everyone looked at him in stunned silence. Only the sound of his Gucci loafers on the marble floor could be heard as he walked past them and into the administrative section. No one knew why the curator had decided to come to work this early. But immediately after he passed, everyone gathered their cups and food items and returned to their work areas.

Luca hadn't noticed anyone at the information desk. His thoughts were solely on getting what he needed for his meeting with Cai Fu, which was an hour away. He entered his office, took a seat behind his desk, and logged into the computer. When the main menu appeared, he scrolled to the line for archival records, clicked on it, and selected the sign-out/return option. Luca knew there were only two possible locations for the documents Cai Fu sought. They were either in Gina Moretti's office or in archival storage. Since it was against policy to remove anything from the premises without his written permission and he hadn't signed such an authorization, he surmised that they had to be in one of those two places. He'd last seen the documents on her desk, when he visited her office the day before she'd gone missing. Therefore, he believed they could still be there. The other possibility was that before she left, she returned them to archival storage. Either way, he needed to make sure the computer records reflected that they'd been returned. That was integral to his plan. Items were always being misplaced in a building that housed more than a million printed books and documents, and it was sometimes a lengthy process locating them. After he accessed the sign-out/return option, he scrolled down until he found Gina Moretti's name. The log showed that two days ago she'd removed nineteen documents from archival storage bin Y-217 and had not yet returned them. Therefore, they must still be in her office.

It took only a few clicks to alter the records. Then he grabbed his briefcase and left the office, walking down the administrative corridor to the last room on the left. Using his master key, he opened Gina Moretti's door. When he did, he was met by the lingering smell of her perfume, which floated lazily in the stillness of the small office. A deep sense of sadness and loss overcame him. He wished more than anything in the world that she was still alive so they could be together and enjoy the enormous wealth he was about to receive. But that dream had come to an end.

He walked to her desk, and when he saw nothing on top, he opened each of its three drawers, expecting to find what he was looking for in one of them. Instead he found only office supplies. He checked the bookshelf to the left of the desk but saw that it contained only historical reference books. In frustration Luca roughly pulled the desk and bookshelf away from the wall, hoping to miraculously find what he was looking for behind them. When that miracle didn't happen, he slammed both back into position and hurried out of the office.

He was in a panic. The clock was ticking. His money was waiting, and he didn't have what he'd promised to deliver. He rushed across the library to the anteroom, where he went behind the information counter and opened the door leading to the archives. He ran past twenty-four aisles of document storage cabinets, sweating profusely from both exertion and fear until he came to the aisle he was looking for. Halfway down it, he found bin Y-217. When he opened it, his legs became limp, and he had to sit down on the floor before he collapsed. The documents were missing.

General Lin rubbed his eyes. He was scheduled to retire next year as soon as the president of China was reelected for a second five-year term and filled his position with one of his cronies. He'd already been told that his resignation was expected at that time.

He thought about the last document, the nineteenth, and its ramifications. It literally rewrote history. If published, it could destroy the party's iron grip on the country and subsequently bring down the government. And that was exactly what he wanted.

> It is the summer of 1936. Comrade Stalin has shown his displeasure with my suggestion to form a separate state in the northwest, and in response, he has publicly acknowledged the accomplishments of my foe, Chiang Kai-shek. He is telling me not to treat him as an adversary but as a friend fighting a common enemy. This infuriates me. Chiang will never be my friend. He hates communists more than those who invade our homeland, and he kills both with equal vigor. I find myself engaged in two wars—one against the Japanese and the other against Chiang. Yet I am in a difficult position, as I need Comrade Stalin's support if I and my army are to survive.

In the past year, we have grown from ten thousand half-starved men to almost eighty thousand soldiers. Comrade Stalin had promised me that he will continue to support my army, and to that end, he will send whatever weapons I require. But soon after I received that communique, I learned the arms that were to be given to me were far less than requested. I don't think he knows or believes that my army has grown so rapidly. But I desperately need weapons, so I accepted what was offered. But getting them turned out to be a formidable task. Comrade Stalin communicated that he could only deliver them in the north, where my enemy stood between me and the shipment I so desperately needed. Chiang did not want me to receive these arms, and therefore, he put all his might into blocking my access to them. He wants us weak and defenseless instead of a formidable match for his army. Therefore, with little choice, I ordered my men to attack his forces and retrieve our weapons. But Chiang's army is larger and better armed than mine. Although my men fought fiercely to try to break through his lines, we were unable to do so. I had no choice but to order a retreat to conserve what precious arms and munitions I had left. I was barely able to escape his grasp. But I know the tiger still searches for me and yearns to devour its nemesis.

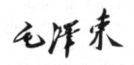

CHAPTER

5

CHIEF INSPECTOR BRUNO WAS SEARCHING Gina Moretti's apartment, hoping to find a clue as to who killed her and why. In his opinion, there was no such thing as a perfect crime. There were always inconsistencies, and these usually proved to be the deciding factors in solving a case. In the past half hour, he noted six. The first was the missing laptop. There was an Apple computer power cable on the desk, exactly like the one he had at home. But the laptop was nowhere to be found. He made a mental note to call Luca to ask if it was in her office. If not, he would have his men check the city's computer repair shops to see if they had it. Another inconsistency—and the one that bothered him the most—was that her purse was on the nightstand. When he saw her body in the Campo Santo Stefano and noticed the lack of any personnel items, he assumed those had been taken by the murderer. Instead he now knew she'd left them behind. Why? Possibly she forgot them. Everyone had lapses in memory from time to time. Did she have one that night, or was there another reason she didn't take her purse? The third and fourth inconsistencies involved the facts that the back door to her apartment was unlocked and the lights were on. Utilities were expensive in Italy, and no one illuminated their residence unless they were home. And when they left, people locked their doors. Did she again have a memory lapse, or as he was beginning to think, was she in such a hurry that it wasn't a priority? The fifth and sixth inconsistencies were that she was walking alone at night and didn't take her cell phone. He knew very few women who'd be comfortable walking by themselves after dark, especially without a cell phone. The only possible explanation for leaving it behind, besides forgetfulness, was that it was out of power. That may have been the case since he found it connected to her charger in the bedroom. He knew that any one of these inconsistencies didn't amount to much in isolation. But taken together, he believed they pointed to Gina Moretti leaving her apartment in a hurry, probably to escape her killer, who eventually caught up with her in the Campo Santo Stefano. It was only conjecture at this point. But in his mind, the fact that she was dead gave credence to this theory.

Bruno decided to try to duplicate the route she might have taken that night and put himself in the position of a woman running for her life. He went out the back door of the residence and started in the general direction of the piazza. He knew there were many ways to get there because Venice's streets were short and interconnected, providing a myriad of paths to one's destination. But he needed to go back to the piazza anyway, and this might give him a fresh perspective.

The Campo Santo Stefano is an elongated square named after the fourteen-century gothic-style church that anchors its northern boundary. The southern border was marked by the austere-looking Palazzo Pisani, home of the Benedetto Marcello Conservatory of Music. In between, the square is edged with numerous shops, restaurants, and bars. When Bruno arrived, he went to the spot where Gina Moretti was killed, not far from a clothing shop near the church. He could still visualize her lying on the cobblestone street, a bullet hole in the center of her forehead. He'd noticed nothing unusual on his way here, assuming he'd somehow taken the same route she did, except that it was quite a distance from her residence. The more he thought about it, the stronger his belief that the route itself wasn't important. The killer didn't happen upon her as she was strolling through the area. He was chasing her for reasons that were not yet clear. And in that pursuit, her route to the piazza could have been very erratic.

Bruno didn't expect any eyewitnesses. At the approximate time the medical examiner said she was killed, the entire area would have been deserted. Evening patrols and security cameras weren't deemed a priority in this outlying concentration of shops. The area's businesses were not only locked and had security alarms, but their doors and windows were protected by steel shutters. Anyone trying to break in would need an acetylene torch. Consequently, police patrols were assigned to areas of the city where tourists congregated. With an absence of law enforcement and no place to hide, no one could have saved Gina Moretti from whoever was pursuing her.

Reaching into his jacket pocket, he took a cigarette from the almost empty pack, lit it, and inhaled deeply. He started toward the northern portion of the square, exhaling the bluish smoke as he walked. He'd taken about thirty steps when he saw a dark brown smear that resembled a footprint. There was another just a couple of feet beyond that. He knew right away that these had come from Gina Moretti's badly cut left foot, which the coroner told him would have been excruciatingly painful and bleeding quite badly. Forensics photographed and noted these blood spots while he was at the crime scene. But they'd found no others in the piazza. Bruno guessed that the moisture on the streets and the foot traffic from curious bystanders or first responders all but obliterated other traces of blood. He was surprised that these were still visible, given the fact that they'd been exposed to the elements and pedestrian traffic for two days.

He looked at his watch and saw that it was getting late. He needed to return to his office and face the mound of paperwork on top of his desk. As he walked back, he thought about the fact that Gina Moretti was wearing shoes when her body was discovered. This morning, seeing her bloody footprints in the square for a second time, he needed to know why she had taken her shoes off. When she did, something cut her foot, which caused her to put them back on anyway. Listening to the sound of his shoes echoing off the cobblestone street, he realized he had the probable answer. After that, she'd have a difficult choice. Leave the shoes off and give her pursuer a blood trail to follow or put them back on and endure the crippling pain and impeded mobility described to him by the coroner. Bruno lit another cigarette. He didn't believe this was a random killing. He returned to his central question. What did Gina Moretti do, or what did she have that was so important that someone wanted to kill her for it? When he had the answer to that, he'd have his killer.

Cai Fu had killed many people in his life. Usually, at the end, when they knew they were going to die, the varnish of lies covering what they were hiding was stripped away, and they usually told the truth. That's what scared him about Gina Moretti. She sounded much too confident that the documents were well hidden and beyond his reach. *Somewhere you'll never find them.* Those words haunted him.

He was certain they were somewhere safe. After speaking with Luca, he didn't think they were in the Marciana. If they had been, he would have gladly handed them over for the vast sum of money he was offered. Instead he believed Gina Moretti took the documents and somehow managed to hide them before he killed her. He'd thoroughly searched her apartment and the alley behind it. He wasn't convinced that she'd stashed them on the way to the piazza. With all businesses in the area shuttered at that hour, the only hiding places available were alleyways. That would have exposed the documents to the elements, something he didn't think would be acceptable to someone intent on protecting them.

He thought back to the night he killed her. His plan had been to drag her out of bed, tie her up, and then interrogate her for the location of the documents. He could be very persuasive. He had no doubt she'd have told him where they were. That plan changed when he saw her lights were on because it meant she was almost certainly awake. He decided to wait until the apartment went dark, and sometime after that, when she was hopefully asleep, he'd enter. But that never happened. Somehow she'd seen him and fled. Looking through the front window, he could see her bolt out the back door. He wanted to run after her, Instead he forced himself to walk at a fast pace so that the sound of his shoes on the street didn't drown out her footsteps. She changed direction often. That didn't affect his ability to follow. With all the noise her heels were making, he could almost pinpoint where she was. Eventually, she'd tire, and he'd catch up. Then suddenly, silence. He stopped and waited for a full three minutes, hoping she was catching her breath. That's when it came to him. She'd heard his footsteps and removed her shoes. Doing the same, he broke into a run, taking routes parallel to the general direction he believed she was headed. The fact that he found her was more luck than skill because the street he was running down ended at the Campo Santo Stefano.

With Luca failing to deliver the documents, he wanted to have a more thorough look at Gina Moretti's apartment. He decided to enter through the back door to avoid prying eyes. As he walked into the alley, he saw a man with salt-and-pepper hair and a black moustache come out of the residence. If he'd turned left instead of right, they would have collided. He didn't know who this person was, but his instincts told him he was a police detective or someone of similar standing. Walking behind him, the man went the Campo Santo Stefano, going directly to the spot where he'd killed the woman. There was little doubt that the person he was looking at was a police officer and probably the one in charge of the investigation. When the man left the square, he followed at a cautious distance, eventually ending up at a Venice police station, where he heard one of the officers who was leaving the building greet him as Chief Inspector Bruno.

Cai Fu returned to the piazza to try to piece together what he had. He'd go back to the apartment later, once the police had finished and look for hidden spaces in the walls, in the ceiling, and under the floorboards. He would have done it sooner, but he wasn't sure how long it'd take the authorities to identify the body and then go to Gina Moretti's residence. It'd be hard to explain his presence if he was caught. And even though he had diplomatic immunity, there'd be no avoiding the one-way ticket back to Beijing he'd receive following his arrest. Ideally, he should have waited a couple more days to thoroughly search the residence; however, General Lin was putting the screws to him, and he didn't have the luxury of time.

Entering the northern end of the square, he selected a shaded table at one of the outdoor restaurants near the church and ordered hot green tea. When his drink arrived, he took a sip and found that it was bitter and much too strong. Italians made a great espresso, but they were still adolescents in the world of brewing tea. Whoever made this had used tea bags instead of leaves and then let it steep too long. He set it aside. His mind drifted back to the other night. *Somewhere you'll never find them.* She'd obviously hidden the documents. The question was this: Had she concealed them before running or after entering the piazza? He supposed it was also possible that she had given them to someone who was waiting for her and who departed before she was killed. But he summarily dismissed that idea because it was unlikely that the person she met would leave her bleeding and in peril while he or she ran off to safety. He thought back to the night she died. Each of the surrounding businesses was shuttered. There was literally nowhere to hide. He was becoming convinced that she hid the documents before she went home that night. If that was true, he'd have to take a new tack. He put some euros on the table and got up. Looking directly across the square, he saw a men's clothing shop. Next to that was a wine emporium, another restaurant, a stationary store, and then something innocuous that he'd overlooked. Could it really be that simple? *Somewhere where you'll never find them.* He believed he was about to disprove that.

It is November 1936, and my army's needs grow
daily as our numbers increase. My men live mainly
on black beans and take shelter in holes that we dig

into the hills. It is getting colder by the week. Most of my men are thinly clothed, and they wrap their feet in straw to protect them from the snow and ice. My wife is suffering greatly. She is expecting soon, and our deplorable living conditions have made her life a misery. Rats infest our living spaces, and it is difficult for us to keep what little food we have away from them. We are cold, living in squalor, and hungry.

If we are to survive, we must again become the aggressor. Any other course of action would let Chiang continue to get stronger while I fade into irrelevance. I have commanded my staff to come up with a bold plan to take the offensive. But when I look at their faces, I see they're skeptical of my order. They think it is a grand delusion. Many believe we are already defeated since we can barely keep ourselves clothed and fed. They ask how we can defeat such a well-provisioned and armed enemy, a question I ask myself daily. Despite the belief that what I'm asking of them is folly, my men prove loyal and accede to my wishes.

Several days later, to their credit and my great surprise and joy, my staff came up with an ingenious plan to cut off the head of the dragon. It is brilliant in its audacity and simplicity. They are going to kidnap Chiang. I have thoroughly reviewed what they've devised, and I believe we have a good chance of success. But we will have to act quickly. Chiang has spies everywhere. If he discovers our intentions, he will be in the wind.

The fact that I might be successful in kidnapping my enemy also carries its own burden, as I risk incurring the wrath of Comrade Stalin. That I cannot afford. My army would perish without his help. But I am out of alternatives, and capturing Chiang is the only way for us to survive. I will speak with Comrade Stalin at the appropriate time. He is paranoid about the Japanese, and I can use this to my advantage. I have given my approval for this operation to commence, and either success or death will come from it. Tomorrow we will see which.

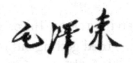

CHAPTER

6

MATT MORETTI GRITTED HIS TEETH. The pain in his lower back was the most intense when he tried getting out of bed in the morning, making it almost impossible for him to sit up. Instead, if he wanted to get vertical, he needed to roll out of bed and lower himself down to his knees. From there, he'd get to his feet by pushing down on the mattress with his muscular arms.

Today's attack seemed worse than most, every nerve in his back deciding to make its presence known at the same time. The truth was that he'd never had a painless night since the crash. He looked at his nightstand and the nearly empty bottle of Johnny Walker Black. He could easily have finished it before he went to bed; however, he'd reset his limit to a single nightly glass of alcohol, and he was determined to keep this new boundary. It was his only chance of maintaining some measure of control over his addiction. It was hard to believe that he'd transformed into the person he was. Six years ago as a US Army Ranger, it was different. His job, as he once told his father and sister, was to protect this country against shitheads who wanted to bring it down. Back then the Distinguished Service Cross and Silver Star, the US military's second and third highest awards, sat proudly at the top of a cluster of medals across his broad chest. He was at the apex of his profession when in the blink of an eye—or more specifically the crash of the MH-47 Chinook helicopter he was riding in—everything changed. He was one of two survivors and the most seriously hurt. His broken back required six operations in as many months just so that he could walk, and it took another year of physical therapy to lose the cane. No one today could tell by looking at his six-foot-three, 230-pound frame that he'd ever come close to becoming an invalid. The doctors initially gave him only a forty-sixty chance of ever walking again. He'd beaten those odds and handed them back his cane upon completing his final rehab session. But his life had taken a dramatic turn. Unable to pass an army physical, he was medically discharged, given a pat on the back, and told to find a civilian job.

Returning to Anchorage, where he and his sister had been raised by their widowed father, he got an apartment and started looking for work. Three months later, with no marketable civilian skills, he was still searching. That's when he took the brakes off his drinking and he started to feel sorry for himself, withdrawing into the comfort and protection of his inebriated shell. With his savings nearing depletion and his father unable to straighten out his head or stop his drinking, he received a call from Doug Cray, the other survivor of the Chinook crash. The intelligence officer's injuries were relatively modest, allowing him to stay in the army and return to work in six months. To this day, he didn't know for sure how Cray had gotten his phone number or had picked this time in his life to call, but he suspected his sister was behind it because the army officer asked if he'd spoken with her lately. Cray told him that if he was still looking for a job, there was an opening at a government agency in Anchorage. Cray gave him the name of the person to contact and said to use him as a reference. It took two days for Moretti to clear his head enough to call and schedule an interview. The following day he had a job, and he cut down his drinking to one glass a day, usually before bed. That was five years ago. Life was still a struggle. If it wasn't staying away from the bottle, it was the daily boredom of pushing papers. Somehow there had to be more.

Major Zhou An's car was in gridlock. Unfortunately, the cluster of government buildings where he was headed was near the Forbidden

City, Beijing's geographic center of congestion. He'd called ahead to make sure his uncle, Wu Jin, would still be there when he arrived, although he didn't tell him the subject of their conversation. It was well known that all cellular and landline conversations within China were subject to monitoring. What he was about to reveal had to remain between the two of them ... for now. As far as his uncle knew, this was a social visit, although that couldn't have been further from the truth. The papers lying on the seat beside him, which he'd taken without permission from a secure facility, were toxic to the government and very likely to the person who was bringing the info to their attention. That's why he needed his uncle. As one of seven members of the Politburo Standing Committee, the most powerful decision-making body in China, he could ensure his survival when the dust settled.

His day started innocently enough when General Lin called and requested the smartest technician in the unit to come to his office. He didn't know why he wanted this person, but a major didn't question a general, at least not if he wanted to maintain his rank. Therefore, he sent his brightest tech, wondering all the while what was going on. Given that he was the senior supervisor in the most clandestine technology organization in China, Unit 61398, his staff consisted of hackers. Their daily focus was to surgically enter the computer systems of foreign businesses and governments without being detected. They were also meant to intercept and analyze international email traffic going in and out of the country. This data would then be transferred to a central repository managed by the army. That begged the question, What was General Lin up to?

Later that day the technician returned, passing by his glass-enclosed office without so much as a word. This was unusual because as an enlisted man, military protocol dictated that upon returning, he'd summarize the success or failure of the services performed to the officer in charge. Pissed, he left his desk and went to the tech's cubicle, where he saw him inserting a flash drive into the USB port, a practice that was strictly forbidden without authorization and an act that would trigger a visual alarm in his office. When he asked what he was doing, the tech told him that he was following the general's orders of not explaining his actions to anyone. Unsettled, he phoned to verify what he'd been told. The response he received was direct and to the point. *Stay in your office, shut up, and what occurred today never happened.*

His attention returned to the mass of cars in front of him. Beijing was considered to have the worst traffic in China, but he'd rarely seen it this bad. There had to be a high-ranking official or foreign dignitary entering or leaving one of the government ministry's ahead, and subsequently, the police were stopping all traffic. Zhou looked at the red light that just illuminated on his control panel. His aging Hafei was beginning to overheat. Since he wasn't going anywhere, he turned the engine off and rolled down the driver and passenger windows to get some cross ventilation. His thoughts returned to his office and watching the technician leave with the USB flash drive in his hand. Bringing up the camera system on his desktop, he saw him take the elevator to the lobby and stop at the security desk. He knew what would inevitably follow. A few seconds later, the guard called to verify whether the flash drive was permitted to leave the building. Something wasn't right. Ignoring the general's orders, he was determined to find out if something illicit was going on. He was certain that if there was, he'd later be blamed for it. He went to the tech's workstation and used his supervisory codes to see what was downloaded. Surprisingly, he was unable to do so because the transaction log showing what the tech had done had been erased. All he could determine was that it was a relatively recent email. There were numerous safeguards to prevent this from happening, but all could be bypassed with the proper access codes, which were entrusted to only a handful of very important individuals.

Getting the same results after searching the backup system, he was ready to throw in the towel when a thought came to him. He picked up the phone and called a friend who worked at the Ministry of Public Security. Each morning they received their most recent email intercepts and any updates. Therefore, they would have the deleted data, at least until tomorrow when the tech's actions would flow to their system and eliminate this information.

The MPS took spying on citizens and foreigners very seriously. They had an estimated two million people performing an eyes-on review of specific internet traffic selected by sophisticated algorithms that looked for anything or anyone at odds with the public good. Because of the avalanche of emails that entered the system daily, he knew they were routinely two to six months behind in their reviews. Therefore, even if one of their filters did select the deleted email for screening, chances were that no one had yet read it.

It took only a few minutes for his friend to give him restricted access to the email database that his unit had accessed. He ran a program comparing both sets of data, which should have been identical, and he quickly found the deleted email. He printed a hard copy and downloaded the file to the flash drive, both of which he now kept in the folder on the passenger seat.

Zhou observed a group of men in the street going from car to car, drivers handing them some form of identification. Behind them traffic appeared to be moving normally at a somewhat faster crawl. This massive traffic jam was the result of a search rather than the security of a government official or dignitary. Whoever they were looking for had to be in a senior position on the party's shit list to warrant blocking the busiest street in Beijing.

When they eventually reached him, he handed his military identification to a young, fit man with close-cropped black hair. He had all the earmarks of someone who was in the military. Since Zhou was in uniform, he was certain that the guy would quickly hand back his identification and wave him on. The man focused for an instant on the folder lying on the front seat and then contacted someone on his cell phone. A moment later he reached into the car to return his ID. Almost instantaneously, Zhou felt an intense pain in his side. Looking down, he saw a knife buried so deep into him that only the handle was visible. That was the last he saw or felt.

The man quickly removed the knife, retracted the blade, and placed it back into his pants pocket. Pushing Zhou's body aside, he got into the car and drove away.

The old man listened intently to General Lin's telephone call and wondered if he'd have the strength to stop him. At ninety-three years of age, he would need to marshal all his energy if he was going to thwart the general's plan and keep the documents within Pandora's box. He was thankful that he'd had the foresight to plant a listening device in his office many years ago and that it hadn't been discovered. Someone would eventually find it, but in the meantime, it was providing a treasure trove of information. The conversation between General Lin and Cai Fu he'd just heard was alarming. It meant that the existence of the documents had been uncovered. But he didn't know where they were. Otherwise, he'd have them. He briefly thought about bringing the general's treachery to the attention of the party. But what had he done other than scheme? If he were to arrest every schemer in government, the halls of the National People's Congress would be empty. Even as the most senior member of the Politburo Standing Committee, Cho Ling knew he had his limitations. The general was too powerful, and he had too many friends in high places to be accused without hard evidence of actions against the state. Therefore, the only way to stop him was to get the originals. Then he'd have nothing but scanned copies of alleged historical papers, which could easily be debunked. Getting them wouldn't be easy. With Cai Fu leading the search, he'd need to be even deadlier. Fortunately, China's deadliest assassin worked for him.

Cho Ling walked from his office to the couch in his living quarters, sat down, and rubbed his weary eyes. He took a pill out of the plastic container he kept in his pants pocket and swallowed it with some water. In a few minutes, his headache would go away. The doctor told him that the medicine wouldn't cure what ailed him. There was no remedy. He had between three and six weeks to live. But it would take away some of the pain. He accepted his fate without remorse. Death was inevitable, and, at his age it was long overdue. He'd outlived a wife and daughter. A granddaughter in her late twenties was his only surviving family member. Now his only goal was to live long enough to retake possession of the documents that he'd given to his nephew, Chang Hao, so many decades ago.

His mind drifted back to 1942 and the death of his parents at the hands of the Japanese when they swept through their home. His older sister, hiding in another village, was the only member of his family to survive. After the war she moved to the city and married a successful businessman and landowner. A short time later, they had a son they named Chang Hao. After the communists came to power, all land reverted to the state. His sister and her husband were labeled as bourgeois, and with others who bore that label, they were sent to the countryside to toil as common laborers and become reeducated in the newly established national priorities. Knowing the hardships and uncertain future that faced them, he provided forged documents and arranged to smuggle their son out of the country. But Chang Hao's mother and father had to remain behind. All bourgeois were being closely watched because the government knew they were frantic to leave the country with their wealth. Therefore, after a tearful farewell, their son left for Hong Kong, and from there, he took a cargo ship to Brazil. There he lived with a married couple who were friends with his parents and had fled China just prior to the communists coming to power. Half a decade later, famine gripped the country, and Cho Ling's sister and her husband died of starvation along with tens of millions of other Chinese people.

Cho Ling remained unmarried for most of his life, except for a brief period in his late twenties when he wed one of Chairman Mao's housekeepers. But she died during childbirth, and he raised his daughter as a single parent for nineteen years until she married a party official in Beijing. Soon afterward, he had a granddaughter. But tragedy struck again when his daughter and her husband perished in an automobile crash. Thankfully, Han Li, his eight-year-old granddaughter, survived. Cho Ling raised her, sending her to special government schools where she excelled at martial arts. Following graduation, she began work at the Second Bureau, which sent foreign agents abroad. That was ten years ago.

Over the years Cho Ling corresponded with Chang Hao, who continued to live in Brazil. Their letters passed through a contact in Hong Kong, and after he died, they used his contact's son. In 1973, he sent him a letter and a package wrapped in brown paper. The paper covered a rectangular brown leather box that was ten inches long, nine inches wide, and two inches high. Attached to the front of it on the top and bottom was a metal loop. A thin strip of steel crimped together with a tool that imprinted a star at the connection point ran through both loops and prevented anyone from opening the box undetected. His letter instructed Chang Hao to hold the package until he asked for it.

Chang Hao eventually tired of Brazil and moved to Venice, where he lived until his death. Cho Ling didn't anticipate his nephew dying before him, and he also never expected him to donate the box containing the documents to a Venetian library. The only explanation he could think of as to why this happened was that he'd once told him that the package contained priceless Chinese documents that must be preserved. Giving them to the Marciana Library to honor his wishes probably seemed logical to his nephew. Now he'd sent his only living relative to put them back in Pandora's box.

General Lin removed the scanned copy of the documents from his drawer and set them on his desk. He thought about the many similarities he shared with Chairman Mao. Both commanded an army, had an insatiable desire to unite their people, and were not afraid to take military action to accomplish their geopolitical goals. When he received the original documents, which would invariably lead to becoming the leader of his country, he'd reverse the government's long-standing policy of military timidity and backing down to other world powers. That was preposterous. China had a boatload of cash in its treasury, and more was coming in daily. Given the political will, he fully believed they could fund a military and develop weapons that would be on par or even superior to that of the United States. What good was power if one didn't use it? America had one weapon—their military. China had two—economic clout and the military. But his party's leadership didn't have the backbone for confrontation. Instead they were only interested in maintaining their political power base, perpetuating an extravagant lifestyle, and exercising absolute control over its citizens to protect their nests. This was an intolerable and treasonous weakness. When he became emperor, things would change. China would bow to no one when he restored his country to the greatness for which it was destined.

He took the fourth document off the stack before him and started to read.

> It is December 1936. The kidnapping was successful. I was ecstatic when told that Chiang was in my custody. I advised my staff that there will be no firing squad. Instead I want to personally put a rope around his neck and pull the trap door open. Everyone must see what happens to traitors who harbor the bourgeois, steal from the people, and kill communists and Japanese with equal energy. I shared with Comrade Stalin my plans to execute Chiang, thereby unifying my country under one flag and one leader. Expecting him to be happy, I was stunned when he became quite angry at me instead. He threatened to withdraw his support if, as he said, a single hair on Chiang's head was harmed. He told me that killing or imprisoning him would only help the Japanese. An absurdity. Nevertheless, Comrade Stalin has ordered me to immediately release him or suffer his wrath. I now know that he doesn't believe that I can defeat the Japanese without the

help of my enemy and his army. I was violently against setting Chiang free, but what choice did I have? I cannot survive without Comrade Stalin's assistance. He provides me the money, weapons, and food that my army so desperately needs. With great reluctance and a loss of face, I've released my enemy, and we are once again a nation divided.

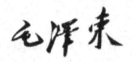

CHAPTER

7

"HOLD THE ELEVATOR," MORETTI CALLED out as he hurried down the hall. "Thanks, Allison," he said to the attractive brunette in the tight pencil skirt who had her finger on the open button.

Allison Davers politely smiled as he rushed inside. Once the doors closed, she turned around, threw her hands up around his neck, and kissed him full on the lips. "And how is the archivist this morning?" she asked, referring to his job at the National Archives in downtown Anchorage.

"Another day in the mines as usual."

"How about if I cook a late dinner for us and massage your back afterward?"

"Are you a qualified physical therapist?"

"No, but I guarantee I'll take your mind off your back pain."

Before Moretti could respond, the elevator reached the parking garage, and he held the door open as she exited. Noticing an elderly lady in her midseventies slowly making her way toward them, he kept his finger on the button until she entered.

"Chivalrous," Davers said with a smile that showed off her brilliant white teeth. "I'm only working half a day. Come across the hall when you get home. You remember my apartment number, don't you? Five seventeen," she said flirtatiously, even though she knew it was unnecessary to remind him. She gave him a quick kiss on the lips before heading toward her car, and he went in the opposite direction to his GMC Yukon. He felt bad about not wanting a closer relationship with her. She was gorgeous, and she was the type of woman who'd make a great wife and mother. They'd been seeing each other for several months, and they slept together once or twice a week. Although they had a great physical relationship, at least in his opinion, he could tell she wanted more.

Several days ago she suggested that they move in together. But he told her he wasn't ready, even though he knew it hurt her feelings. What he didn't say was that he first needed to get his head on straight. That meant that he needed to stop drinking and recognize that his current job was not going to give him the same sense of fulfillment as being an army ranger. And until he bridged and accepted this gap in life's expectations, neither he nor anyone he was with would be happy.

This morning he had an early meeting with a reporter from China who wanted to write an article on the National Archives. Requests such as this were common and assigned equally among the staff. What made this interview unusual was that the Chinese journalist specifically requested him.

Moretti entered the building and touched his security card to the scanner at the employee turnstile. Nonemployees were required to go through the metal detector on the opposite side of the lobby. He proceeded straight to the break room, where he poured himself a cup of coffee before going to his office. He'd just logged into his computer, and he was about to check his emails when the front desk called and said that a Mr. Wu Bai from China's *People's Daily* had arrived. He looked at the wall clock and saw that the reporter was fifteen minutes early. After taking a quick sip of coffee, he left to retrieve his guest.

Wu Bai didn't fit his mental image of a reporter. He was a lean six foot two with broad shoulders and a narrow waist. His black hair was short, and he had what army rangers called knowing eyes, the result of a tightening of the eye muscles. When he looked at someone, his eyes gave the appearance that he was contemptuous of the person he was speaking with. The fact that they were coal black added to this impression.

"*People's Daily*," Moretti said after Wu Bai handed him his business card and he reciprocated.

"I write international feature stories. Since our readers particularly enjoy anything relating to the United States, my editor wants an article on the US National Archives, comparing it to its counterpart in China. He also wants a human interest component."

"Is that why you asked for me?"

"I looked at the staff biographies on the website. Your military background would make my article more interesting."

Moretti didn't know whether to believe him or not. It wouldn't be the first time someone lied to him about what they were looking for in an interview.

"Before we get started, can I offer you a cup of coffee or tea?"

"Tea would be nice."

"I'll be right back."

He went to the break room and returned a short time later, handing the reporter a Styrofoam cup with a tea bag floating in the hot water.

Wu Bai set the cup on the edge of Moretti's desk without taking a drink. Removing a digital recorder, notebook, and pen from his black soft-sided briefcase, he put the recorder next to his tea and turned it on.

"Can you tell me what the National Archives does?"

"I'd be happy to. Essentially, we centralize the government's record keeping and systematically protect our nation's important documentation."

"Do you maintain a copy of all government records?"

"No. We only keep 1 to 2 percent—those that are historically or legally important. For example, we're the keeper of the Declaration of Independence and the Bill of Rights, archive military and naturalization records, and miscellaneous items of national importance, such as the check for the purchase of Alaska. We'll also restore documents as necessary. Electronically, our system contains ten billion pages of textual records; twelve million maps, charts, and architectural drawings; twenty-five million still photographs; and so on. All in all, we have 133 terabytes of electronic data, and we add 1.4 billion pages to the archives yearly."

Wu Bai thanked him and changed the subject. "Let's talk a little about you and your family and why you went from being a soldier to a librarian."

"I'm an archivist," Moretti corrected, "not a librarian."

"My mistake, an archivist. What's the difference?"

"An archivist collects, organizes, and preserves unpublished records that have been determined to have long-term value. Archives are not unlike museums, and archivists are their curators. A librarian provides and maintains published materials, both physical and electronic, which may or may not have value."

Moretti didn't like the person sitting in front of him. He couldn't put his finger on exactly why. Perhaps it was antipathy. Whatever the reason, he wanted to get through the interview as quickly as possible. "Getting back to your question, my father was an American executive with British Petroleum, and my mother was a librarian. They met in Italy and married six months later."

"You were born in Italy?"

"No. My father was transferred before then to Houston, where Gina and I were born. We're twins. We lived there for ten years before moving to Anchorage. My mother died the following year of ovarian cancer."

"I'm sorry to hear that," Wu Bai responded in a tone that lacked any semblance of emotional sincerity.

"Any other siblings besides Gina?"

"No." Moretti made his answers concise, hoping the reporter would get the hint and leave.

"Are you close?"

Moretti wondered why the reporter asked this question, and he thought about telling him that it was none of his business. But he decided to hold back instead. "Very," he replied, and Wu Bai smiled when he answered.

"And you speak often?"

"I haven't spoken to her for a couple of weeks, but yes, we speak fairly often."

Wu Bai continued asking questions about his sister until Moretti cut him off, saying it would be better if he contacted her directly.

"Why did you join the army?"

"Living in Alaska since I was ten, I wanted to travel and see a bit more of the world before I settled down."

"Interesting. What did you do in the army? Were you also an archivist?"

"I was a ranger."

He noticed Wu Bai seemed surprised, probably because his website biography only noted that he was in the army.

"Why did you decide to leave? You're obviously too young to have retired."

"I was injured in a helicopter crash and was medically discharged."

"You're lucky to have survived."

When Moretti didn't respond, Wu Bai continued his questions for another ten minutes before announcing that he was finished. He put his digital recorder, notebook, and pen back into his briefcase and thanked Moretti for his time.

Moretti wasn't convinced that the person he'd just escorted to the exit was a reporter. His entire demeanor was unlike anyone who'd interviewed him in the past. In fact, the more he thought about it, the more it seemed like an interrogation. Excluding his questions on the National Archives, which were well explained on the website, half the interview consisted of personal inquiries, most involving his sister. The man was after more than just the story he was purportedly going to run. Moretti also had no doubt that if he called the phone number on his card, *People's Daily* would verify his employment. But there was one person who couldn't be fooled, and he decided to call him now.

The day Cai Fu set aside his tea and looked across the piazza while sitting at an outdoor restaurant at the Campo Santo Stefano, he noticed a drop box to the right of the entrance to the FedEx office. He realized it was the perfect way to get the documents to safety or hide them so they could be retrieved later. Given the two choices, he believed Gina Moretti sent them to someone she trusted with an address she could easily recall. The other alternative, placing them inside the container, where they could be discarded or damaged, seemed too risky. Accessing her social media site with the assistance of a technician in China, he determined from her numerous comments that the person she'd trusted most was her brother. That's when he decided to schedule a meeting with him, using the subterfuge of being a reporter. Time was of the essence, which is why he went to Anchorage before continuing his search in Venice. If she did send him the documents, then he needed to get to them before they were made public. But if they were in the drop box, then they'd hopefully be at FedEx—at least for a short time—until someone figured out what to do with them. It wasn't nearly a perfect solution, but given the situation, it was the best he could come up with.

Unfortunately, his meeting with her brother turned up nothing. While he'd gone to get him tea, he searched his office. There was no sign of either a FedEx package or the documents. And he didn't seem to be affected by the fact that he was Asian, something that would have elicited an unintentional response of some sort, given the fact that what he'd received would have been in Chinese. He briefly considered kidnapping, interrogating, and then killing the former army ranger just to make sure. But that would be careless, especially since his sister was recently murdered, and he didn't want the US government authorities to initiate an investigation. Still, he had to be certain, as the search of his office wasn't definitive.

He flagged a passing cab and asked to be taken to the airport. He needed to return to Venice. But before then, there was one thing he needed to do.

The last decade has been a period of tumultuous change for me and my country. The war with Japan and my continuing struggles with Chiang have consumed every second of my existence. I have ignored my diary for far too long, and now I will summarize the most import aspects of the past ten years.

In October 1938, Comrade Stalin told me that he implicitly trusted Chiang's ability to stop the Japanese advance since his army was nearly ten times the size of mine. But he put too much faith in numbers and not enough in the spirit of ordinary citizens fighting for a leader they believe in. Chiang's forces continue to be defeated time and again. Most pitifully, they were surrounded in Chongqing, where they cowered in the face of the Japanese onslaught. Unable to lead his men to victory, he attempted to slow down the enemy's advance and ordered the destruction of all dykes on the Yellow River. The resulting floods killed more than five hundred thousand of my people and displaced more than five million. I cried when I heard the news. Chiang cares little for farmers and peasants and recklessly uses them as pawns. His concern is only for the bourgeois. Even with such wanton destruction, the Japanese continued their advance. Since Chiang did not control the sky, the enemy's air force flew mission after mission over Chongqing. The death toll was horrific, and the suffering was unimaginable.

Famine followed Japan's advance across my country, but nowhere was it felt more than in the province of Henan. In 1940 and 1941, their crop output was poor, and food reserves were completely consumed. The following year the drought arrived, resulting in very little wheat to harvest. However, Chiang still demanded the normal tax paid in grain from all farmers. In many cases, the payment due was the entire crop, and in some instances, it was greater than what they had reaped. When this occurred, they not only gave up their harvest but also sold their possessions to cover the tax. As a result, many of my people were reduced to eating elm bark and dried leaves, and hundreds of thousands died of starvation.

On the land that I controlled, I reduced rents and taxes so that my people could have enough to eat, and I ordered those provisioning foods for my men to pay for all they took. Unlike Chiang, this army will not condemn its citizens to misery and starvation by appropriating what does not belong to us. As a result, the people rallied around me, and my Chinese Communist Party grew. From a mere forty thousand members in 1937, we number more than eight hundred thousand three years later. My army has swelled from forty-five thousand to more than five hundred thousand.

I know Chiang's hate for communism will not go away because he cannot discriminate between fighting the Japanese and communists. He sees both as equally evil. I have never trusted him, but for the sake of my country, I ordered my army to fight alongside his men. Letting down my guard in such a manner turned out to be a grave mistake. In December 1940, he demanded that my New Fourth Army leave both Anhui and Jiangsu provinces. With Chiang's much larger forces threatening them, I gave my commanders permission to withdraw and leave these two provinces to his soldiers. If my adversary wants to spill his men's blood, then so be it. But as my men peaceably withdrew, his army ambushed and killed thousands of them. I was foolish to have trusted such a vile and dishonorable person, and I have now terminated all mutual endeavors with him.

Given the size of my army, I decided to conduct guerilla warfare against the Japanese. This turned out to be an effective strategy, far exceeding even my grandest expectations. Chiang says this tactic is only suitable for peasants and refuses to employ it. Thousands of his men die because of this pride. He will never accept that the Japanese are too powerful and too well trained to engage head-on. As a result, while he weakens by the day, I grow stronger. But this joy was tempered by the fact that the famine made it increasingly hard to feed my men. My people suffer. My army suffers. I suffer.

In late 1941, shortly after the United States declared war on Japan, representatives from the American government contacted me. Although they support Chiang, they offered to supply me with money and supplies. They said that with 40 percent of Japan's troops in China, the fiercer the fight in my country, the more time they'd have to rebuild their Pacific fleet. This was welcome news as our Soviet allies, who were completely consumed with fighting German invaders, have been unable to provide me with the logistical and monetary support I required.

My spies tell me that Chiang spends more time coddling the American imperialists than he does fighting our common enemy. He senses that the

United States will eventually be victorious and therefore will decide the spoils of war. Representing himself as the military leader of China, he discounts my army as nothing more than a gathering of peasants who could surrender to the Japanese at any time. He also fueled their fear of communism by comparing us to the Soviet Union. The Allies believed Chiang and invited him to a conference on postwar goals.

At the end of 1943, the Allies issued the Cairo Declaration, which stripped Japan of the territories they illegally seized. In this promulgation, Korea's independence was once again restored, and Taiwan was designated an inseparable part of China. My spirit soared. I hungered for the Allies to win the war and for Taiwan to be returned to us so that we could again be a united country. But when the war ended, America reneged on its promise and did not support China's unilateral right to Taiwan. Instead it left its fate to those living there. Although I do not like uncertainty, I believed those on that small island would want to be part of our great nation. But Chiang and the Americans felt such an outcome was in neither of their interests. With an endorsement from the United States, giving him credit where none was due, these misinformed turncoats welcomed Chiang as their liberator. I knew it was the hen welcoming the fox. Chiang cares only for the wealthy and bourgeois, and he despises peasants. He doesn't realize that ordinary citizens are the backbone and fabric of China, while the bourgeois merely steal the eggs and tell the hen to lay more.

Before long, the people realized their mistake as I knew they would. Chiang took all the eggs and ruled the hens with an iron fist, ruthlessly killing all who opposed him. Ten thousand, I estimate, lay dead by his commands. And for what reason? All they did was tell the truth, saying they had no jobs and no future, given the government's corruption and its ignorance of the people's needs. Chiang's army recognizes this, and many of his troops have deserted and joined me, bringing their American weaponry with them. Now the tide has begun to turn. My army rapidly grows stronger, and I eventually forced Chiang to retreat south. I have him on the run.

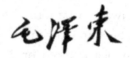

CHAPTER

8

MAJOR DOUG CRAY WAS DEEP in thought, trying to finish a report that was due before the end of the day for the two-star commander of INSCOM, the US Army Intelligence and Security Command at Fort Belvoir, Virginia. Functionally part of the NSA, it gleaned intelligence from satellite, electronic, physical, and every other means of surveillance at the nation's disposal. It then analyzed and sent this data to battlefield and combat units. At an even six feet tall and with sandy-brown hair, blue eyes, and a jogger's body, Cray looked more like a college professor than a counterintelligence officer, his slight Bostonian accent adding to the misconception. Today he was all thumbs on the keyboard, and it was going slowly.

The phone on his desk rang with an obnoxious buzzing sound that someone had probably convinced the government that it needed and that Uncle Sam undoubtedly paid a premium to implement.

"INSCOM, Major Cray."

"Doug, it's Matt."

"It's good to hear from you. How are you doing?" Cray asked, relieved it wasn't his boss calling to accelerate the delivery of his report.

"Still glued to my chair, the same as you."

"Matt, I'm just finishing something. Can I call you back?"

"If you give me two minutes, you won't have to."

"Go."

"This morning I received a visit from a Chinese reporter by the name of Wu Bai, who claimed to work for *People's Daily* in Beijing. My instincts tell me he's not a reporter. His mannerisms, bearing, and even the way he asked his questions seemed to hint at a military underpinning. I was hoping you had him in your system."

"Sure, we always make our classified databases available to civilians."

"I'm serious. Why would a Chinese reporter show up in Anchorage to do an article on the National Archives and include me in it? That's a little thin. There's a building full of veterans working at our headquarters in DC, and many of them have a chest full of medals."

"He asked for you by name?"

"Yes, but hardly spent any time inquiring on my military service. He did, however, ask a lot of questions about Gina."

"Maybe he wanted a free trip to Alaska, and you were the excuse to get him there."

"He just didn't seem like the tourist type."

"What other reason could he have? You've been out of the military for what, five years? You're not exactly a fountainhead of top secret information."

"I guess you're right."

"Look, I know this is important to you. Let me see if I can get someone to authorize me to do this search. No promises."

"No promises," Moretti repeated.

"Give me the name and physical description of the person who came to see you."

After the call ended, Moretti stood to get another cup of coffee when his cell phone rang. Looking at the number, he was surprised to see it was his father, who'd largely become a recluse since his mother died. When he answered, he could hear him sobbing.

"Dad, what's wrong?"

"Gina's been murdered," he managed to get out.

It took him a moment or two to process what he'd been told.

He had difficulty comprehending that his sister was gone, and he didn't want to believe it. He felt nauseous, and he grabbed his chair as his legs began to buckle.

"Murdered?"

"The US consulate in Venice told me that she was shot and killed two days ago. Since she had no identification on her, the police were only able to confirm she was the victim once her boss reported her missing."

He had a hundred questions, but now wasn't the time. "I'll be right over," he said, not waiting for a response before he ended the call.

On the way to his father's house he bought a bottle of Johnny Walker Black. He was becoming increasingly depressed by the thought that he'd never again see his sister, and he needed a drink badly. He wanted to take a pull in the parking lot of the liquor store, but he decided against it because he'd likely stay there until the bottle was drained. If that happened, he didn't know if he'd even make it to his father's house. It was better to wait thirty minutes until he got to his Eagle River home.

When he arrived, his father told him everything he knew, including the consulate asking if a family member would be escorting her body back to the United States.

"I'll do it," the junior Moretti said as he poured himself another drink while his fathers remained untouched.

"You might want to go easy."

The younger Moretti nodded and put the stopper back in the bottle. Today was easily the worst day in his life. His sister was one of the few people he could always count on. After the helicopter crash, she'd been his biggest source of encouragement as he underwent numerous surgeries and grueling physical therapy sessions. He remembered their last call less than two weeks ago when they'd discussed getting together in Venice. He should have told her then how much he loved her and appreciated all she'd done for him. But since leaving the army, he'd built such a thick shell over his emotions that expressing his feelings wasn't easy.

Moretti took out his cell and booked the 4:45 Delta flight. With a connection in Frankfurt, he'd arrive in Venice the following day. As he was making these arrangements, he received two calls from a blocked number, both of which he ignored. Once he was off the phone, he answered the caller's third attempt to contact him.

"Moretti."

"Matt, it's Doug Cray. I have something for you."

He wasn't in the mood to talk to anyone; however, Cray had gone out of his way to do him a favor, and he felt guilty for making him go to this much trouble only to put him off. "What have you got?" he asked.

"Not over an unsecure line. Do you have encrypted phone at the Archives?"

"Sure, but—"

"Call me at this number when you get to it."

Moretti walked into the kitchen, found a pad of paper on the counter, and wrote down the number given to him.

"Dad, I have to go," he said, walking back into the family room.

"Are you okay to drive? I can take you to the airport."

"I'm fine. I'll call you a little later." They embraced briefly, and he left the house.

Once inside the Yukon, he lowered both the driver and passenger side windows, and he stayed at the speed limit. He didn't feel drunk, but that didn't mean he could pass a Breathalyzer test. He'd consumed nearly half a bottle of scotch in a short period of time, and therefore, he was probably pushing the legal limit. He wondered what was so important that Cray could only discuss it over a secure line.

Moretti entered the National Archives and proceeded to the administration office, where the STE (Secure Terminal Equipment) phone was located. It resembled any other phone, except that the person using it could only speak to a similar phone that had the same encryption key. He picked it up and dialed the number he'd been given. After a click, indicating that both phones were now synced, Cray came on the line.

"Thanks for calling me back. Matt. I first want to let you know how sorry I am to hear about Gina. I didn't know about her death when you called me earlier today. I found out from my CO when I spoke to him about you. Apparently, she was in a State Department notice that was circulated through various government agencies."

"Thanks. She was a kind and gentle person, and I don't know why anyone would want to kill her."

"I'm sure the Italians will catch them."

"Yeah," Moretti replied, unconvinced.

After an awkward pause, Cray broke the silence. "As I said, I spoke to my CO. Since what you told me involved the Chinese which, if you'll pardon the expression, always makes him see red, he gave me permission to search our database for Wu Bai. I got a hit."

"What did you find out?"

"Assume that everything I'm about to tell you is top secret. Don't take notes, and don't talk to anyone about this conversation. Are we square?"

"Got it."

"Wu Bai isn't his real name. It's Cai Fu, and he's a major in the Second Department of the People's Liberation Army. That's their intelligence section."

"I knew he wasn't a reporter."

"He sometimes uses Wu Bai as an alias. Homeland Security doesn't know this, which is why he was able to enter the country without our knowledge. That won't happen again. The question is this: Why did you get a visit from a Chinese intelligence operative?"

"I wish I knew."

"We're going to figure that one out together. Here's the interesting part. He's an assassin."

"Since I'm not dead, what does he want from me?"

"That's the question, isn't it? What makes this even more bizarre is that he's assigned to the Chinese consulate in Florence, Italy. Yet he flies halfway around the world, leaving from Venice I might add, to spend less than an hour with you. Why?"

"Are you thinking that he may be involved in Gina's murder?

"It raises the bar on coincidence."

"I agree. You don't send an asset like Cai Fu unless it's important. And as you pointed out, since you're still alive, his mission wasn't to kill you. Why does a killer want to spend such a short amount of time asking you seemingly meaningless questions? Unless it wasn't so meaningless."

"I'm leaving for Venice later today to bring my sister home. Let's discuss this further when I get back."

"Keep in touch while you're there. If I find out anything more, I'll let you know. Write this address and phone number down," Cray said. "It's the US consulate in Venice. They have an STE." He gave him the information, as well as the phone number of the duty officer at Ft. Belvoir, who could get ahold of Cray at any time. "One last thing. We saw Cai Fu's name on a passenger manifest. He's returning to Venice, so you may run into him while you're there. If you do, don't say or do anything stupid."

"How do you guys get this information?"

"Because we're nosy and have ten acres of supercomputers under my feet to intrude on everyone's privacy."

After his call Moretti drove back to his apartment building. He knocked on Allison Davers's door to cancel dinner, but she wasn't home. He didn't have time to wait around until she arrived, and he didn't want to write a note and slip it under the door. That seemed too impersonal. He'd have to remember to call her later. He went to his apartment, packed a carry-on bag, and grabbed his passport. Twenty minutes later he was on his way to the airport.

Moretti's apartment building was the first in a line of four on the street. They were all five stories, rectangular, and white, and they occupied the top of a hill that faced downtown Anchorage. The contractor had apparently decided that, while variety may be the spice of life, replicating the same design saved money. Across the street from his building, two men pulled their rental car to the curb and waited for the right moment. They'd been told their task had to be finished before Moretti returned from work. Although they didn't know exactly when that was, they set their hard stop for leaving the premises at five o'clock, which gave them more than enough time.

Ten minutes after they arrived, a car pulled into the parking entrance. This was exactly what they'd been waiting for. They followed it down the ramp, watching as it stopped beside the parking kiosk. The window on the driver's side slid down, and a woman inserted and removed her access card. When the security gate opened, they followed her into the garage and found a parking space. The two men tried to keep a low profile, which meant that they didn't want anyone to see them. Therefore, they stayed in their rental until the woman stepped out of her car and walked toward the parking elevator sign. She was tall and in her late twenties. She wore a pencil skirt that accentuated her shapely legs, and she had long brunette hair. In her left hand, she carried a plastic grocery bag. Letting three minutes pass, both men left their car. Unfortunately, they didn't know that the developer had purchased the cheapest and therefore the slowest elevator possible. When they went around the wall that blocked a view of the elevator, they saw the woman waiting for the elevator doors to open. They obviously hadn't delayed long enough. The woman briefly looked at them and then entered. What could they do? If they didn't enter behind her, she'd wonder why, which would make their presence even more conspicuous. Each man seemed to have the same thought and followed her inside, keeping their heads lowered as they did. But there was only so much they could conceal, as both were undeniably Asian. The brunette pressed the fifth floor. This put both men into temporary state of confusion. That was exactly where they wanted to go. Finally, one of them leaned forward and pushed the button for the floor below. After a reasonable wait, they'd walk upstairs.

They got off on the fourth floor and waited nearly ten minutes before proceeding to the fifth floor. No one was in the hallway as they made their way to apartment 501, and with no response to either the doorbell or repeated knocking on the door, one of the men removed two slender steel tools from a leather pouch and picked the lock.

The residence had just under a thousand square feet of floor space, which consisted of a living room, kitchen with a small eating area, and bedroom with a connecting bathroom and shower. One man started with the bedroom, while the other relocked the door and went to Moretti's desk, which was in the far corner of the living room and had a Dell computer and detached keyboard on top. Removing a tiny black box from his jacket pocket, he connected its cable to the computer's USB port and then pushed the power switch. While the computer was going through its start-up sequence, he took off his jacket, placed it over the back of the desk chair, and loosened his tie. There was no air flow within the apartment, and it was so hot inside that beads of sweat were beginning to drip down the side of his face and onto his shirt collar. The login screen eventually appeared and then disappeared almost immediately. He now had unrestricted access to the computer. The man disconnected the black box and inserted a flash drive in its place. It took only five minutes to download the data, remove the data stick, and shut off the computer. He was about to go and help his partner when he heard someone knock on the door. He froze, hoping they'd think no one was home. But then there was a second and much harder knock.

"I know you two are in there. Open up," Davers said, "or I'll call the police!"

That got a response. The door opened, and in front of her were the two men she'd seen on the elevator. *What are they doing on the fifth floor and in this apartment?* she thought.

"Can I help you?" one of them said in perfect English.

"What are you doing here?" she asked, entering the apartment before the man could stop her.

"Pardon me?"

"You don't live here. How did you get in?"

"Mr. Moretti left the door open for us," the man answered. "He told us we could crash here before our early morning flight to Seattle."

Davers didn't want to push the issue, and she was starting to rethink the wisdom of barging into an apartment with two strangers. She should have called the police instead. They were clearly lying because she and Moretti were having dinner tonight. What she needed to do was return to her apartment and call the authorities. She was about to do that when she let out an involuntary gasp and her eyes suddenly widened. The man who answered the door turned to see what caused this reaction and saw that the Glock tucked in the small of his partner's back could be seen in the mirror behind him.

"My mistake. I'll leave you two alone then," Davers said as she started to back away.

The man quickly stepped behind her and closed the door.

"I have a better idea," he said.

> The People's Republic of China was born on October 1, 1949, when I declared China to be a country with a single leader. I have defeated and vanquished my enemy, Chiang, who escaped with five hundred thousand of his troops and followers. I want to obliterate him, but the American imperialists' mighty fleet stands between me and what he refers to as the Republic of China. I told the Americans that this is a Chinese matter and that they should not involve themselves with our internal issues. But they don't listen. They see China as militarily insignificant and communism as a threat to their

way of life. Therefore, it was of no surprise that the Americans have refused to force Chiang to return the gold he looted from our national treasury in Shanghai less than a year ago. The theft of our entire reserves has impoverished my country and made us even more reliant on our Soviet comrades until we become strong enough to rid ourselves of all foreign influence.

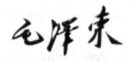

CHAPTER

9

HOMICIDE DETECTIVE JOHN LESTER WAS having a late lunch at the Lucky Wishbone restaurant when his cell phone rang. Unfortunately, his two-hundred-pound, five-foot-ten-inch frame was wedged tightly in a booth, and he was unable to take the phone out of his pocket without first sliding into the aisle and standing up. The other patrons in the restaurant looked at him with annoyance, and his cell continued to ring until he was finally able to put a beefy hand on the answer button. He told the caller to hold while he grabbed a ten-dollar bill out of his pocket, slapped it on the table, and then took one last bite of his half-eaten hamburger before heading for the front door.

"John, are you there?" the voice on his cell phone repeated as Lester tried to swallow the burger and answer at the same time.

"Yeah, I'm here," he finally said, opening the front door of the restaurant and walking toward his car. Twenty years of experience on the force with ten in homicide told him that when his cell phone rang, he wouldn't be finishing his meal.

"We received an anonymous call reporting a homicide at 130 Benson Street, apartment 501," the dispatcher said.

"Are units on the way?"

"Two cruisers are at the scene."

"Tell them not to go in until I arrive. I'll be there in five minutes."

Pulling behind the two patrol cars, he reached under the front seat and removed a plastic bag before joining the four officers who were standing near their vehicles. Each had worked with him in the past and greeted him as he approached. They walked up the short flight of steps that led to the front entrance of the apartment building, and he pressed the button labeled *manager* to the right of the door. A woman with a hoarse, gravelly voice answered, and Lester identified himself and told her why he was there. A metallic click followed, and all five entered the building.

An elderly woman met them in the lobby. Lester asked if she was the manager, and when she nodded, he pulled out his ID and showed it to her. Four uniformed officers standing with him was all the verification she needed, and she barely glanced at his credentials. Since Lester had already told her that he was there to investigate a reported homicide in apartment 501, she brought the master key with her, led them to Moretti's apartment, and unlocked the door. On their way Lester said he was surprised that she was so calm, learning that a homicide had allegedly taken place in her building. The response he received was not what he expected when she said that quite a few elderly couples lived there and that three to four of them died in their residence each year on average. Whether or not this was a homicide, there was still a body.

Before Lester entered the apartment, he noticed that the manager was waiting, the look on her face telling him that she wanted to see what was inside. That was the last thing he needed in an investigation, someone who might blab about what she saw on social media. She'd be a dream witness for a defense attorney, who'd seed the jury with reasonable doubt after asking her a variety of skillful questions on what she'd seen.

"Thank you. We'll take it from here," Lester said in a dismissing tone.

Disappointed, she turned and made her way back to the elevator. When she was out of sight, he opened the plastic bag he'd taken from his car and gave a pair of latex gloves and paper shoe covers to each of the officers before putting on his. Opening the door to the apartment, he immediately saw the body of a young woman a couple of paces in front of him. Two bullet wounds were closely grouped on the left side of her chest, and her hazel eyes were staring blankly at the ceiling. He directed the two officers nearest him to search the apartment, and he told the other two to start knocking on the residents' doors, beginning on the fifth floor and working their way down, asking if anyone in the building saw or heard anything unusual. He then called the dispatcher and requested a medical examiner and forensic identification crew. He'd just put his cell phone back in his pocket when one of the officers asked him to come into the bedroom. There was no need to ask why because there was a suppressed Glock pistol lying on top of the box spring.

General Lin blew a cloud of blue smoke across his desk and put his lighter back in his pocket. It irked him that his country's leadership was so corrupt and focused on capitalism. They'd abandoned their ancestral values and adopted many of the traits and mannerisms of foreigners, particularly those from the West. China had once been the greatest nation on earth when it was ruled by an emperor who held that position for life and answered to no man. He wanted to become that iron ruler. That was his destiny. It was naïve to believe that everyone would agree to return to dynastic China. But with the support of the army, it would happen. The catalyst would be the documents. Although rumors of their existence had been circulating for decades, most equated these stories to sightings of the Loch Ness monster. They wanted to believe it was true, but they knew it probably wasn't. Even he doubted they were real—that is, until a chance encounter with an old and destitute man living in the streets of Beijing changed that.

He remembered walking through Tiananmen Square and seeing an old beggar in the tattered remnants of an army uniform, worn during the time of Chairman Mao. His aides tried to steer him clear, but he resisted and took some money out of his pocket and dropped it into the man's alms bowl. The old one looked up after hearing the clink of metal and noticed the rank of the person standing over him. He said his name was Cheng Fa and that he had a great secret he needed to share with someone in authority. Believing this was just a ploy to get more money, he considered walking away. But the beggar had once been a soldier, and he wanted to do something for him. Therefore, he told his aide to take him to a noodle shop across the square and buy him whatever he wanted, and then he'd join them when his meeting was over. Later when he entered the shop, he saw several empty bowls on the table. Cheng Fa had apparently been very hungry. He was in the process of reaching forward and handing him some money before he left when the beggar grabbed his hand and asked if they could speak privately. His initial inclination was that he'd wasted enough time and had a myriad of things he had to get done before the end of the day. But his curiosity got the better of him, and he told his aide to give them some privacy and direct anyone who wanted to sit near them to other tables. When they were alone, he took two cigarettes from a pack he carried in his jacket pocket, lit both, and handed one to the beggar. He then heard the story that would change his life.

Cheng Fa was recruited into Chairman Mao's army when they passed through his village in 1934. He was seventeen at the time and big for his age, standing a head taller than most. Because of his size, he was assigned as one of the chairman's bodyguards, and he continued to serve him in various capacities until Mao's death in 1976. Since his parents had long since died and he had no known family, he returned to Beijing and spent his days begging for money. The general had heard similar stories, and although it troubled him that men who'd once served their country were now reduced to being indigents, there was nothing he could do about it. He started to get up from the table, and he was taking money from his pocket when the beggar placed a hand on his arm and asked him to stay and hear the rest of his story. Staring him directly in the eye, Cheng Fa was unflinching and held his gaze. After a long interlude and for reasons he probably still couldn't explain, he sat back down.

Two years before he died, Mao went on a secret trip. None of his staff—except for an aide who accompanied him—knew the destination or the purpose of this journey. The fact that the chairman was so infirmed at the time told him that what he was doing must have been extremely important and that he didn't want anyone in the party or the government to know about it. Mao was gone for only a short time, but when he returned, he informed his staff that Premier Chou En-Lai would arrive that evening. In preparation, he ordered Cheng Fa to polish the floor in his study. He'd done this often, and he knew it would take several hours to bring the aged wood to the high shine the chairman expected. Three hours later, all that remained was to polish the crawl space under the desktop. He got to his knees and started rubbing the wax onto the wood when his rag suddenly snagged. Loosening it from a tiny splinter, he noticed that this floorboard was jagged along its edge and that there was an almost invisible gap behind it. He removed a folding knife from his pocket and placed the blade into the gap, eventually prying away two floorboards. Beneath them was a hidden chamber that concealed a rectangular leather box. Unable to control himself, knowing that he was unlikely to be disturbed for some time because the chairman was taking a nap in preparation for his meeting, he lifted the box from its hiding space. Inside was a stack of papers, most of which appeared to be written in the chairman's hand. Glancing quickly through them, the first few seemed unremarkable. But as he approached the end, his hands began to shake. If either the chairman or his aide knew of this intrusion, he didn't know whether they'd kill him or trust that he'd keep quiet. But he didn't intend to find out. He returned the box to its hiding place, quickly polished the small square of floor, and left the study.

The beggar gave him a summary of what he'd read. At first, he believed Cheng Fa was lying. But what cast doubt on that assumption was the fact that some of what he'd heard was only known to higher-ranking military officers and government officials. And if this was true, perhaps the remainder of his story was as well.

He summoned his aide, telling him to take Cheng Fa to a nearby barracks, get him cleaned up, and make sure he had a bed for the night. During this time, the beggar was to be isolated, and he would speak to no one. The aide acknowledged his orders and left with the old man.

When he returned to his office, he had his staff search for Cheng Fa's Army records, but they couldn't be located. That wasn't surprising. During that era the army was more concerned with survival than with paperwork. Recalling the last part of their conversation, he thought of a way to indirectly verify what he'd been told. Speaking to the army commander at the PLA guard station outside Mao's former home in Shaoshan, which was now a museum, he told the lieutenant colonel what he needed. A short time later, a return call confirmed that Mao did have a secret compartment under the floor beneath his desktop. Even the commander, who had been stationed there for several years, didn't know about this hiding place until today. Now that he knew what Cheng Fa had said was probably true, he had to make sure no one else found out. Calling his aide, he directed him to kill the beggar and get rid of the body. A moment later there was a single gunshot.

Twenty years passed, and despite his nearly constant efforts to find the documents, he'd never had a single clue as to their whereabouts. Until now.

> It is the summer of 1953, and the war in Korea has been raging for three years. This takes its toll on my country and moves us deeper into poverty. I must find a way to end this struggle in a way that does not make me appear weak to my enemies. This carnage is the fault of American imperialists who took Korea from the Japanese and then stupidly divided it in half as if they could so easily divide a culture. The Americans understand nothing. They believe that the People's Republic of China is a threat to their national security, and they have

correspondingly placed their military forces in both Korea and Taiwan in order to hold a knife to my throat. This is an act of aggression. In the early days of the war, I agreed to supply North Korea with its necessities. I had no choice. The Allies under General MacArthur, who protects my enemy Chiang in Taiwan, captured most of North Korea and would soon be at my border. The Americans would like nothing better than to rid themselves of me and raise their imperialistic flag over my country's capital. Therefore, in the winter of 1950, I ordered my forces to attack them, knowing that MacArthur's forces would be severely disadvantaged by the harshness of the weather. My Ninth Army infiltrated North Korea and surprised them at the Chosin Reservoir. We targeted their drivers and trucks so that they couldn't easily escape. Anyone who wanted to survive had to go south on foot.

President Eisenhower became so angry with my support of North Korea, that he hinted that he might use nuclear weapons against my troops. I do not believe he will, but many in the military disagree. The Americans also torment me by continuing to allow Chiang to make raids on my country. Although these are of little military consequence, they've made me look impotent. The only way to counter this was to end this war in a favorable manner and get the Americans to control Chiang. Any other outcome, and I'd lose face. Therefore, I sent word to the American president that he has my support in ending this bloodshed. Thankfully, he was as anxious as me. On July 27, an armistice was signed, and a new border divides Korea. My people consider this to be acceptable, although it wasn't the military victory they'd hoped for.

Destitute from years of war, I must now face the many severe challenges to the survival of the People's Republic of China. The imperialist nations know this and act as sharks circling their prey. I desperately need a champion who will help our economy and breathe life into my nation's hollow core. In the past, that was Comrade Stalin, but no more. It's been nearly five months since his death, and our relationship with the Soviets dissipates more with each passing day. I've been told that Comrade Khrushchev will succeed him, but I don't know much about this man. I only know that I need the help of the Soviet Union now more than ever.

I vow that one day I will unify my country so that our survival is no longer dependent on the scraps we receive from foreigners, and that our military will be the equal or the juggernaut to both our friends and our enemies.

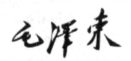

CHAPTER

10

AFTER THE MANAGER IDENTIFIED ALLISON Davers as the victim and pointed out her apartment, Lester and one of the forensic techs went across the hall to begin their search. During this time Todd Travers, his longtime partner, arrived and was asked to escort the manager downstairs and get anything from her that might be helpful to their investigation.

Davers kept her apartment extraordinarily neat. Not a speck of dust could be found anywhere. The cans in her cupboard were perfectly stacked so that the labels faced forward, and the items inside the refrigerator were similarly obsessive-compulsively arranged. Lester had never seen anything like it. Therefore, it came as a surprise when he saw a plastic bag containing groceries on her kitchen counter. The fact that a person with her personality hadn't put them away, especially since half the bag had perishable food, told him she must have seen or heard something that diverted her attention just after she entered the apartment. Whatever it was, it immediately caused her to go across the hall. That's when Moretti killed her, at least according to the prevailing logic. After all, a dead body and probably the murder weapon were in his residence. But it somehow seemed too simple. It was as if someone put a spotlight on him and said, "Here's your killer. Stop looking." Twenty years on the force had taught him that getting to the truth was usually far more complex. The problem he had was the anonymous caller. There was no way they could know about the murder unless they were in the apartment. The medical examiner told him that Davers was killed exactly where she fell. She wasn't murdered somewhere else and moved to Moretti's residence. Furthermore, the building sat on a hill, making it impossible for someone standing outside to look into the apartment and see the murder.

Lester spent the next hour searching the apartment. He'd just finished, and he was leaning against the kitchen counter when Travers returned and handed him several sheets of paper.

"What's this?"

"A list of everyone who inserted their key card into the parking garage kiosk from six o'clock this morning through just a few minutes ago. It shows Moretti entered the garage an hour before Davers."

"Then we can prove he was in the building at the approximate time of her death."

"Not really. The parking system doesn't require residents to use their card to exit the garage. An electric eye automatically slides the barrier aside when it senses an approaching vehicle."

"What about the building's security cameras? I saw one above the front entrance."

"There's only two. The one you saw and the other in the parking garage elevator. I've reviewed the recordings from both," he said, holding up two DVDs. "The elevator camera shows Moretti leaving with a carry-on bag before Davers arrives home."

"But we don't know for sure if he left the premises."

"No. It's possible to take the elevator to the parking garage and then use the interior stairway to get to a particular floor. To complicate matters, the manager explained that the data from the parking garage kiosk is never accurate. There's a pressure pad preventing the access gate from striking a car. The residents and apparently more than a few visitors know this. Therefore, there's often one or more cars behind the person inserting their key card. I looked at the kiosk. It's old, and any pro would know how to get around it. But I haven't gotten to the good part."

"Which is?"

"Two Asian men followed Davers into the garage elevator. They get off on four, while she goes to five. It turns out they're the only three who entered the building for the next thirty-four minutes."

"I'm guessing the ME will tell us that she was killed during this time. Did you ask the manager if she knew the Asians?"

"She has no idea who they are. She's been here since the building first opened and prides herself on knowing every tenant. Oh, and both men left thirty minutes after they arrived."

"Let's run their photos and see what we get. Then we'll try to get their prints off the elevator buttons. We know they touched the 4 and P buttons, although there are probably so many people who've put their fingers on those buttons that I'm not expecting much."

"Just know that both men kept their heads down and away from the elevator camera. All we have is a side view."

"They're beginning to sound like pros. See if you can get the manager to print out their photo from the surveillance camera and give it to the officers going door to door. Even though we only have a partial view of their faces, someone may recognize them. Get one of our computer techs to try to reconstruct a head shot. Those geeks can do almost anything. We'll then input what we have into the facial recognition program."

"I'm on it," Travers said as he left the room.

Lester took a seat on one of the barstools behind the kitchen counter. What were the two Asians doing in the building? Were they visiting someone, or did they have something to do with Davers's death? He was running his hands across his crew-cut salt-and-pepper hair when he noticed a forensic technician walking past him with an iPhone in a sealed plastic bag and a chain of custody document in the same hand.

"Hold on a second. Let me have the iPhone," Lester said, taking the chain of custody document from his hand, signing it, and handing it back. He grabbed the plastic bag and went across the hall to Moretti's apartment, where Davers's body was still waiting to be transported to the morgue. Putting on a pair of latex gloves, he unzipped the body bag, removed the iPhone from the evidence bag, saw that it was already on, and pressed Davers's right index finger to the round fingerprint ID button. A moment later, the home screen appeared.

"Let's see what we have," he said to himself after placing her hand back in the body bag and zipping it back up. He started with the activity log, looking for calls made and received in the past two days. Each item was a name instead of a phone number, meaning that every call she made or received during that time was from someone on her contact list, and Moretti was not one of them. Moving on to her most recent emails and messages, he also found nothing that stood out. When he went to check her photo album, he was surprised to see that it mostly contained videos. He wouldn't have time to review them all now, but he could look at a couple of the most recent ones. The first one he selected was ten seconds in length, and it showed Matthew Moretti going down the hall toward the elevator, at least he believed it was him since the man came out of Moretti's apartment. He could tell the video was made by pressing the iPhone's camera lens to the peephole in the door. Even so, the picture quality was remarkably good. The next video was of a couple arguing as they passed her apartment. He couldn't hear what they were saying, but their facial expressions and hand waving indicated they were having a major disagreement. Lester guessed that Davers loved spying on people and that the remainder of the video library was more of the same. He next pressed the camera icon to look at what didn't yet make it to the album. Her most recent video was by far the most interesting.

Mark Kincaid, deputy chief of the Anchorage Police Department, was watching the video on Davers's iPhone for the second time. When it finished, he picked up Lester's preliminary report, turned to the last page, and reread it.

"What you're going to be telling me and the rest of the

department is that two unidentified Asians are the primary suspects in Davers's murder?"

"I believe so. I can't prove it yet, but that's what my gut tells me. All I know for certain is that the murderer wasn't Moretti, although it's possible he could have been involved. As I indicated, a parking lot camera at the airport recorded his car arriving at 4:11 p.m., his face clearly visible in the shot, nine minutes after Davers entered her apartment elevator."

"He could have had someone else kill her."

"Hire a killer? There's no insurance policy. They're not married, and they haven't bought so much as a coffeepot together. I don't see it."

"But one of the Asians is the murderer."

"The ME estimates Davers's time of death as somewhere between 4:00 and 5:00 p.m. That's consistent with the building's video monitor, which shows them entering the garage elevator on the fifth floor at 4:45 p.m. They arrived on four and left from five. Why?"

"Because they're going to Moretti's apartment, which happens to be on five?"

"Exactly. And they can't get off there because Davers might start asking them questions, such as who they're going to see."

"That's what I'm thinking." Lester wished he'd brought a cup of coffee with him. He could have used the caffeine right about now. Three hours of sleep wasn't getting him very far. His thoughts returned to the present when he heard Kincaid asking him a question.

"And we weren't able to get prints off the elevator buttons?"

"None that's usable."

"What about in the apartment?"

"Moretti and Davers. No one else. There's also no prints on the Glock, even though ballistics confirmed it as being the murder weapon."

"When will you speak with Moretti?"

"His flight landed in Venice, and I've left a message on his cell.

I also gave his father my name and number and asked him to pass it to him the next time they speak."

"What about getting the Venice police to help?"

"I'm not so sure. I need Moretti cooperative and not defensive."

"It's a strange coincidence that his sister is murdered and that his neighbor is too a couple of days later. The one common denominator seems to be Matthew Moretti."

"And we don't know why that's proved lethal to both."

"Find out."

It is October 16, 1964. It's been eleven years since the death of Comrade Stalin and nearly as long since I made my last entry. I have no excuse for this lapse except that my duties consume every waking hour of my day, exhausting me to the point where I tell myself I will write about these events at some future date. But today I'm energized, and I will briefly summarize what's occurred before I get to the joyful occurrence that caused me to put pen to paper again.

Comrade Khrushchev has not proved to be the friend to China that I expected. He wants us to abandon our claims against Taiwan and become more conciliatory toward the imperialist warmongers in the United States. I can only believe the reason for this is to curry favor with the West at the expense of my country. He has no diplomatic skills. His rhetoric is offensive, and he speaks to everyone in a condescending tone. I detest the man. In 1961, on the second day of my visit to the Soviet Union, he lectured me on the mistakes I made in the Great Leap Forward. My goal was sound in wanting to transform my country from a nation of farmers to an industrialized society. Otherwise, we will never take our rightful place alongside other great nations. Comrade Khrushchev does not understand that transformations can be painful and require sacrifice. People will die, and people will live; however, our country will eventually become stronger.

Three decades ago Soviet agriculture was collectivized. I have more recently done the same, reflecting my belief that we are a communal society where everything is shared and nothing is private. Yet Mr. Khrushchev now wants me to abandon the ideals of communism and adopt the policies of the West in providing material incentives for those who are deemed more productive in our society. I believe the fact that I refuse makes him afraid that the purity of Chinese ideals will spread to other nations under his control and undermine his authority. My country is surrounded by our enemies—Korea, Japan, Taiwan, and now the Soviet Union. All have a knife at our throat. The only way to survive is to be strong.

In my Twelve-Year Science Plan, following the death of Comrade Stalin, I directed our technicians to develop nuclear weapons. Comrade Khrushchev initially agreed to give me a sample atomic bomb, a facility to help enrich the uranium, and all the technical data I needed to build nuclear weapons to protect my country from the imperialists. But with Comrade Khrushchev, a promise is like a leaf that changes direction with the slightest breath of wind, and he withdrew all technical advisers from our country without fulfilling his promises. I had no doubt that this withdrawal was to appease the West. But I surprised him. We acquired sufficient knowledge to develop our own nuclear bomb, and on this day, October 16, 1964, we showed him our strength. Let him now begin to fear us. We are no longer a son of the Soviets and a stepchild of the world. Today we have become equal to the father.

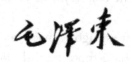

CHAPTER

It took Moretti nearly a day to get to the Venice's Marco Polo Airport. With only a carry-on bag, he quickly passed through customs and immigration and entered the main terminal. From there he followed the signs to the water taxi, which eventually took him outside and down a long covered walkway that sloped to the lagoon. Each of the waiting craft was constructed of mahogany and was approximately thirty feet in length and a little more than seven feet wide with an enclosed cabin on the aft part of its deck. Stepping onto the dock, he walked onto one of the boats, gave the driver his destination, and went into the cabin. Once he was seated, the taxi slowly backed into the lagoon.

Following him was a stunning five-foot-eleven Asian woman in her late twenties. She had porcelain skin, an athletic build, long brunette hair, and brilliant black opal-colored eyes. Han Li watched as Moretti's boat picked up speed and began distancing itself from the airport before proceeding to the adjoining water taxi. Boarding, she told the driver to follow the boat that just left. Forty minutes later, as his craft pulled aside the dock at the Hotel Bauer Il Palazzo and tied up, she asked to be taken to the Gritti Palace Hotel, which was farther up the Grand Canal. There she stepped onto the dock and strolled through the meandering streets to the Bauer, giving Moretti time to register and go to his room before she arrived.

When she walked through the revolving door, the lobby was empty. Finding a room didn't turn out to be an issue because, as the desk clerk told her, budget-conscious travelers didn't tend to stay at hotels in this price range. Looking at the rate she—or more correctly, the Chinese government—was paying, it was understandable why.

Her room on the fourth-floor proved to be lavish beyond all expectations. But in her opinion, the most spectacular feature was the view. She threw open the two French doors that led onto the balcony and gazed across the Grand Canal to the seventeenth-century Basilica di Santa della Salute, or La Salute as it's referred to by locals. Constructed from Istrian stone and brick covered with marble dust, the massive octagonal basilica had two domes and a pair of bell towers that rested on a platform of more than a million wooden piles. She would have liked to spend more time gazing at the city, but there was a lot she still needed to accomplish. Going back inside, she didn't bother to change. Instead she went down to the hotel lobby and sat at a table in an adjoining sitting room. This gave her an unobstructed view of the elevator, the outside entrances, and the exits. She'd been seated for only a few minutes when she saw Moretti get off the elevator and approach a well-dressed man standing near the revolving door leading to the Campo San Moise. They shook hands and exchanged a few words, after which the man handed Moretti a business card and pointed to a table not far from where she was sitting. They spent the next hour talking. Ordering a hot tea and taking a hotel pamphlet off the table and pretending to read it, she tried to observe them while appearing to be unobtrusive.

When their conversation ended, each went their separate way, with Moretti going directly to the hotel elevator. As the doors closed, Han Li looked at the digital indicator, which told her the floor the elevator was currently on. When it stopped at two, she dashed up the adjacent stairs, taking them two at a time, reaching the second floor just as Moretti entered a room halfway down the hall on the right. Visually locking on it, she walked toward his room, eventually discovering that he was in 204. She turned around and went back downstairs, preparing herself for what she'd have to do next.

At seven o'clock that evening, she was sitting in the same chair at the same table off the lobby when Moretti got off the elevator. She watched with some trepidation as he made a beeline straight toward her table and took a seat directly across from her.

"I feel introductions are in order," he said. "My name is Matt Moretti."

"Han Li," she replied in a voice that sounded as if it came from the lips of Angelina Jolie. She kept her face expressionless. In her original plan, he'd notice her sitting by herself and come over and speak with her or at least make eye contact. That would make him less suspicious than if she was the aggressor. But as time was short and she only had today to enlist his help, the outcome was all that was important. Tomorrow he'd be on his way back to the United States with his sister's remains, and everything she had to accomplish would either become harder or impossible.

"Why would a beautiful woman like you want to follow me?"

That was not the response she expected.

"How did you know I was following you?"

"A tall and attractive Asian lady is hard to miss. You were outside the entrance to the main terminal as I walked to the water taxi. I thought you might be waiting for someone. But as I was leaving the dock and looked through my cabin window, I saw you get into a boat by yourself. I was curious as to why you didn't take a taxi sooner. Later I saw you in the lobby. Again, by yourself. I thought you were waiting for someone since you rejected the advances of several men. But that assumption became doubtful when I finished my meeting and saw that you were still alone. No man in his right mind would keep a gorgeous woman like you waiting. He'd call, send a boat, or have you join him somewhere else. That's when I suspected you were tailing me. When I returned to my room I left my door open a crack, to see if I was being paranoid. You walked right past it, noted the number, and then turned around. The only way you could have been in the hallway that quickly was if you sprinted up the stairs. If you were staying on my floor, you would have gone to your room."

"You're very observant. And now you want me to tell you why I'm following you and exactly what I want."

"You can answer those questions at dinner. Should we say eight o'clock on the deck at De Pisis?"

"Eight o'clock."

Cray was sitting at his desk in one of the micro offices assigned to an officer at Fort Belvoir with the lowly rank of major when someone opened his door without first knocking. He was about to give that person hell when he looked up and saw two stars on the shoulders of the man standing in front of him. He snapped to attention.

"At ease," Major General Thomas Scharlau, commander of the US Army Intelligence and Security Command, said as he took a seat in the gray steel chair in front of Cray's desk.

Scharlau was not known for exchanging pleasantries before getting down to business. His management style was *my way or the highway,* and he'd sent more than a few officers down that road in the thirty years he wore the uniform. At six feet ten inches, the former University of Illinois basketball player towered over those around him.

"Have you heard from Moretti?" he asked, looking at Cray with steely gray eyes that seemed to pierce right through him.

"Not yet, sir. I left a couple of messages on his cell, but he hasn't returned my call."

"We need an invitation to the party, Major, and your friend is the only one who can get it for us. The Chinese are up to something, and whatever it is, I want to know. Moretti's sister is murdered in Venice, which is only a two-hour train ride from the Chinese consulate in Florence, and one of their intelligence officers, who's also an assassin, flies halfway around the world to see her brother. I don't believe in coincidences. Do you, Major?"

"No sir," he answered. *Even if I did, I wouldn't say so.*

"I don't either. It'd take a Methodist to believe this was. Something big is going down, and I don't want my Johnson slammed in the door from being the last to find out. Your friend is going to be my bait to catch the Chinese at whatever they're up to. Did you run the photos of the two Asians you received from the FBI?"

Cray knew he meant the photos the FBI received from the Anchorage PD, requesting their help in identifying the images taken from both an elevator and iPhone camera. Earlier, he'd flagged Moretti's name. If it appeared in any local, state, or federal computer system, that data would be surreptitiously forwarded to him. Neither the FBI nor the Anchorage PD knew he had their photos, and they probably never would.

"Yes, sir. We're still running them through our system."

"Good. While you're at it, call the Sixty-Sixth Military Intelligence Brigade in Wiesbaden, Germany, and have them dispatch someone to Venice. Let's see if they can find out what Cai Fu was doing there and if he had any involvement in the death of Gina Moretti."

"Yes, sir."

"Until I say differently, you're on this full time."

He was going to point out that Gina Moretti's death was a civilian matter and that Matthew Moretti, while formerly a military officer, was now a civilian. If any US government agency was to investigate, it'd be the FBI and not the Sixty-Sixth. But he wasn't about to tell that to a two-star general. If he did, his next intelligence assignment would likely require a parka and a set of snowshoes.

"Yes sir," Cray said as an automatic response to whatever the general said.

"And make sure you get in touch with Moretti. You know what eventually happens to bait?"

"Yes, sir." *The bait always dies*, Cray wanted to reply. But they were talking about his friend, and he couldn't bring himself to say it.

"It gets eaten, and I want to find out what he knows before the Chinese start munching on him. Let me know when you contact Moretti."

Han Li walked onto the outdoor deck of the De Pisis restaurant and saw Moretti sitting at a table for two overlooking the Grand Canal. She was dressed in an Asian-style black dress with a slit up the left side to nearly the middle of her thigh. It clung to her athletic frame, and exposed one of her long and shapely legs. More than a few men's heads turned as she passed by, and more than a few wives were now making their husband's lives difficult.

As she approached the table, Moretti stood and pulled out her chair so she could be seated. He was wearing a dark blue blazer, tan slacks, and a white open-collared dress shirt. In front of him was an empty drink glass containing a few lingering drops of scotch.

"You look stunning," he said as she sat down.

There was an open bottle of Prosecco in an ice bucket to the side of the table. When one of the waiters saw Han Li take her seat, he poured two flutes of the sparkling wine and left. She and Moretti silently looked across the table at each other. He already knew from his conversation with Cray that Cai Fu was a Chinese agent and assassin. He was willing to bet that the beautiful brunette sitting across from him was also one. What he wanted to know was what she was after and if either she or Cai Fu had been involved in the death of his sister. But before he got a chance to ask, the first question came from Han Li.

"How did you select this hotel? It's beautiful."

"I didn't pick it. The US consulate reserved a room for me here. That's who I met with earlier today."

"Pricey for a government worker."

"I'm not paying for the room That's being taken care of by the government. Not to change the subject, but I'm guessing you're not a tourist."

"I work for the Chinese government, and I was sent to Venice to enlist your help," she responded without breaking eye contact.

"Why would you need my help?" Moretti said, surprised at her directness.

Han Li took a sip of Prosecco. "To recover Chairman Mao's

personal diary, a set of documents that was stolen in the midseventies by Chang Hao, who eventually smuggled them into Venice. It seems that he bequeathed them to the Marciana Library upon his death."

Moretti saw the waiter approach to take their order and then waved him away. This was starting to get interesting.

"Why don't you ask the Italians to return the diary, documents, or whatever you call them? That should be simple enough."

"My government never publicized their existence. If they did, the people would want to see them. That must never happen."

"Why?" Moretti asked, finding it hard to believe that such a seemingly important historical document from their nation's founder was being treated as toxic.

"It would prove very distressing to my country's leadership."

"How distressing?"

"Catastrophically so. Do you know what our people want?"

Moretti shook his head.

"A government they believe acts in their best interest. This gives them faith in our leadership."

"By that you mean the president of China?"

"The Chinese Communist Party," Han Li corrected. "The documents comprising Mao's diary would destroy their trust in the party."

"Which makes it even more confusing as to why you need my help."

"Your sister was a respected employee of the Marciana and, as far as we know, the last person to have the documents in her possession. She emailed a scanned copy to a friend in China, who agreed to translate them. Shortly thereafter, both your sister and her friend were killed."

Moretti was speechless by what he'd just heard, and then he was angry. He didn't know if he should believe her or if he was being manipulated. Trying to suppress his anger, he leaned forward on his elbows and locked his eyes onto hers. "I have a few questions before we go any further. To begin with, who do you work for in the Chinese government?"

"Let's just say I work for my government and leave it at that."

"Try harder."

Han Li seemed to think for a moment before responding. "I work exclusively for a senior government official."

"Try harder."

"I'm an agent who's sent to do things my government wants to keep secret."

"You just told me that releasing these documents would be catastrophic. That sounds like a motive for murder."

"My government didn't kill your sister."

"Prove it."

"We didn't know that the documents were in Venice until we learned that the most senior general in the People's Liberation Army had a copy of them and was seeking the originals. That was after your sister was murdered."

"The party is omnipotent in China. Why can't you arrest this officer, force him to talk, and then look for them yourself?"

"He has too much influence. Besides, we don't know how many others know of their existence. If we get the originals, we can claim that all copies are forgeries."

"If I understand correctly, Cai Fu works for this general, and you're both in competition to find the originals. If you get to them first, the documents won't see the light of day. And if he gets to them before you and gives them to this military officer, what happens?"

"The general will show them to the people and there will be a revolution, peaceful or otherwise, that will sweep him into power. He'll be the reformer and the Chairman Mao of the twenty-first century."

"I don't see it."

"Believe it. The person I report to knows the inner workings of my government better than anyone. This is his scenario."

"No offense, but I really don't care about what happens in China.

All I want from you is the identity of the person who killed my sister. Do you know that name with absolute certainty?"

"Cai Fu."

Moretti had a sinking feeling in the pit of his stomach when he realized that a little more than a day ago, he'd sat across from the person who'd killed his sister. He downed the glass of Prosecco in front of him and then took the bottle out of the ice bucket and refilled it.

"Why do you need my help?"

"To get the documents back."

"How? I don't even know what they look like."

"But you can get me a meeting with the library's curator. I believe they're still in the Marciana."

"I don't know him."

"But the fact that your sister was a respected employee of the Marciana would almost guarantee that he'd take a meeting with us."

"Then what?"

"Just get me in front of him. That's all you need to do."

"There's two problems. Tomorrow morning I'm going to the US consulate to sign the forms necessary to release my sister's body. After that, I'm accompanying her remains to the airport. You'll have to find someone else."

"There's only you."

"Then you have a problem," Moretti said, drinking what was in his flute and then pouring himself the last of the Prosecco.

"What if I tell you that Cai Fu is here and that I'll help you find and kill him if you work with me?"

Moretti's expression turned hard. His jaw tightened, his eyes slightly narrowed, and he straightened in his chair.

"How do you know he's here?"

"He wants the documents just as much as I do. Where else would he be?"

"That's not an answer."

"The same way we knew your flight number and arrival time in

Venice. We constantly access the passenger lists for both international and domestic airlines and compare those names against individuals and their aliases that we've flagged. That's how we knew he went to see you in Alaska with his alias, Wu Bai, and that he returned to Venice."

"He's not leaving this city alive."

"And how are you going to kill him? He's a trained killer who will be well armed."

Moretti didn't say anything. He just stared in the distance. He realized she was right. He didn't have the resources to find him, especially in a city the size of Venice. Not to mention that without a weapon, he had little chance of surviving the encounter. Han Li was a government agent with all the resources that entailed. She could help find him and supply whatever weaponry was required. With no other options, he shook his head in acceptance. "Now tell me how we find him?"

"That's easy. You don't have to. He'll find you."

He was about to ask her to explain, but he decided to defer the question. Having eaten only airline food for the past day, he was famished. He signaled the waiter to come to their table, and without any idea about what he wanted, he asked that the server select their courses and the wine.

The waiter excused himself and returned several minutes later with a 2005 Collio Rosso Riserva from the Colmello di Grotta vineyard of the hotel's owner, Francesca Bortolotto Possati. He opened the bottle and poured a small amount for Moretti, who found it to be better than any wine he'd tasted before. When he nodded his appreciation, the waiter poured a glass for Han Li and then did the same for Moretti.

The first course of tartare of Piedmont beef soon arrived, and both of them eagerly devoured the food in silence. When the dishes were cleared and the waiter refilled their wineglasses and left, Moretti spoke. "How can you be so sure that Cai Fu will come after me?"

"Because he doesn't leave loose ends. He's an assassin. When he finds out we're working together—and he will—he'll want to kill both of us."

"Then why do I need you if he'll come to me?"

"To survive. What are you going to do when he finds you? Because you're not going to see him first. You're dealing with a professional assassin. Even with a weapon, the odds of you killing him would be less than even."

Moretti didn't respond.

"I said I'd help you kill him in return for working with me."

"And Cai Fu is in Venice?"

"I'm sure he believes there's two links to the documents—you and the Marciana. Both are here."

"I need a weapon. Do you have access to a gun and a knife?"

"I have both on me."

Moretti looked at her questionably. Examining the skin-tight fit of her dress, it was hard to imagine where she was hiding them.

"I'll need them."

The waiter arrived a few seconds later with their main course—grilled rib of beef with vegetables seasoned in olive oil, garlic, and chili pepper. When they'd finished, the waiter cleared their dishes, leaving them to enjoy the remainder of their wine.

"I'll go to the US consulate tomorrow and sign the forms. After that, we'll visit the curator."

She told him that worked.

They decided to pass on dessert and coffee, and Moretti signaled the waiter for the check. When it came, he looked at the total in disbelief.

"I think this one's on your employer," he said, pushing the bill to her. "This restaurant is a little out of my price range."

Directly across the Grand Canal, a rail-thin Asian man in his midtwenties photographed the dinner meeting. To the casual observer, he appeared to be a tourist taking pictures of Venice's nightlife. He carried a Leica S Medium Format DSLR camera and a zoom lens with 37.5-megapixel resolution. This made his images of Moretti and Han Li extraordinarily clear. And with the Leica's internet capability, he could simultaneously send his photographs to both General Lin and Cai Fu. When he received an email confirmation that the pictures he'd taken had been received and no further images were required, he put his camera inside the shoulder bag and left.

CHAPTER

12

MORETTI LEFT HIS CELL PHONE in his room while at dinner, and upon returning, he saw he'd missed a call from his father, an unknown Anchorage number, and Doug Cray. Each left a message. However, he couldn't remember how to retrieve his voice mail from a foreign country, and therefore, he decided to return the calls in the order received and find out what each had to say.

His father started the conversation by saying that he'd been visited by detective John Lester, who was investigating the death of a woman in his apartment. The junior Moretti had difficulty believing what he'd heard and wondered if he'd had too much to drink, which seemed a rhetorical question since he was an alcoholic. He thought he now knew the identity of the unknown caller.

"This has to be a mistake."

"The detective showed me a photo of the body and asked if I recognized her. But I didn't."

"And he believes I'm the killer?"

"I wouldn't say that. He said he has a photo of you entering the airport parking lot at the approximate time of the murder. But he still wants to question you."

"The woman who was killed, did he give you her name?"

The answer he received caused his knees to buckle, and he grabbed the edge of the desk to steady himself. He immediately thought of Cai Fu. If what Han Li told him was correct, he killed Gina, and there was little doubt that he'd also murdered

Allison. When an assassin flies five thousand miles for a phony interview and several hours later someone is murdered, that's not a coincidence. The reasons for each death were still unclear, but if Han Li was to be believed, it probably involved the mysterious documents. Although Allison wouldn't have known about them, her relationship with him somehow contributed to her death. However, he couldn't discount a second possibility, which was that Han Li was manipulating him and was the puppeteer for both deaths. Each assassin had their agenda, which apparently involved getting to the documents first.

Moretti spoke with his father a while longer, and after the conversation ended, he decided to call the unknown number that appeared on his phone. As he thought, it belonged to the Anchorage detective. Lester began by extending his condolences and then told Moretti their conversation was being recorded. For his first question, Lester inquired when he'd be returning to the United States. In response he was told that he'd sign the necessary forms at the consulate tomorrow and then escort his sister's remains back to the United States shortly thereafter. If Lester seemed surprised at the delay in returning to the United States, he gave no indication. Instead he said that he'd like him to come to police headquarters as soon as possible after his return. The detective then asked several questions to solidify his whereabouts at the time of the murder. Moretti thought that everything was going exceptionally well and that their conversation would end after only a few more questions. Then Lester asked if he owned a handgun, specifically the suppressed Glock that was found under his mattress. This caught him by surprise, and he was literally at a loss for words. When he finally spoke, his response seemed like a cliché, telling the detective that the gun wasn't his. Lester chuckled, and in a tone that said, "I'm not buying it," he said he'd never heard that before. Moretti knew he was in much more trouble than he originally thought. In speaking with Lester, he naively believed that because he was at the airport at the time of the murder, he was no longer a suspect. Now he realized that wasn't true. The detective wanted to see if he was involved, even if he didn't pull the trigger.

Walking across the room while he was talking, he went back to the minibar and grabbed whatever miniatures were in front of him. In this case, it was Jack Daniels. He poured four bottles into his glass and downed a third of it before he built up the courage to ask if he was going to be arrested and extradited back to the United States. Becoming increasingly paranoid, he fully expected the Venetian police to barge into his hotel room and take him away. He was in the process of downing another third of the liquid when Lester told him that he was officially considered a person of interest, meaning that he was part of a criminal investigation but not formally accused of a crime. He asked for Moretti's hotel name and room number. Then he ended their call by telling him not to fly anywhere other than the United States, or he'd issue an order for his arrest.

Cray was not in a good mood. He had Scharlau chewing one side of his ass and the commanding officer of the Sixty-Sixth on the other. Each wanted data he didn't have. Only Moretti, who he'd spoken to briefly after his arrival in Venice, could give him the information he needed. He rubbed his bloodshot eyes and ran his hands over his weary face. Having not eaten all day, his energy level was low, and he needed to get something besides coffee into his stomach. He decided to go the cafeteria on the ground floor and bring something back to his office because it didn't look like he'd be going home anytime soon. He'd just gotten up from his desk when his phone rang. Looking at the caller ID, he saw it was Moretti.

During their conversation Moretti detailed his dinner conversation with Han Li, as well as that with Lester. Cray never heard of Mao's diary, but it seemed to explain a great deal about what was happening. After hanging up, he went to see Scharlau. What he hadn't told Moretti was that an hour ago he received the results of a photo recognition search on the two Asians who broke into his apartment. Both were Chinese diplomats assigned to the

San Francisco consulate, and they were likely Allison Davers's killers. He hadn't told Moretti because he wanted to keep this information within their command until they knew who was ultimately behind the killings. With this and the information Moretti provided, the pieces of the puzzle were gradually coming together. He just hoped his friend would still be alive when they finally put the last one in place.

General Lin looked at the photos he'd received from Venice, and hoped the person with Moretti wasn't the person he expected it to be. Since everyone over the age of sixteen had a resident identity card, he'd send her picture to the Second Department's facial recognition section to see if they could give him a name. But if his assumption was correct, this person's image and everything about her would have been deleted long ago. She was a legend within the intelligence community. She was simply referred to as *hei guafu*, meaning black widow. Some said she didn't exist, but he knew better. The previous general secretary had told him about her, but he had refused to give specifics. He didn't know who she worked for within the government or what she looked like. If he couldn't find the image in front of him within the database, he'd have to assume it was her. With something as important as the future leadership of China at stake, who else could it be? He didn't scare easily, but he was a realist. If hei guafu was in Venice, the government knew the documents were there and possibly where they were hidden. He took his cell phone from his pocket and dialed Cai Fu.

Han Li heard the knock at the front door, took the gun off her nightstand, and placed it in the pocket of the hotel robe she was wearing. Looking through the peephole, she saw Moretti and opened the door.

"Lost?"

He ignored her remark and walked past her into the room. "I just spoke to the Anchorage police. They found my neighbor's body in my apartment, and the killer conveniently left the murder weapon behind."

Han Li was surprised, but she didn't let her expression show it. "And the police believe you're the killer?"

"Fortunately, no. They have a photo of me at the airport at the time she was murdered. But they're not convinced I wasn't somehow involved."

Moretti took a seat on the straight-backed chair next to the desk, while Han Li remained standing.

"She must have been in the wrong place at the wrong time."

"Meaning?"

"The killer may have been searching your apartment for the documents, and she either saw or confronted them."

"That's possible. She lived directly across the hall from me. Why would they think I have them?"

"Your sister trusted you. One look at your social media account told me that."

"You looked at my Facebook account?"

Han Li ignored the question. "Your sister wasn't carrying the documents the night she was killed. Nor were they in her apartment, which he would have thoroughly searched. The fact that Cai Fu is still looking tells me he doesn't have them."

"And you believe he thought she sent them to me?"

"Without a doubt."

"How can you be so sure?"

"He came a great distance to see you, probably so he could search your office."

Moretti thought back to when he went to the break room to make a cup of tea.

"When he didn't find the documents, he decided to go through your residence. Eliminating or confirming you as the recipient was important and something he'd want to direct firsthand."

"Why didn't he kill me in Anchorage?"

"Why would he? You didn't have the documents, and you

weren't a threat to him at the time. Killing you so close to Gina's death would draw unwanted attention."

"But now you believe he's changed his mind and wants to kill me."

"He's seen us together and therefore now considers you a threat. This evening I saw someone across the canal taking photos of us. I could see him under the lights at the end of La Salute, pointing his camera in our direction. One might assume he was a tourist, except he was there during our entire dinner and only took photos in our direction. Since only one person in my government knew I was in Venice, we have to assume he's here to photograph you and everyone you meet."

"Will they recognize you?"

"No, but they'll put it together. Neither Cai Fu nor the person he works for is stupid."

"Then I'll kill him when he shows up."

"He knows we're staying at the Bauer, which is in the middle of a huge tourist area. The crowds make it easy for him to camouflage his movements, and we'll never see the kill shot. We need to check into a less conspicuous hotel, one where we'll see him before he sees us. Do you understand?" Han Li didn't wait for Moretti to respond. Instead she grabbed her clothes off the chair next to her bed and went into the bathroom. She returned dressed in a pair of tight-fitting jeans and a black long-sleeved sweater, holding a small handgun in one hand and a pocket knife in the other. The look of recognition on Moretti's face told her he was familiar with both weapons.

"A Boberg XR9-S. This 9 mm semiautomatic pistol will put a very big hole in someone," Moretti said, taking the weapons that were handed to him. "And this looks like a Tac Force Speedster, a spring-assisted knife I used in the rangers."

"We copied and improved on it," she said. "The blade is sharper and much stronger."

"I'm sure the company will appreciate the intellectual property payments they receive from your government."

Han Li ignored his remark. "These weapons will give you at least some chance of killing Cai Fu when you encounter him."

"I take it you didn't bring these on the plane with you?"

"I wasn't flying commercial."

Without further comment, Han Li slung her carry-on bag over her shoulder. They descended the stairs to Moretti's room, where he gathered his personal items.

"Where are we going?" Moretti asked once they'd checked out of the hotel and were standing outside.

"To see Dottore Pietro Luca, curator of the Marciana Library. He's the only surviving link to both your sister and the diary," she said, pulling her cell phone from her back pocket and taking off at a fast pace.

"It's almost midnight. I don't think he's going to be all that happy to see us at this hour," Moretti said as she watched him try to keep up with her.

"He'll see us because your sister worked for him, and you'll have his sympathy. And getting me in front of Luca was part of our bargain as you'll recall."

The streets were empty as they threaded their way to the area where Luca lived. Finding his residence, however, even with it marked by a checkered flag on Han Li's cell phone, proved challenging. Although the buildings in Venice were usually numbered, they didn't necessarily follow in sequential order. Luca's street address was 5225. They found it at half past midnight. It was directly across the street from another dwelling that had an address of 7126.

Luca lived in a beautifully restored nineteenth-century residence in a row bordered by a canal on one side and a narrow cobblestone street on the other. The massive wooden door was covered with a shiny coat of black paint, and it had a large brass ball knocker in the center, one that Moretti repeatedly banged for no less than five minutes before he heard footsteps coming from inside. From the information Cho Ling provided, Han Li knew that Luca was a bachelor and lived alone. She hoped he was by himself tonight.

The door opened a crack, and a man in his forties of medium build and a graying goatee and mustache looked at them with a frown on his face. He had thinning salt-and-pepper hair parted on the left, and he wore a dark blue silk robe with matching pajamas. His black UGG slippers seemed out of place given the elegance of what he was wearing.

"We're sorry to bother you, Dottore Luca, at such a late hour," Moretti said. "But we need your help."

"Who are you? No, don't tell me. It doesn't matter. Come to my office after ten, and we can talk," Luca said as he started closing the door. But at six foot three and 230 pounds, Moretti easily pushed it open.

"My name is Matthew Moretti, Gina's brother. We know it's late, but it's very important that we speak with you."

Luca took a long look at his face. "You don't look much like your sister."

"Perhaps this will help," he said, taking his passport out of his pocket and showing it him. "And this is my friend, Han Li," he said, motioning to her.

After examining the passport, Luca handed it back and stood aside, inviting them into his home. Guiding them up two flights of well-worn wooden stairs, they entered a large seating area on the top floor. They each took a seat in one of the three thickly cushioned club chairs at the far end of the room. Luca asked if either of them would like something to drink, and when they declined, he removed a cigarette and lighter from his robe pocket.

"Do either of you smoke?" he asked. "It's a filthy habit, but I enjoy it nevertheless." When they said they didn't, he lit his cigarette, took a deep draw of smoke into his lungs, held it for a second, and then exhaled. "Your sister was a wonderful person, and we'll all miss her very much," he said, leaning forward in his chair.

"Thank you. She told me many times how much she loved working at the Marciana," Moretti responded.

"You said you needed my help. How can I be of service?"

"I'm in Venice to accompany my sister back to the United States. I apologize for the late notice, but I have a request. Some time ago a series of documents, which comprised the diary of Chairman Mao, was stolen from the Chinese government. I've just learned from Ms. Li that they were recently donated to the Marciana Library."

"You must mean the Chang Hao documents. I had no idea that they were stolen or that they were the dairy of Chairman Mao because they haven't yet been translated."

"We require your help because the Chinese government would like them returned."

"If it can be substantiated that they've been stolen, then a formal request should result in their return. The Marciana will not keep anything that's been illegally taken from their rightful owner," Luca said, looking directly at Han Li.

"Then I would like to have them returned privately and with a minimum of outside involvement."

"I can't just give them to you. There's still legal formalities that have to be followed."

Han Li couldn't allow that to happen and quickly thought of a way to tempt the curator. "What if I arrange for an exchange? My government would give the Marciana some very important European historical works more in keeping with your library's focus in return for the Chang Hao documents. I believe exchanges are common between libraries."

"They are," Luca admitted.

"And who would approve such a transaction?" she asked.

"As curator, I would," he replied, putting out his cigarette in an ashtray on the end table beside his chair. "Would you both please excuse me? I need to go downstairs and get a fresh pack before we continue our discussion."

Luca went to his second-floor bedroom, closed the door behind him, and dialed Cai Fu, who was staying at an apartment the consulate kept as a safe house in Venice. He explained that Moretti and Han Li were there inquiring about the documents. No one spoke for several seconds until Cai Fu told him to make sure they spent the night and to unlock the front door. He'd be there in less than an hour to handle the situation. They spoke for a while longer. Luca provided directions to his residence and indicated that the guest room would be on the second floor. After the call ended, he grabbed a pack of cigarettes off his nightstand, went back upstairs, and retook his seat. "I believe an exchange would be in both our interests," he said. "But it's late, and we all need to get some rest. Stay as my guests, and in the morning, we'll have an early breakfast and discuss the details."

"You'll show us the documents tomorrow?" Han Li asked.

"I believe they're in the Marciana's archives. However, they seem to have been misfiled."

"They're missing?" Han Li asked.

"Technically, but I firmly believe they're in the archives. Misfiling is not uncommon in libraries of our size. As a rule, no employee can remove documents or books without my written permission. Your sister was a stickler for the rules. Therefore, I believe they're misfiled."

"Then how do we find them?" Han Li asked.

"We search. They shouldn't be too difficult to locate, as they're the only documents we have that are written in Chinese. We have a computer record of the last items returned to the storage cabinets. We'll start there in the morning."

Exhausted, Han Li and Moretti agreed, and Luca led them to the guest quarters on the second floor. The room was small and sparsely furnished with only a standard-size bed and one small armoire inside.

"The bathroom is halfway down the hall and on the left. We'll meet here at nine o'clock if that's suitable?"

"That's fine," Han Li responded.

"Then I wish you both a good night," Luca said before he left and closed the door behind him.

"Which side of the bed would you like?" Moretti asked, stretching his arms and yawning.

Han Li didn't reply. Instead she took a pillow and comforter and threw it to him. "The hardwood floor should be good for your back."

The lights were out by the time Cai Fu and one of his agents arrived at Luca's residence. Both carried a Beretta 92FS suppressed handgun with two spare clips of ammunition. There was no conversation or comradery between them. The agent was a worker bee, and he'd been told that he was there to assist and follow any instruction given to him without question. Both excited and terrified, Cai Fu knew that killing China's top assassin wouldn't be easy, even with his high skill level. Going after her would not be unlike entering an enclosed room to grab and kill an extremely large cobra. He knew that if he was close enough to kill, then he was close enough to be killed. But once she was dead, he'd be the reigning legend and the most feared person in the country.

Moretti and Han Li heard the creaking of the front door followed by the sound of stressed wood, and they immediately emerged from a light sleep and got out of bed. There was no mistaking the sound. Each of them had heard it when Luca opened and closed the heavy portal that guarded the entrance to the residence, and they also recognized the groaning of wood when the strangers ascended the stairs.

Eventually, footsteps passed their room and continued down the hall. Opening the door slightly, Moretti poked his head out and looked down the faintly lit hallway. Two men, each with a suppressed gun in their hand, were just entering Luca's bedroom at the end of the hall. Even though he was looking at their profile from the rear, he knew without a shadow of a doubt that one of them was Cai Fu.

When Cai Fu saw Luca sitting up in bed with his reading light on, he was furious with himself. He'd made a mistake in not asking the curator which room Moretti and Han Li would be occupying, believing the guest bedroom would be farthest from the stairway. Turning around to go back down the hall, he was startled to see what should have been his two victims rushing toward him. Moretti was carrying a small handgun in the palm of his hand, and he was raising it to fire. He quickly slammed the door shut, just as the bullet ripped through it no more than a foot from where he was standing. Luca's eyes widened, and he made the sign of the cross before leaping onto the floor and scampering under the bed.

Cai Fu and the agent stood on opposite sides of the door with their backs against the wall. The assassin saw only a small pistol in Moretti's hand and none in Han Li's—a negligible amount of firepower in a confrontation such as this. Exposed and completely vulnerable in the narrow hallway, they'd have no way of avoiding the deadly cascade of bullets he was about to send their way.

Throwing open the door, his finger on the trigger, he expected to see his adversaries. Instead the hallway was empty. Because only a few seconds had elapsed since they were out of his sight, he didn't believe they'd had time to reach their room. This meant that they had to be behind the door halfway down the hall. Cautiously working their way toward it, he and the agent positioned themselves on either side, and when Cai Fu whispered, "Xianzai," both emptied their clips into the portal. Shards of wood flew in every conceivable direction, producing a ruptured opening through which they expected to see two bodies riddled with bullets. Instead all he saw was the shattered remains of a porcelain sink and commode. He knew he'd once again made the wrong choice. He was frantically trying to reload his Beretta when he looked up and saw Moretti with his gun pointed directly at the center of his chest only ten paces away. Han Li was close behind. Expecting that his killer had now concluded that he had murdered his sister, he abandoned his efforts to reload or hide, standing motionless and waiting to die. But instead of firing, Moretti inexplicably kept his gun centered on his chest, looking him directly in the eye with all the malice he expected and stopping a short distance away. At the instant he thought he'd feel a bullet entering his body, Han Li flew in front of him. Since that effectively blocked any shot that Moretti had, he turned and bolted down the hall to Luca's bedroom. His agent wasn't as lucky. She delivered a kick to the side of his head that produced a loud cracking sound. The agent flew into the wall across the hall and slid lifeless to the floor.

Cai Fu was almost to Luca's bedroom when Moretti, who was in full stride, tackled him from behind, resulting in both tumbling into the room. Both guns left their hands and flew in opposite directions. And when Moretti tried to get up and retrieve his, he let out a scream, grabbed his back, and fell back down. He watched as the American struggled to get up, eventually rolling over on his stomach, grabbing the bed, and pulling himself to his feet. During this time he casually retrieved his gun, inserted the spare clip, and racked back the slide. Aiming it at the center of Moretti's chest, no more than five feet separating them, he smiled. "Pity," he said as he started to tense his finger on the trigger. At that instant a bullet grazed the left side of his head just above his ear, causing him to turn away in pain. Out of the corner of his eye, he saw Moretti hobble out of the bedroom as Han Li squeezed off several more rounds in his direction, whereupon he crawled to the door and slammed it shut with his foot. He looked around the room and quickly realized that his only means of escape was through the double doors leading onto the balcony. He raced there, and he was just about to open them when he thought about Luca. He not only knew too much, but he could also help Han Li retrieve the documents. Without a moment's hesitation, he got down on his knees and looked at the trembling curator, who was lying on his stomach under the bed. His pleading eyes did nothing to prevent the assassin from firing two rounds into his head, after which Cai Fu went onto the balcony and jumped eight feet to the street below.

When Han Li and Moretti entered the bedroom and saw the balcony doors open, they turned and ran outside, but Cai Fu was nowhere to be seen. Returning to Luca's bedroom, it didn't take them long to find the curator under the bed, the right side of his head missing.

"We have to go," Han Li said. "We don't want to be here when the police arrive. They'll blame us for Luca's death."

"No one's calling the police, because the neighbors didn't hear a thing, except for possibly my shot. They were using suppressors. Even the rounds you fired came from a silenced weapon."

"Cai Fu will call and give them the name of Luca's killer."

"I'm guessing it won't be his."

"It'll be ours."

"Because?"

"That's exactly what I'd do."

Lin Bogang tapped out a cigarette from the pack on his desk and lit it with the Zippo lighter he took from his pants pocket. After deeply inhaling the smoke, he slowly exhaled through his nose, picked up the printout from his desk, and leaned back in his chair.

It is May 1966. Since the failure of my Great Leap Forward program, I've been increasingly marginalized by all within the government, and I'm now an outcast within the party. It is the lowest point of my life. Decisions regarding my country's future are routinely made without consulting me. Former comrades, once taking advice without question, now doubt all that I say. I have been cast aside.

I know that Chiang hungers to retake this great nation, and those who still confide in me say that he is confident the Americans will support him in this effort. But I fully believe the American imperialists will never support such a move. They are mired in Korea, and they are getting more deeply involved in Vietnam by the day. If they support Chiang in an invasion of our land, they know we will fight to the last person to protect our sovereignty. Such an action would cast the entire region into war. As the Americans are so fond of saying, it will cause a domino effect. We can count on the Soviets to come to our aid, not because of any love for my country but because they must protect their borders by keeping the United States off our land. Supporting an invasion of our homeland by Chiang may lead everyone to World War III. But Chiang is foolhardy and may try this folly without American support, feeling that the time is right and that this opportunity may never come again. His logic is not faulty. Our country has never been weaker. We have been at war for so long that we've not reaped the strength that comes with peace.

Since my party will not listen to me, I've asked our country's youth to answer my call, and they've enthusiastically responded as I knew they would. From their ranks I have formed the Red Guard to purge all those who have adopted bourgeois elitist attitudes, and I have given strict orders for the police not to interfere with their efforts, lest they be prosecuted themselves as counterrevolutionaries. To save my country, I've ordered capitalists, intellectuals, counterrevolutionaries, educated youths, and other revisionists to be sent to the countryside. Members of the Red Guard will carry out my command, by force if necessary. Let us learn about the ideological strength of this great nation from the peasants. If we are to continue toward unequivocal equality and stand alongside Western powers, then we must throw off the shackles of our past. If not, then Chiang will someday come onto our shores and conquer us because of our own divisiveness.

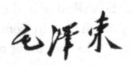

13

HAN LI WAS CORRECT. CAI Fu phoned the police. He refused to give his name, and he informed them that Matthew Moretti, following an angry dispute, shot and killed Pietro Luca, accusing him of being responsible for his sister's death. The duty officer wondered if this was a crank call, especially since the caller's number was blocked. He wasn't about to wake Chief Inspector Mauro Bruno at such an early hour without verifying what he'd been told. Subsequently, he ordered two patrolmen to check out Luca's home, believing that waking the curator was a far better career move than summoning his boss without proof of a crime.

It took Bruno thirty minutes to pull himself together and walk to Luca's residence following his call with the duty officer. When he arrived, the two officers who verified the murders were waiting for him outside and saluted as he approached.

"The bodies are on the second floor, Chief Inspector," one of the officers said.

Bruno sighed and took the pair of latex gloves and shoe covers that the other officer handed to him. When he entered the residence, the first thing he noticed was the burning metallic smell of gunpowder that permeated the air, not to mention the fact that the scent became stronger as he walked onto the second floor. Halfway down the hall, a man lay on his back in front of a shattered wooden door. Turning on the lights, he was about to approach the corpse when he noticed a door to his right. Since the body wasn't going anywhere, he decided to have a look inside. Opening the door and turning on the light switch to his right, he entered what he believed to be the guest room. The bed was unmade, the sheets thrown back, and the pillow still crunched, indicating that someone had recently slept in it. There was also a comforter and pillow on the floor beside it. Otherwise, the room was bare of personal items. Perhaps the lab could get some fiber and hair samples from them. He closed the door and continued down the hall to where the man was lying outside of what used to be the bathroom door. Next to him was a suppressed automatic pistol and numerous shell casings. Bruno reached down and picked up the gun. There was no ammunition clip inside. Nor did he see one on the floor. Gently rolling the man to his left, he found not only the empty clip but a full one as well. He returned the corpse to the position in which he'd found him and stood. The suppressed handgun explained why his neighbors hadn't called the station and reported hearing gunshots. But what he couldn't explain were a great many casings on the floor, far too many to come from the single empty clip he saw. Bruno peered inside the bathroom where the pedestal porcelain sink and the commode were little more than rubble. The bathtub, an old cast-iron model from the last century, was unscathed.

Following the officer who'd discovered Luca's body, he continued to the master bedroom at the end of the hall, where he saw the curator's lifeless body underneath the bed. Since his Rolex and wallet were on the nightstand, the detective knew this wasn't a robbery. Therefore, it could have been exactly what the caller had said it was, namely a dispute in which Moretti held Luca responsible for the death of his sister and killed him. But if that was true, who was the dead man in the hall, and did Moretti also murder him? That also begged the question as to how the American had obtained a suppressed weapon since he arrived in Venice barely twelve hours ago. Bruno doubted he had the necessary connections to arrange for such a purchase, especially in a city as small as Venice, where dealers were leery of selling arms to an unknown person who may very well be with law enforcement. But the biggest question was how the caller knew Luca was dead—that is, unless he was present. Was he the killer and trying to frame Moretti? Bruno was thinking about these various scenarios when he heard someone calling his name from downstairs. Recognizing the voice, he told the medical examiner to come upstairs.

When they left Luca's residence, neither Moretti nor Han Li knew where they were going. They only wanted to get as far away as possible before the police arrived and cordoned off the area. They would've gotten farther except Moretti had a hard time keeping up with the gazelle in front of him because of his bad back, causing her to slow down to a fast trot. They continued this pace for fifteen minutes until they came to a Best Western hotel and decided it was as good a place as any to hide, get some rest, and figure out what they'd do next. Fortunately, Han Li had a backup passport and credit card in her spy bag. Telling him to wait for her signal to enter the hotel, she walked across the street and pressed the intercom, which was just above the room key slot next to the front entrance. Through the hotel's large plate glass window, he saw a clerk come from a back room to the registration desk a moment later. He'd apparently released the lock because Han Li was now able to open the front door. It appeared as if she was crying as she handed the man her passport and credit card. The clerk reached under the counter and retrieved a box of tissues along with what he assumed to be a registration form. After she'd completed it, he gave her a room key and returned her passport and credit card. Five minutes later when the clerk returned to the back room, she opened the front door and waved him across the street.

Once inside their room, Han Li sat on the sofa while Moretti went to the minibar and emptied the five miniature bottles of scotch into a glass. He drained half the liquid before a taking a seat on the couch.

"What did you tell the clerk? I saw him giving you a box of tissues."

"I knew he'd be suspicious about why I was by myself and wanted a room at three in the morning. I told him I'd found another woman sleeping with my boyfriend and decided to get a hotel room for the night until I could figure out what I was going to do."

"Good story."

"I thought so." Moretti was in a bad mood and hoped the amount of alcohol he was putting into his body would help him forget that he'd screwed up. He had the Boberg pointed at the center of Cai Fu's chest but waited a second too long to pull the trigger, wanting to savor the moment instead of just getting the job done. He thought about his sister in the morgue and felt a wave of guilt come over him. She deserved better—much better—and he needed to take her home so that she could have a proper funeral. His father and her friends also needed closure, and he was being selfish in single-handedly taking that away from them because he wanted his revenge. He knew that if he left Venice without getting it, the fact that Cai Fu was still alive would eat at him for the rest of his life. Looking down at his glass and seeing that it was empty, he went back to the minibar. Since he'd drunk all the scotch, he took four miniatures of Ketel One, the bottles closest to him, and poured them into his glass. He took a long drink of the clear liquid and returned to the sofa.

Just as Han Li said, looking for the documents seemed to attract Cai Fu. If he had any chance of confronting him again, he needed to help her. She believed they might still be at the Marciana. But with Luca dead, gaining access to the library seemed to be an insurmountable problem. And if Han Li was correct—and he believed she was—the police were probably looking for them. He took a swallow of Ketel One and leaned back on the sofa. He was about to take another when he stopped his glass short of his mouth and then set it down on the side table.

"You told me on the way here that you wanted to search my sister's office. I think I can arrange that."

"How?" Han Li asked in a voice that was more skeptical than reassuring. "With Luca dead, the police will be at the Marciana questioning employees and asking them if they've seen us."

When he told her his plan, she was silent for a moment before responding. "It's imaginative, very Hollywood, and will probably get us captured or killed. Unfortunately, it's also the only option we have."

They agreed to get started early after they'd gotten a few hours' sleep. While Han Li went into the bathroom, Moretti got up from the sofa and pulled the comforter and a pillow off the bed and onto the floor. He'd just lain down when she came out wearing a hotel robe and carrying her clothes, which she threw on the sofa along with the robe. Moretti's fatigue seemed to momentarily disappear when he saw her wearing a black bra and matching boyshort panties. She had a body that would make a Victoria's Secret model envious, with a perfectly flat stomach and well-formed breasts that were decidedly larger than he'd expected from someone of Asian descent. He watched as she got under the covers and turned off the lights by hitting the master control switch on the nightstand. What he saw was seared into his memory and on constant replay. He knew he was in for a restless night. He thought about taking the initiative and getting under the covers with her. He was single. She was single. But he quickly decided that was a bad idea, recalling how easily she'd crushed a man's skull. He wrapped himself inside his comforter and closed his eyes, even though his imagination kept him awake long after.

Leaving the hotel at nine, they went directly to the Marciana Library in Saint Mark's Square, which would open to the public in an hour, and they watched as employees entered the building through an open door in the rear. The security check was as casual as Moretti expected. His sister had told him that it was virtually nonexistent. Halfway down the corridor, a guard was reading a newspaper while sitting at his desk. The man's eyes never left the paper unless someone addressed him. The Hollywood plan was to enter the building with the employees and then search Gina's office and leave the library before it opened. They both acknowledged the entire plan was a house of cards, but with no other option, they entered the corridor and started toward the guard. The temptation was to walk fast and get past him as quickly as possible; however, they kept their pace casual and unhurried just as those before them, and the guard never looked up as they passed his desk and continued to the end of the corridor and through a set of double doors.

In front of them was a long flight of concrete stairs, and at the top there was a single doorway. When they opened it, they found themselves next to the information desk in the vestibule. In front of them were two long halls, one with a sign indicating that it led to the library room and the other with a sign that read Uffici Amministrativi, their first piece of good luck, which they badly needed.

The administrative wing consisted of ten offices, five on either side of the hall, each with a brass plate affixed to the door giving the name and title of the occupant. They passed Pietro Luca's office, which was the first one on the right, and continued to the end of the corridor. The last office on the left was nameless. Moretti wondered if this was his sister's office and what he'd find inside if it was.

He hoped the door would be unlocked, but when he turned the knob, he had no such luck. Seeing no one in the hall, he was about to kick it in when Han Li gently pushed him aside, removed a credit card from her back pocket, and deftly inserted it between the door and the frame. Almost instantly, the lock popped with an audible click.

The office was no more than a cubicle, measuring ten feet on a side. It was dominated by a small wooden desk old enough to qualify as an antique that was flush against the wall opposite the door. Behind it was a wooden chair of similar age. To the left was an empty three-tier bookshelf squeezed in between the desk and the wall. Moretti didn't seem to notice any of this. His eyes were focused on a single white cardboard box on top of the desk that bore the name Gina Moretti. He took a deep breath and slowly walked to it as if drawn by some invisible force, and then he slowly removed the top. Looking inside, he saw his sister's personal items and began removing them one by one and placing each on the desk. He wasn't looking for the documents. He just wanted one last glimpse at his sister's life. But Han Li was focused on nothing else, and they weren't there.

"We'd better leave," she said, the disappointment evident in her voice.

Moretti knew she was right. They'd been lucky so far. He began putting the items back into the box, which he knew would accompany her back to the States, but he placed three inside his jacket pocket as immediate remembrances. One was a dog-eared purple address book. The second was a computer flash drive. The third a train schedule where his sister had drawn flowers on the back cover. The address book was particularly important because he'd given it to her in high school. He was surprised she still had it, especially in this digital age. He wasn't going to leave that behind. The train schedule was only important because of the flowers, which made it deeply personal. He'd debated about taking the flash drive. It obviously didn't have any sentimental value; however, it might contain pictures or personal information his sister had placed on it, and he could look at it on his computer.

"We didn't think it would be in her office," Moretti said. "This narrows your search, at least regarding the Marciana."

"Which we have no access to, except for the areas open to the public."

"There's nothing more we can do here. Let's go back to our hotel. It's a couple of minutes past ten, and the front doors should be open."

Han Li agreed, and they made their way to the vestibule and down the double staircase that led to the main entrance and Saint Mark's Square.

Mauro Bruno ordered a second cup of espresso and lit his third cigarette of the morning. Exhausted from a lack of sleep, he needed the caffeine to stay alert. He'd arrived fifteen minutes ago at a café directly across from the Marciana Library. On the table in front of him was an enlarged copy of both Moretti and Han Li's passport photos. He was trying to determine what the two had in common. So far, he'd found nothing other than the fact that they'd stayed at the Bauer and checked out together late last night. That was peculiar because they'd arrived earlier that day. What was so important to cause them to leave a five-star hotel at that hour? They'd already paid for their rooms. Neither was staying at another hotel in the city. Nor had they purchased any train or airline tickets or rented a car. He told his staff to begin circulating their pictures. They were somewhere in Venice, and he wanted to speak with them.

He was waiting for the Marciana to open so that he could begin questioning Luca's staff to see if they'd heard or seen anything that might indicate why Luca was murdered. He had a strong feeling that both Gina Moretti and Pietro Luca were killed for the same reason, and he needed to find out what that was. He wasn't ready to issue an arrest warrant for Moretti because the only indication that he was Luca's killer came from an anonymous caller, which didn't prove anything. Even if he was in Luca's house, it wouldn't surprise him. After all, his sister had worked for the curator, and getting together was a good way for both men to get closure. It would also explain where he and possibly Han Li had spent the night since he was sure two people slept in the guest bedroom. He'd know soon enough since the fingerprint analysis he requested from Rome would be completed shortly. He was about to take a sip of espresso when Moretti and Han Li walked out of the Marciana Library. Although he was thirty yards away, he was sure it was them. He put some money on the table, and he was about to approach them when he saw a tall Asian man walking parallel to the couple, intently watching their every move. Curious, he backed off. The more he looked, the more he realized that the man wasn't watching them. He was watching her.

He couldn't blame him. She was very attractive. He took out his cell phone and clicked several pictures of the tall Asian, zooming in on his face the best he could. For the moment at least, he decided to put off bringing Moretti and Han Li in for questioning. With their photos circulated to all transportation agencies and hotels, he'd find them again. Something else seemed to be going on. The dead person in Luca's home, Han Li, and the man he was watching were all Asian. It was just too much of a coincidence.

It is September 12, 1969. Yesterday I met with Soviet prime minister Alexei Kosygin, who was returning from the funeral of my friend Ho Chi Minh. It seems like only yesterday that I last spoke with Comrade Ho. Now he is lost to the ages, where I will join him in the not too distant future.

Ever since Comrade Stalin died, my country's relations with our once close ally have deteriorated. The Soviets have decreased their support to my nation and have philosophically moved closer to the West. Because of this, I did not hold a formal reception for Comrade Kosygin. Instead I met with him informally at the Beijing airport.

Since their politburo replaced Comrade Khrushchev with Leonid Brezhnev as first secretary and installed Alexei Kosygin as premier, the Soviets have become more belligerent. Our two countries continually fight along our common border, and many in my party fear that they will attack our nuclear weapons facilities. As a result, I have taken care to disperse our weapons and will ensure they're unleashed on any aggressor nation. I told Comrade Kosygin that any use of force against my country would be considered an act of war, and if our nuclear bases were attacked, we would respond in kind with the full might of our weapon systems. I do not believe that he understood the depth of my commitment before that moment or the intensity of my resolve to defend our country's right to possess nuclear weapons. In response, Comrade Kosygin asked what I would need to settle the differences between our countries. I was prepared for this question, and I replied that the Soviet Union must agree to an immediate cease-fire and status quo along our historic boundaries. After some thought he agreed and suggested that both countries conduct settlement conferences to resolve this issue in perpetuity. I fully supported this.

I never believed anything would come from these talks. Negotiating is not in the Soviet nature. They are used to obtaining what they want through force, or the threat of force. They do not compromise. Their goal was to destroy our nuclear weapons and then to dictate settlement terms to a weaker country. But after seeing that I was determined to have a nuclear war, if that was what was necessary to protect my country, he seemed to understand and adopted a more conciliatory tone. The Soviets will not risk a military confrontation to try to strip us of our nuclear weapons. They know our resolve is great, and if there is a conflict, we will inflict great harm on the Soviet Union.

I have but one goal for the remainder of my life, and that's to unite China. To my consternation, however, Chiang moves increasingly closer to the West and away from our country's historic roots. He is corrupting present and future generations, and soon those he governs will forget they are Chinese and not Taiwanese. They will not remember that they are cut from the same fabric as their mainland brothers and sisters. When that happens, it will be too late for us to unite and speak with one voice. That is why today I have decided to embark on a plan that will forever bring my people the stability, greatness, and respect they deserve.

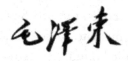

CHAPTER

14

CAI FU EXPECTED MORETTI AND Han Li to go to the Marciana
following Luca's murder, because it was the most logical place for
Gina Moretti to secure the documents and keep their exact location
secret, even from the library's staff. In a building with more than
one million written works, finding anything within it was next to
impossible if one didn't know exactly where to look. That's why he
wanted to see if she gave her brother instructions where to locate that
needle in a haystack. Although Luca said that Moretti assumed that
he knew where the documents were located and Han Li offered to
barter for them, he thought that exchange might have been staged.
More likely the American was visiting Luca to get his assistance to
enter a nonpublic area of the Marciana so that he could retrieve the
documents from a hiding place that only he knew. Nevertheless, if
Mao's diary wasn't in the library, then he'd fall back to his alternate
theory, which was that she somehow managed to FedEx it to someone
she trusted, which now meant someone other than her brother.

He arrived at the library at eight, and a little more than an hour
later, he saw Moretti and Han Li enter the Piazza San Marco. Given
that the police would obviously be looking for them following his
call, he didn't know how they'd get inside before it opened. That's
before he saw them going through the employee entrance, a move
he considered brilliant.

He considered himself good at reading people. Therefore, an
hour later when he noticed them walking empty-handed out the

front entrance and their mannerism didn't seem to say, "I've got it," he knew they'd failed to retrieve the diary. He wondered if that was because they couldn't access the area where he'd been instructed that it was hidden or because it wasn't there.

This morning he had an idea that would provide needed clarity. Luca previously told him that the documents were apparently misplaced and that he'd ordered a search to try to find them. What if they'd already been found and returned to their assigned storage space? Could that be the reason Moretti and Han Li didn't recover them? Were they looking in the wrong place? Alternately, maybe they weren't misplaced at all, and Luca intended to negotiate a higher price? He'd find out the answer in a few minutes. He continued to follow Moretti and Han Li until they were almost out of the piazza, more to get a rare glimpse of China's most famous assassin than anything else before walking to the Marciana.

He strode up the two ascending staircases to the vestibule's information desk, where he asked how he could see one of the library's documents and was directed to the anteroom. More relaxed, knowing that Moretti and Han Li didn't have the diary, he took a detailed notice of his surroundings for the first time. He wasn't fond of Western art, but he had to admit, as he passed through the main room, that it was spectacular. With seven incredible paintings by various Venetian artists across the ceiling and row after row of deep-brown shelves packed with a variety of leather-bound books below, it was the most elegant area he'd seen in any library. The anteroom he continued into was smaller but just as magnificent with Titian's painting of Wisdom dominating its ceiling.

The clerk at the information booth, a heavyset woman in her early sixties, had a bored look on her face as she robotically handed him a request form in response to his question. He looked at the paper he'd been given, apologized in nearly perfect Italian, and seemed embarrassed as he told the woman that he didn't know the exact name of the documents he wanted, only that they were in Chinese and that they were previously shown to him by Gina Moretti.

"Signorina Moretti, ah," the heavyset woman said with a sigh of sadness.

"Yes, I heard. I'm very sorry. She was a good friend of mine, and I translated these documents for her. Before I return to China, I wanted to take another look at them to ensure that my interpretation was perfect."

"I'm sure I can get them for you," she said, taking back the request form. "Let me check my computer and see where they're stored. Please have a seat at that table," she said, pointing to one a few feet away.

"Thank you," he responded, trying to control his elation.

The heavyset woman went through a doorway directly behind her workstation. He had a copy of the documents at his apartment, sent by courier from the general, who duplicated them from the scanned copy in his possession. The substitution wouldn't be perfect, but it'd be close enough. Once he verified that the Marciana had the originals, he'd return and make the switch. He heard the approaching footsteps and turned around as the heavyset woman approached. She'd been gone for some time.

"I'm sorry, signore. I can't find them. My computer shows they should be in a specific drawer within the archives, but they aren't there. I'm certain they've been misfiled because nothing can be removed from this building without written authorization, which would be noted. Perhaps you can extend your stay in Italy by a couple of days while we search for them. The weather is quite lovely."

He wanted to scream. Everything he dreamed about—a promotion to colonel, a plush assignment in Beijing, and all the perks of rank—was so much vapor. He had little confidence that she'd ever find them. Instead he now believed that Gina Moretti sent them by FedEx to someone, and he knew how to find out the identity of that person. *Somewhere you'll never find them*. I don't think so.

Moretti entered the hotel room with Han Li, and while she went straight to the bathroom and closed the door behind her, he sat down in front of the desk. After removing from his pocket the three items he'd taken from his sister's office, he took the laptop from his carry-on bag and powered it up. Inserting the flash drive, he hoped to see photos and videos of his sister, bringing a small part of her back into his life. But when he clicked on the icon, the drive was empty. Disappointed, he put the computer aside and looked at the other two items. He picked up the train schedule. It was dog-eared, and on closer inspection, the flowers were drawn in the open spaces and seemed to be more doodles than drawings. Unfolding it, he saw nothing written or underlined inside. Lastly, he opened the purple address book. As he started flipping through it, he saw that there were about a hundred hand-written entries and that more than half the names were unfamiliar. Moving his computer back in front of him, he logged onto the hotel server and did a Google search of each of those names, finding information on two-thirds with one standing out. He grabbed the desk phone from its cradle and dialed the number given on their home page. After five rings, he was sent to voice mail. The recording, given first in German and then in English, was from a man identifying himself as Franz Ludewig, who said to leave a message at the beep so that he could call back shortly. There was a long tone followed by a second recording, also in German and English, which said that the message box was full. He hung up.

Han Li had come out of the bathroom and was standing behind him, staring at the website on his laptop. After a short discussion, she made a call to her superior in China. They were going to Vienna.

Bruno returned to his office, sat down at his desk, and ran his fingers through his hair. Word of Luca's murder had gotten out, and the lobby of the police station was filled with reporters who wanted to know more. *If only there was more to give them.* Three murders in the space of a few days in a city that was considered one of the safest in the world? How was that possible? That thought brought him back to the dead Asian and Cai Fu. Perhaps he'd been too hasty in discounting the tall Asian's involvement. Thinking it was better late than never, he called one of his detectives and sent him a message with a picture of the tall Asian, dispatching him to Saint Mark's Square with instructions to follow the man when he came out of the Mariana. Hopefully, he was still inside. In any event, he'd send the photographs he'd taken to Rome and see if the immigration department had a record of his identity.

He looked at the pile of papers on his desk. Somehow, no matter how much time he spent, the stack never seemed to decrease in size. Taking a deep breath, he put on his reading glasses and grabbed the paper on top. A half an hour later, his cell phone started to vibrate. The call was from the detective he'd sent to the Marciana, who reported that he'd been following the tall Asian and was just passing the Hard Rock Café. He directed the detective to continue following the man and report back every fifteen minutes. *Maybe something, maybe nothing,* he thought.

He went back to his paperwork, and fifteen minutes later, he received a call that made his jaw muscles tighten when the detective told him that he'd lost the tall Asian. As the man was making excuses, Bruno hung up. Phoning Rome for the second time this morning, trying to get the results of the fingerprints they'd taken at Luca's home, as well as the photo of the tall Asian, he tried to push along the glacial speed of getting information from Rome's bureaucracy. The fingerprint clerk promised he'd have the results within the next two hours. He didn't necessarily believe him, but there was nothing he could do about it.

He believed that Moretti and Han Li had slept in the guestroom and that their prints would be there, but he needed to know who else was in Luca's home and why. He tapped a cigarette out of the pack in front of him and lit it. He wasn't getting anywhere on the three murders, and if he didn't start making progress soon, the police chief and the mayor would both be sitting on the couch across from his desk, informing him they'd just submitted his paperwork for retirement.

Cai Fu was walking past the Hard Rock Café when he stopped and looked inside, staring at his reflection in its large plate glass window and that of the man following him. This was the second time he'd looked for a tail, and both times this person had waited for him to move before continuing behind him. He didn't know why he was being followed, only that he couldn't accomplish what he needed to do with anyone looking over his shoulder. The street he was on was narrow, and it would take some time to lose the man if he continued in the direction he was going. He decided to return to Saint Mark's Square, where the heavy crowds within the large area would give him an edge. Retracing his steps, he bypassed the Marciana and walked straight toward the Basilica adjacent to it. Just as he was about to enter, he took a hard right, walked halfway up a steep staircase, and waited. It didn't take long before the man ran past him and into the Basilica. He waited a few seconds to make sure he didn't return, and then he went back down the stairs and left the area.

He spent the rest of the day in the consulate's apartment, waiting for early evening to arrive before going to the Campo Santo Stefano and entering the FedEx office a few minutes before their 7:00 p.m. closing time. Only one clerk was working. He was a man in his midtwenties. He was medium height and perhaps thirty pounds overweight with a neatly trimmed black beard. He was standing behind a counter that divided the single-room facility. Behind the clerk were three rows of steel shelves, each five feet in height, containing various packages and boxes. He was engrossed with waving his handheld scanner over the airbill bar codes on the various packages stacked around him, and he didn't hear Cai Fu approach.

"Buona sera," he said to the clerk, startling him. "I'd like to know if you have a package my assistant placed in the drop box outside your shop the other night. She may have forgotten to put an airbill on it."

"I found no such package," the clerk responded curtly before resuming scanning of the airbills.

"In that case, perhaps you can check and see if you have a record of it being sent. It still hasn't been delivered."

"Do you have the airbill number?" the clerk asked without raising his head.

"No, but it was put in the drop box early the morning of April 2nd by my associate, Gina Moretti."

The clerk put the scanner down and raised his head. "The signorina who was murdered in the piazza?"

"I'm afraid so."

"I'm very sorry to hear that, signore. But without the airbill number, there's nothing I can do. It's company policy," the clerk replied and again resumed what he was doing.

Cai Fu went to the front door and reversed the sign that hung on the inside of the glass window, changing it from *aperto* to *chiuso*. He then locked the door and pulled the shade down over the window before walking back to the clerk. "Perhaps you can make an exception," he said as he took his gun from his right jacket pocket and a suppressor from the left.

The clerk raised his head when he heard the metallic sound of the suppressor screwing into the handgun, and his eyes went wide.

"I want to know the name and address of the recipient of the package sent by Signorina Moretti. And no, I don't have the airbill number. But perhaps you can still help me."

He motioned with his gun for the man to go to the computer, which was a few feet to his left. The clerk complied and started punching keys. A minute later, he brought up the activity log for April 2.

"Si, I have it here. A FedEx box weighing three and a half kilos. It has already been delivered."

"Print off the name, address, and any other information you have on the recipient."

The clerk hit several keys, and a few moments later, the laser printer next to the computer delivered a page with the information.

"Now erase everything about this package from the computer."

"I can't," he stuttered with trembling lips. "Only corporate headquarters can completely erase it. Surely, you understand. Otherwise, employees and their friends could have their packages delivered for free by erasing the airbill number and delivery information."

That made sense. But there had to be something the clerk could do to prevent someone from retrieving the information he'd just received.

The man was almost in tears as he stared at the gun, and then he seemed to think of something and quickly raised his hand. "Perhaps there is a way," the clerk said. "I can't erase the entry, but I can transfer the entire data file to a folder that's designated for interoffice shipments. The only way someone would be able to find this information is if they look inside that folder and trace that specific airbill number. We transfer a great many packages between offices, so I don't think anyone will ever notice it."

"Do it."

The clerk's hands flied across the keyboard as he transferred the shipping information.

"What time will someone arrive to pick up these packages?" Cai Fu asked, nodding toward the envelopes on the counter.

"At eight o'clock this evening."

That was forty minutes away.

"Pity."

"What is?"

"That you won't be alive when they arrive."

> It is March 1970. My health is failing, and I know that I have little time to attain my lifelong dream of a united China. I believe that if I am to unite China, then I will need the help of the Americans.

I am encouraged that this may occur because for the past year our diplomats in Warsaw have been communicating with them. The US ambassador to Poland, Walter Stoessel, told them that President Nixon was "seriously interested in having concrete discussions with China." I immediately instructed our representatives to respond that "if the Americans wished to send a representative of 'ministerial rank' or a special presidential envoy to Beijing for the further exploration of fundamental principles of relations between our countries, then we would be prepared to receive him." In acknowledgment, the Americans have asked Pakistani president Yahya to be their intermediary in making this possible, and he confirmed to me that in preparation for such a meeting, the United States would be removing two destroyers from the Formosa Straits. This is a welcome sign, and I asked President Yahya to tell the Americans that I was encouraged by their initiatives. But I also let it be known that these discussions were not being held out of fear. After he relayed this and to make sure there were no misunderstandings or miscommunications at this critical juncture, I decided to avoid intermediaries and directed that all discussions should now be directly between Beijing and the White House.

My highest spy in Taiwan has informed me that Chiang has learned that the Americans want to establish a dialogue with us and that he is very angry. He's written to the American president and asked him not to pursue these talks, saying that I cannot be trusted. I believe he knows that if the United States does establish relations with us, then it's only a matter of time till they abandon their blind support for him. President Nixon responded to Chiang, saying that "I would be remiss in my duty to the American people if I did not attempt to discover whether a basis may not exist for reducing the risk of a conflict between the United States and Communist China."

Still, I am not without those within my country who will oppose such talks and will want to sabotage any relations with the United States. Just the other day our military, without my authority, tried to intercept an American aircraft a hundred miles from our coast. Thankfully, they were not successful. Otherwise, all efforts to establish relations between us would have been undermined. As reassurance of my intent to move forward and begin a conversation between our nations, I passed a private message for Pakistani president Yahya to give to President Nixon, indicating that China would welcome an envoy from the United States. I also stated that when we meet, I want a meaningful discussion about America's withdrawal of troops from Taiwan.

The Americans responded that my terms were acceptable and that they will publicly announce their intentions to diminish their presence in East Asia as tensions there lessen. Upon receiving this, I scheduled a meeting with Edgar Snow, who first interviewed me decades ago. On December 18, I will inform him that China will welcome Nixon as either a president or as a tourist. Today I feel that I am closer than ever to reuniting my country.

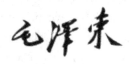

CHAPTER

15

As HIS DRIVER WOVE THROUGH Beijing traffic, General Lin returned his cell phone to his pocket and stared out the black Audi's passenger window. The call he'd just received was from one of his informants in the Second Bureau, advising him that a diplomatic pouch was being sent to Venice and contained two forged passports. One was for Matthew Moretti, although he would be given an alias, and the other was for a Chinese woman whom the informant could not find in the national name or facial recognition databases. He suspected she was hei guafu. This caused him a great deal of concern. For this to happen, someone very high up within the government had to be supporting them. Thankfully, the informant understood his propensity to learn all that was going on within the Second Bureau, and he had installed tracking software on the phone included in the pouch so he could track their whereabouts.

Producing a US passport was a big deal, and there were very few government officials who were powerful enough to order its issuance this quickly. That number dwindled even more if that person also had the authority to use hei guafu, someone whose services he didn't even have access to. Outside of the president, only the Politburo Standing Committee had these dual powers. He knew all seven of its members. Six were bureaucratic and nonconfrontational. The seventh, Cho Ling, was the opposite. They'd clashed many times, and he was anxiously waiting for him to die so he could persuade the other members to adopt many of his points of view that this irritable person, the unofficial chairman of the committee, had refused to consider. But the man seemed to be eternal. On several occasions he'd politely suggested to the president that Cho Ling deserved to retire and enjoy his remaining years in luxury. But this always fell on a deaf ear. If he was responsible for the passports and employing hei guafu, then he also had the president's ear. The longer Cai Fu took to retrieve the documents, the better the chance that they'd discover his involvement. The major needed much more encouragement, and as he removed his cell phone from his pocket and dialed him, he explained what would happen if Han Li and Moretti got to the documents first.

Moretti tried getting himself up off the floor, where he'd spent the night wrapped in a comforter, but he was having difficulty. His lower back locked up again, and he had difficulty standing. He reached up and grabbed the mattress, got to his knees, and then pulled himself into a standing position. After taking a few robotic steps and stretching, his flexibility increased. He walked past Han Li, who was speaking on the hotel phone, and then he went to the minibar and grabbed two miniature bottles of Chivas Regal. He brought them into the bathroom and closed the door behind him.

When he came out, room service had come, and a large plate of scrambled eggs, sausage, roasted potatoes, and toast along with a pot of coffee was now waiting for him. Han Li had already started on her fruit plate, and she was pouring herself a cup of green tea. Both ate with little conversation, and when they finished, the two discussed their plans for the day.

Last night when he came across Franz Ludewig's name in his sister's address book and looked at his company, Document Restoration and Authentication, his mind went into overdrive. He believed he knew where the documents were, and it explained how the Marciana thought they'd been misfiled when, in fact, they were being restored or verified by an expert in another city. But to confirm this, they needed to go to Vienna. That was the rub because he believed Cai Fu was in Venice. And if he was, then leaving the city would negate any chance he had of killing him. That's when Han Li came up with an idea. Looking at the Marciana's website and with tomorrow being Saturday, she saw that the library would be closed from midday through Sunday. She reasoned they had enough time to go to Vienna, which was only 374 miles away, and ask Ludewig if he had the documents since his website noted that his shop was open all day. If he didn't, then they had plenty of time to return before the Marciana opened Monday morning. When Moretti said that worked, Han Li got on the phone with her contact in China and arranged the rest. A water taxi was now standing by to take them across the canal, where a rental car and courier would be waiting.

They tried dialing Ludewig's business number one last time, hoping he was an early riser; however, there was no answer, and his voice mail box was still full. After checking out of the hotel, they walked several blocks to a dock on the Grand Canal, where the water taxi was waiting with its engines running. A rotund man in his late forties wearing a blue-and-white-striped nautical shirt and black trousers was on the aft deck. He gestured for them to enter the boat's cabin, and once they were comfortably seated, he cast off and worked his way through the morning traffic. Twenty minutes later they crossed to the other side, and the driver gave them a helping hand as they stepped from the taxi onto the dock. In front of them was a short, thin Asian man leaning against a white Mercedes E550. He appeared to be in his early twenties, and he wore loose-fitting baggy pants and a plain black T-shirt. White earbuds extended down to an iPhone that stuck out of his back pocket. His clothes were extremely wrinkled, looking like he'd slept in them for the past month. A gray backpack was at his feet. As Han Li and Moretti approached, he bowed and walked away.

After picking up the backpack, Han Li went through its contents. There were two passports, two driver's licenses, several credit cards, a cell phone, a small flashlight, and a stack of euros bound with a rubber band. Han Li handed Moretti his identifications, and when he looked at the photo in them, he saw that whoever had forged these had Photoshopped a head shot his sister had posted on her Facebook page. His new name was Matthew Grogan.

Han Li divided the euros unevenly and handed him the smaller stack. Both put the cash into their pockets. He then placed their bags in the trunk before getting into the passenger seat and entering Franz Ludewig's business address into the cars navigation system. They'd be in Vienna by late afternoon.

Mauro Bruno was chain-drinking espressos from the police station's break room. After spending the night at the murder scene of the FedEx clerk in the Campo Santo Stefano, the same square where Gina Moretti was killed, he needed all the caffeine he could get to stay alert. It was the second night in a row he hadn't gotten much sleep, and he wanted nothing more than to go home and drop into bed, although he knew he had no chance of that happening with four unsolved homicides.

When he'd finally gotten the fingerprint and photo analysis back from Rome, he learned that the tall Asian, whose name was Cai Fu, was a Chinese diplomat assigned to their consulate in Florence and that the dead Asian in Luca's home also worked there. That was a problem. He couldn't bring anyone with diplomatic immunity in for questioning. There was a reason the tall Asian was in Venice, and not at the consulate in Florence, and he wanted to know why. He took the last cigarette out of the pack on his desk, lit it, and blew a cloud of smoke across his office. He stared at the photo of Cai Fu and looked at his coal-black eyes. *Was he the killer?* He considered a person's eyes the gateway to their soul, and he had seen those of more than a few killers. These were no different. If so, why would a Chinese diplomat want Luca dead? He didn't know the answer to that question, but his instincts told him that the man had killed him. The suppressed handgun found with the dead Asian and the large number of rounds fired seemed beyond Moretti's capability. He was about to go for another espresso when he received a text. The security office at Marco Polo Airport, one of the transportation hubs where he'd previously sent photos of Moretti, Han Li, and Cai Fu with instructions to text the location of the diplomat and detain the others, reported that the Chinese diplomat had purchased a ticket on the next flight to Vienna and gave him the time of departure. He wanted to have one of his detective's follow him, but he needed permission from his boss since the travel would be outside of Italy. That wasn't going to happen since Cai Fu was a diplomat, and the career bureaucrat who needed to permit the trip wasn't going to risk criticism by approving the request. He was thinking about who he knew in the Viennese police department when the officer at the front desk told him Captain Justin Davidson was here to see him. He'd forgotten about the meeting.

Last night he received a call from Davidson, requesting they meet to talk about something he could not discuss over the phone. Since the request was from the US military, he agreed without requiring further explanation. An officer led Davidson into his office. The US Army captain was dressed in civilian clothes and wore a dark blue suit, an ecru open-collared shirt, and black loafers. He was a little more than five foot eight with a medium build and sandy-blond hair that he'd parted on the left, making him look more like a California attorney than someone in the military. Bruno stood and shook his hand.

"Would you like coffee or an espresso?"

Davidson politely declined, and reached into his jacket pocket to produce his military credentials. Bruno saw that he was assigned to the Sixty-Sixth Military Intelligence Brigade in Germany, and he became even more curious as to what the captain wanted. Returning his creds, he motioned him to the couch, which was just to the right of his office door as one entered.

"And how may I be of service to the US military?" Bruno said without preamble.

"I believe we may be able to help each other, Chief Inspector. But before we begin, can we agree that what's said here remains solely between the two of us? What I'm about to tell you is very sensitive, and in the hands of those with political aspirations, it would create a number of very undesirable side effects if publicly known."

Bruno told him he agreed. More than once political interference and currying favor with the press had created roadblocks to his solving a case.

"Also, as this is a two-way street, I'd like you to reciprocate by sharing what you have."

"Assuming you tell me something useful."

Davidson smiled. "Shortly after Gina Moretti's body was identified, a Chinese agent by the name of Cai Fu visited her brother, a former military officer who's now an archivist at a branch of the National Archives."

Bruno sat up straight when the diplomat's name was mentioned.

"Saying that he worked for *People's Daily*, a Chinese newspaper, he arranged to interview Moretti for an article he said he was writing. During the meeting Moretti became suspicious and didn't believe the man, who called himself Wu Bai, was actually a reporter. When Cai Fu left, Moretti called a friend of his at the Army Intelligence and Security Command in the hope that he could shed light on who had really visited him. What he learned was that Cai Fu, alias Wu Bai, is a major in the People's Liberation Army's Second Department, which is their intelligence section. And in addition to conducting espionage, he's an assassin. We know for a fact that he killed Pietro Luca, and we suspect that he also murdered Gina Moretti."

"How do you know he killed the curator of the Marciana?"

"I'll get to that in a moment. This is Cai Fu," he continued, taking a photo from his jacket pocket. He handed it to Bruno, who glanced at it before giving it back.

"I can understand the US government's peripheral involvement in Gina Moretti's death since she was an American citizen. But why is the military involved? Isn't this a State Department matter?"

When Davidson didn't immediately respond, Bruno took this opportunity to reach inside his desk and pull out a pad of paper and a pen. Since this conversation was providing him with a substantial amount of useful information, he decided to take notes and not rely on his memory.

"The military isn't officially involved," Davidson said after a pause. "We take great pains to stay below everyone's radar. Between us, our intelligence arm has an intense interest in finding out what the Chinese are up to."

"Which doesn't involve me. I'm only concerned with solving four murders."

"And how's that going?"

"Less than desirable."

"What if I could help?"

"And how would you do that?"

"My command has substantial resources at its disposal. I can arrange for you to have access to relevant information that resides in our databases. This might substantially help your investigation. More importantly, I'll ensure you have political cover."

"I don't need it."

"You're wrong because that's exactly what you'll need if those above you find out you're working with us. The political cover I'm offering and will give you at the proper time is a letter from our government revealing that your prime minister asked you to keep your working relationship with the United States and certain investigative details secret. The letter will also name Cai Fu as the killer of Gina Moretti and Pietro Luca."

"Has the prime minister already agreed to this?"

"That's not an issue that need concern you. I told you what my government is prepared to do, and we're true to our word."

Bruno realized that Davidson was right about the political cover. With a letter from the United States identifying Cai Fu as a murderer and the prime minister asking him to keep that secret, he had a career-saving "get out of jail free" card. Without it, he'd probably be made the scapegoat and forced to retire, especially in lieu of the fact that the government was unlikely to accuse a Chinese diplomat as the murderer who put four victims in the morgue.

The chief inspector was still thinking about the letter when Davidson again spoke.

"We've only known each other for a few minutes, but I believe you're someone who likes to see the scales of justice balance. I suspect you believe that Cai Fu will get away with murder and that because of his diplomatic status, there's no way to bring him to justice. Let the US government deal with him. I promise you that eventually, the scales of justice will balance. Anyway, what do you have to lose since you can't prove Cai Fu's the killer or even accuse him and not solving these crimes will eventually lead to your retirement?"

Davidson was correct. He was unlikely to come out of this whole, left to his own resources. At least, with the American's help, he had some chance of retaining his career.

"And in return, all you want is to be kept informed on the progress of my investigation?"

"Yes."

With little alternative, he said they had a deal.

The captain smiled. "Perhaps this would be a good time for me to provide you with what else I know. You asked me earlier how we knew Cai Fu killed Pietro Luca. We know because we received a call from Matthew Moretti, who was staying at Luca's home."

"I already know that because his fingerprints were in the guest bedroom. Does he work for you?"

"No, but he's helping us. You may have noticed that he's in the company of a Chinese national."

"Han Li."

"Very good. But what you might not know is that she's seeking Moretti's help to retrieve a series of documents comprising Mao's diary, which she claims was stolen from her country. According to her, they were smuggled out China decades ago and eventually ended up in Venice, where they were recently bequeathed to the

Marciana Library. The Chinese government wants them back, and they've sent Han Li here to retrieve them."

Bruno's mind was in overdrive, and he was furiously taking notes. But while this filled in many of the blanks he was drawing in his investigation, it also created additional questions. "Why doesn't China ask the Marciana to return the diary? No reputable library would keep something that's stolen."

"Because if made public, it would deeply embarrass the Chinese government. A formal request would mean that prior to the documents being delivered, a copy of what was turned over would be made and eventually translated. Therefore, in trying to keep below the radar the Chinese government, in the form of Han Li, enlisted Matthew Moretti to help her retrieve them."

"Because his sister was employed by the Marciana."

"And the fact she was probably hoping that because of the relationship, Luca would agree to quietly return the documents. Which is why they were at his residence. However, they learned from Luca they were not in their designated storage area, and had been misfiled. They were supposed to go to the Marciana with him this morning and search for them, but as you know, that never happened."

"That doesn't explain the killings or Cai Fu's involvement."

"Someone in China, a person in authority, is trying to get ahold of the documents first. He wants to use them to discredit the country's current leadership and then leverage that into becoming China's new leader. Cai Fu is his henchman, and he killed Gina Moretti, believing that she had the documents. She didn't. The fact is that we're not entirely sure where they are."

"Then why kill Pietro Luca?"

"Cai Fu killed him, we believe, to prevent him from helping Moretti and Han Li."

"Did Mr. Moretti kill the Asian in Luca's home?"

"Han Li did."

"This is … complicated." Bruno's cell phone began to vibrate. He looked at the text message and set the phone back on his desk.

"Do you know where Mr. Moretti and Han Li are?" Bruno asked.

"At this moment, driving to Vienna. They believe the documents may be there."

"And not the Marciana?"

"Gina Moretti may have sent them to someone she trusted in Vienna. That's all I know at this point. Does what I've told you help your investigation, Chief Inspector?"

Bruno placed his pen down on his desk. The answer to that question was obvious and didn't warrant a response. He took a fresh pack of cigarettes from his desk and extracted one. After he lit it and expelled a lungful of smoke toward the ceiling, he told Davidson about the FedEx clerk, which he believed was connected to the other murders. He also told him about seeing Cai Fu this morning outside the Marciana.

Davidson didn't take notes. Instead the electronic device sewn inside the lining of his jacket was transmitting everything that was being said to the Sixty-Sixth. A written record of their conversation would be on his desk by the time he returned to his office.

"There's one more piece of information that I wish to share with you, Captain."

"Which is?"

"At this moment Cai Fu is at the airport, waiting to board a flight to Vienna. It appears that Mr. Moretti may run into him there. Of course, I have no authority to follow him to another country. But the US government doesn't have my constraints. If you're so inclined, I can have a police boat take you to the airport. His Alitalia flight is scheduled to leave the gate in …" Bruno looked at his watch and then finished, "Ten minutes."

"I'll never make it."

"Let me see," Bruno said, picking up his cell phone and punching in a number from his contact list. Bruno spoke in a low voice to the person who answered. When the call ended, he stood and walked to where Davidson was seated. "My mistake. It seems the Alitalia flight to Vienna has a mechanical problem. I believe they should have it fixed by the time you arrive at the airport. Would you like a cup of espresso before you leave?"

It is July 11, 1971. Two days ago, under a cloak of secrecy, I sent a plane to Pakistan for what I hoped would be the catalyst to unify my country. It carried Chang Wen-chin, head of the West European and American Department of my country's foreign ministry, and three of my most trusted navigators. They were there to escort Dr. Henry Kissinger and his Chinese-speaking assistant, Winston Lord, to Beijing. The Americans and I wanted to keep this meeting secret so that we could freely exchange our views away from prying eyes. It's a new beginning for both of us, and we need to control expectations.

President Nixon announced that he was sending Dr. Kissinger to Pakistan to hold talks with President Yahya Khan. When he was due to return home, the Americans made a press announcement that Dr. Kissinger had developed a sudden illness and that his doctors wanted him to remain in seclusion in Pakistan until he could regain his strength. President Yahya, who has been acting as a bridge between me and the United States and who has been very supportive of America's initiative to reestablish a dialogue with my country, personally coordinated this deception.

When Dr. Kissinger's plane arrived in Beijing, I had Marshal Yeh, who accompanied me on my Long March and has been a trusted friend for many decades, at the airport to greet him. I did not come personally as I have been experiencing heart and lung problems, which makes leaving my home difficult. Instead I arranged to see Dr. Kissinger later in the day. Our meeting was more cordial than expected, and for the next two days, we exchanged views on a multitude of topics. One of these discussions addressed whether the Americans, Soviets, and Japanese were planning to carve up my country and divide it among themselves. Dr. Kissinger assured me that this was not the United States' intent. On the contrary, he said America wanted to untangle itself from its conflicts in Asia and avoid regional wars. I believed him, as I've heard that the American people are weary of their involvement in Vietnam and want their government to end the war. It was to that end that I offered to help America negotiate a solution to their folly. I will use this as a bargaining chip on future matters that more deeply affect my country.

I convinced Dr. Kissinger that I felt it was time to set aside our differences, ignore what's previously been said about each other, and establish a formal relationship between our two nations. After some discussion, he suggested that I meet with President Nixon in the spring of 1972 and that we issue a joint communique announcing it. The notion of my sitting down with the Americans will be difficult for my people to accept. Many have grown up with a lifetime of teachings pointing out the corruption and moral turpitude of America. They will wonder why I am now talking with my declared enemy, a country who has caused my people to struggle for many years because of their embargo and their open support for our enemies. I will respond by telling them that I am more concerned about the Soviets, who eye me and my country as an increasing threat to their sovereignty. I will also explain that détente with the United States will prevent the Soviets, as well as Chiang, from taking military action against us until we become stronger and more self-reliant.

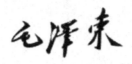

CHAPTER

16

CAI FU LANDED AT THE Vienna International Airport nearly two hours late. Once off the plane, he cleared customs and immigration and exited the terminal. He noticed that a blond-haired man in a dark blue suit seemed to be keeping pace ten yards behind him. He wasn't completely sure that he was following him until he walked outside and took a seat on a bench and saw through the terminal window that the man was in the baggage claim area, apparently waiting for his luggage. What made this suspicious was that the flight attendant announced the number of the carousal where they could retrieve their checked luggage, and that was half a terminal away. And if he could see him through the window, the reverse was also true.

Less than thirty seconds after he sat down, the person he'd been waiting for walked to the other end of the bench, put down his briefcase, and tied his shoe. His contact then stepped away, leaving a black leather attaché behind. Picking it up, he followed the signs to the ground level of the P4 parking garage, which housed the car rental agencies. Sixt was the first cubicle as he entered, and he took a place in line while the blond-haired man went to Avis several counters away, which didn't have a queue. Five minutes later he worked his way to the agent, and after filling out the necessary paperwork, he was given the keys to a beige Volvo S60 sedan. The car was in the first row of the rental car parking area, and after placing the briefcase on the passenger seat and adjusting his mirrors, he pulled out of his space. At the exit as he was showing his rental papers to the guard, he checked his rearview mirror and noticed that the blond-haired man was two cars behind him in a white Toyota Camry.

It took forty-five minutes to get to Vienna's Schonbrunn Palace and enter its adjacent parking structure. He'd used this location several times before because there were no surveillance cameras and the garage, which was mostly used by locals and employees, was relatively empty at this time of day. Parking on the third level, he took his time getting out of his car, doing so only after the white Toyota passed him and proceeded to the deck above. Taking what he needed, he left the car and walked through the exit doorway and waited to the side of the staircase, where he couldn't be seen. Seconds later he heard the door on the floor above slam open and rapidly descending footsteps. Holding out his foot just as his pursuer was stepping onto the metal platform, he saw the blond-haired man hit the deck hard and fall on his face. When he turned over, he was staring at a suppressed handgun.

"Why are you following me?"

"You've got an active imagination, buddy. I just dropped off my wife and kids at the entrance to the Schonbrunn, and I'm rushing to meet them." Davidson started to get up, but the man standing over him shook his head. The meaning was clear, and the American remained lying on his back.

"You were three rows behind me on the flight from Venice. You were at the car rental counter at the airport without a wife, children, or luggage. And you followed me here in a white Toyota. Did I miss anything?"

"I don't know what you're talking about."

"Pity."

The suppressor was still hot when he detached it from his gun and placed both in his jacket pockets. He searched Davidson, and taking what he found, he left the Schonbrunn garage and drove to another parking structure that also lacked a video surveillance system.

Examining what he'd taken from the dead man, he first picked up his passport, opened it, and saw that he'd killed Justin Davidson, a twenty-eight-year-old who seemed to have traveled extensively, judging by the number of international stamps. Next he looked at the black vinyl credential case, indicating that Davidson was a US Army captain assigned to the Sixty-Sixth Military Intelligence Brigade in Germany. He stared at the military ID card in disbelief. Why was he on America's radar? He wasn't a terrorist, at least not the type the United States was currently hunting. And neither Gina Moretti nor her brother were all that important to garner this level of surveillance, at least not as far as he knew. But then he thought about what Moretti might have learned from the assassin calling herself Han Li. If she confided to him about the documents and he passed that information to his government, it could explain the surveillance. He had a great deal of respect for US intelligence agencies. Despite criticism from Congress, they were the best in the world. It wouldn't take them long to determine he was Wu Bai, especially if they ran a facial recognition program off his photo on the *People's Daily* website. Taking the cell phone and cash, he locked the car and took the stairs down to the street level. On his way, he broke the SIM card in half and threw it, the cell phone, the passport, and Davidson's ID into a nearby trash container. Leaving the parking garage, he increased his stride. Franz Ludewig's shop was less than a block away.

It took only five and a half hours to drive from Venice to Franz Ludewig's shop, Document Restoration and Authentication. Han Li suggested calling prior to their arrival, but Moretti thought it'd be better to surprise him. If the man was involved, then he wouldn't have time to put together a story or hide the document beforehand. She agreed.

They found a parking space in front of the small business establishment, which was directly across the street from the Ritz-Carlton Hotel. The shop looked like it'd been there for more than a century, but it didn't seem out of place in a city that was a mixture of many architectural styles that traced its roots as far back as the Celts and Romans. The outside wall of the storefront was half-timbered, a combination of old wooden beams with masonry in between, that surrounded a large window showcasing a variety of historical books. Although the front of the shop was only three car lengths' wide, when they entered, they were surprised to see that it was more than twice that in depth and quite modern. The wall to the left of the entrance contained a long row of black metal cabinets, each with twenty-five drawers two inches in height and about three feet in depth. The right wall was lined with thick oak bookshelves, worn from decades of usage, stuffed with leather- and cloth-bound books in various states of wear. The center of the room was dominated by three black metal tables pushed together end to end, all of which were empty. In the far right corner was a door, which Moretti assumed led to Ludewig's office.

A bell chimed when they'd entered. Not long after, a short rotund man opened the door in the corner of the shop and came forward and greeted them. He appeared to be in his late seventies, and he was wearing a three-piece gray suit with a white shirt and light blue tie.

"May I be of assistance?"

"I hope so," Moretti replied, looking at the man who was nearly a foot shorter than him.

"My name is Matthew Moretti. I'm Gina's brother."

The man's face lit up. "I'm Franz Ludewig, but please call me Franz. I'm happy to meet you," he said, extending his hand. "She's told me so much about you."

Moretti shook his hand. Remembering that Han Li was behind him, he quickly introduced her as his friend.

"Don't stand there. Please come into my office. I insist." Before they could reply, he ushered them through the open doorway.

A cherrywood desk dominated the back of the room and faced the door. Behind it was a large double-hung window with raisable upper and lower sashes. It was flanked on both sides by thick red pull drapes. In front of the desk were two brown leather chairs that were worn unevenly from years of use. Against the wall to the left of the door as one entered was a similarly worn brown leather couch.

"Can I get you some coffee, hot chocolate, espresso?" Ludewig asked, motioning them to the chairs in front of his desk.

Moretti and Han Li both shook their heads in the negative and sat down.

"Well then," he said, sitting down behind his desk. "How is your dear sister?"

"I'm afraid that's why we're here," Moretti said. "She's dead."

Ludewig was taken aback and tried to speak, but no sound escaped his mouth. Finally, he responded with a feeble. "I'm sorry. Was she ill?"

"She was murdered. The police have an idea as to who was involved and are working to catch those responsible."

"Your sister was an angel. The world is a sadder place without her light to warm us. It's too bad Italy doesn't have capital punishment. I would like to see whoever did this to her hanged."

Moretti watched closely to see if he had any prior knowledge of his sister's death. If this was an act, he deserved an Academy Award.

"As would I. I'm here because I was hoping you could help me. I'm trying to clean up my sister's affairs, and I'm looking for a group of Chinese documents that she may have sent you. I want to ensure they're safely returned before I take my sister back to the United States for burial."

During their drive to Vienna, he and Han Li agreed that this would be their story as to the reason they wanted the documents.

"Yes, I understand. But that's already been taken care of," Ludewig said, causing Moretti and Han Li to move to the edge of their chairs. "Your sister phoned me less than a week ago and asked if I'd evaluate the authenticity of these documents and the single signature on eighteen of them and the two on the nineteenth. There was no note with them when they arrived, but I knew what she wanted from our earlier conversation. I verified the age of the paper and ink, as well as the peculiarities of penmanship that the author had, which I obtained from the internet. I'm not bragging, but I determined the document's authenticity in less than two hours."

"You said the nineteenth had two signatures. Whose were they?" Moretti asked.

Before the old man could answer, Han Li interrupted and said, "Were they authentic, Herr Ludewig?"

"Yes, all were authentic. I brought them to a colleague of mine, whose wife is a professor of history at the University of Vienna. She obtained reliable copies of these individual's signatures, and with the help of a handwriting expert I hired, we confirmed they'd signed the documents. I should also tell you that strangely enough, your sister sent me her computer and backpack in the same box that contained the documents," Ludewig said, turning toward Moretti. "I believe she thought the backpack would act as a cushion and further protect the contents. She probably forgot she'd left her computer inside. I sent back both with the documents."

"You don't have them?" Han Li asked.

"Why, no, not anymore. But don't worry. I took exceptional precautions. Since the signatories make these quite valuable, I chose to send them by another carrier, one who'd guarantee moisture and temperature control during the shipping process. People don't understand how even a small amount of atmospheric variance can destroy the quality of a document. I was frankly surprised your sister chose to send them by FedEx. But then again, she didn't know with certainty their authenticity. Either that, or she had budget constraints."

"Where exactly did you send them?" Moretti asked, just as the front doorbell rang.

"To the destination your sister provided me, of course, but not, as I said, by the same carrier."

"And that destination was?"

Ludewig held up his forefinger, indicating that he would answer that question as soon as he attended to his customer. He left the room, leaving his office door open.

Han Li and Moretti soon heard Ludewig apparently getting into an argument, repeatedly saying *nein, nein* to the person he was speaking with. His voice was strained, and he was becoming increasingly irritated. Finally, he seemed to have reached the tipping point, saying *nein* in a loud and forceful voice that indicated a note of finality. The response by the man he was speaking with was a single word—*pity*. Immediately, there was the unmistakable sound of a suppressed handgun followed by something heavy hitting the floor. Realizing what happened, Moretti raced to the window behind Ludewig's desk, opened it, and climbed out followed closely by Han Li. Both ran as fast as they could until they entered a tightly packed area of retail businesses, souvenir shops, and tourist attractions. Looking back and seeing that no one was following them, they transitioned to a fast walk. Moretti's back was beginning to tighten, and he was starting to limp. He stopped to stretch his muscles beside St. Stephen's Cathedral, a large gothic edifice that was built in the twelfth century, when a splinter of stone struck the side of his face. He didn't have a chance to think about what happened because the next thing he knew, Han Li tackled him to the ground just as a three-round burst hit the stone behind where his head had been a moment earlier. Looking in the distance, he saw Cai Fu aiming a gun in his direction. Picking himself up as another three-round burst hit just in front of him, he took off behind Han Li. His back was tight, preventing him from taking long strides, and she was increasing the divide between them until he saw her look over her shoulder and stop. She took her cell phone from her pocket and threw it into a nearby trash receptacle just as he came alongside. She then took off like a jackrabbit, keeping the distance between them at roughly ten yards and constantly changing direction as if in a maze. Ten minutes later, Moretti yelled at her to stop. He put his hands on his knees and took in deep gulps of air.

"The phone?" Moretti asked between gasps when she ran back to him.

"That's probably how he was able to follow us. In any case, keeping it wasn't worth the risk."

He nodded in agreement. "You were right. I didn't have to find Cai Fu. He found me."

"Fortunately, you survived. Next time you won't be as lucky. We need to get indoors."

"Where do you suggest?"

"There," she said, pointing to the Hotel Bristol, which was in directly front of them.

With his back in full spasm, he wasn't about to argue.

Once through the entrance, they saw a sign indicating that the ballrooms were down the hallway to their left. He followed Han Li, who went in and out of several before settling on one at the end of the hall.

"Why is this any different from the rest?" he asked.

"It's the only one with a rear exit."

"Good call."

"Let's talk over there," she said, pointing to a table near the exit.

He agreed. With the way their luck was running, they'd probably have to bolt out the door and run for their lives at any moment.

"We have to go back and search Ludewig's shop," she said.

"No argument from me. We need to look at his records and find out where the documents were sent or if he was lying to us and still has them. But I'm guessing now's not a good time since his business is probably crawling with police or soon will be. Which also brings up the question of our rental car, which is parked directly in front of his shop. The police will run a database search of every license plate in the vicinity. When they do, they'll have a photo of us from the border crossing."

"We don't have a choice."

"As I said, I agree. But just to be clear. We have different agendas. You're after the documents, and I'm after Cai Fu. Fortunately, being with you seems to draw him like a bee to honey. I wish I hadn't gotten rid of the Boberg before we crossed the border."

He stood and bent over to stretch his muscles. As he tried to touch his toes, he saw a visitor's map on the floor. Picking it up, he located where they were and saw that Ludewig's shop was directly across the street from the Ritz-Carlton Hotel and not far from various landmarks. One caught his attention and gave him an idea.

When he told her his idea, she thought it would almost certainly get him killed. On the other hand, it was just bold enough to work, and if he was killed in the process, it would solve her problem. His usefulness was coming to an end, and when it did, she'd either put a bullet in his head or let Cai Fu do it. Her orders were clear and unequivocal. Moretti had to die. The fact that he didn't know the contents of the documents was meaningless. He knew enough to embarrass her government, which was more than enough reason to send him back to the United States in a coffin next to his sister.

CHAPTER

17

CRAY WAS WAITING OUTSIDE SCHARLAU'S conference room, biding his time until the door opened and he could speak with his boss. Earlier, he was informed by his counterpart at the Sixty-Sixth of Davidson's death and the circumstances surrounding it. He'd come to brief the general as it was now known that Cai Fu was the killer. The captain's discussion with him, picked up by the electronic device sewn inside the lining of his jacket pocket and transmitted by satellite to the operations center at the Sixty-Sixth, had been transcribed and was now in the folder resting on his lap. The officer on duty, who was monitoring the transmission, heard the agent whisper Cai Fu's name just before the sound everyone in the room later said they knew was the discharge of a suppressed handgun. The duty officer followed protocol and immediately dialed 112, a number used within all EU member states to summon emergency services. The person answering, initially confused as to why someone in Germany would be reporting a crime in Austria, nevertheless connected the caller, whose ID was blocked, to the Viennese Federal Police, where he reported an armed robbery in progress and provided Davidson's location.

The authorities were eventually able to identify the body but only after speaking with Mauro Bruno, whose business card was found in the breast pocket of his jacket. The Viennese police also spoke with the commander of the Sixty-Sixth, Colonel Vincent Pappas, telling him that they believed this was a robbery since the killer took his wallet, along with any cash he may have had.

There was an age-old saying. *Don't shoot the messenger.* But in the military, Cray knew that the inverse was frequently true. Therefore, he wasn't looking forward to speaking with Scharlau. The Austrian government had already reached out to the State Department, trying to get ahead of the situation. They believed that a US military officer visiting their country as a tourist was robbed and killed, and they'd do anything to keep the murder of a foreigner quiet. It was bad for tourism and foreign business alike. Therefore, reaching an agreement that a significant favor could be extracted from the Austrian government in the future, the State Department turned to the Department of Defense, who arranged for Davidson to be "killed" in a training mishap in Germany. No one on the US side of the barter liked it, but since the officer was already dead, they hoped that somewhere down the line they could get something of value in return.

Scharlau's door opened, and he escorted a brigadier general, one rank lower than him, out of his office and then told Cray to come in. The major relayed what he knew along with the fact that he'd been unable to contact Moretti, even though his cell phone was communicating with a tower in Vienna's Ringstrasse. At the end of their meeting, which lasted only twenty minutes, Cray left with sweat running down the sides of his face. He'd just been ordered to call the Viennese police to have Moretti and Han Li arrested.

They stood in the shadows a hundred yards from Ludewig's shop. Moretti believed now that they'd discarded the cell phone, Cai Fu had no logical way of locating them, which was a necessity for his plan to succeed. Therefore, they needed to find him instead. He presumed that the Chinese assassin would conclude that there were three possibilities for the location of the documents. Either Ludewig had them hidden in his shop; had left a clue, intentional or not, as to where they were; or had given Mao's diary to him and Han Li. Therefore, Cai Fu would have no alternative but to search the shop, which is why they were waiting for him.

Prior to taking their position, they looked closely at the

surrounding area. There were only two locations that provided the requisite vantage point to unobtrusively observe when the police left the premises, and no one else was around, giving Cai Fu the opportunity to break in unobserved. One was the Ritz-Carlton Hotel, and the other was the office building next to it. He selected the office building for himself and Han Li, figuring correctly, as it turned out, that Cai Fu would not want to hide in a recessed doorway of the secured building with the possibility of being noticed by a roving police patrol or passersby rather than in a room at the Ritz.

An hour after he and Han Li settled into the doorway, a police officer exited the shop and placed a strip of yellow police tape across the door prior to leaving in his patrol car.

He sprang into action. Leaving his hiding place, he walked with a limp, given the soreness of his back, past the front of the Ritz, hoping that Cai Fu would see him and give chase. Carrying a large brown paper bag that he'd found near a trash container and stuffed with folded newspaper, he hoped that the promise of what he was carrying would be irresistible to the Chinese assassin. While he was leading him on this wild goose chase, Han Li would have time to search the shop for the documents, and if they weren't there, at least find the name of the shipping company Ludewig used.

As it turned out, Moretti was correct because just after he passed the hotel, Cai Fu ran out the lobby door and followed him. Han Li watched, and once they were out of sight, crossed the Ringstrasse and went to the rear of Ludewig's shop. However, the office window, through which they escaped, had been locked. So much for the easy way in. Walking to the front of the building, she noticed, as expected, that their car was no longer there. Fortunately, there was nothing within it that she needed.

At this hour there was very little foot traffic since the merchants had already locked up and gone home for the evening. Verifying that no one was within sight, she took a credit card and used it to slice through the police tape that ran over the door frame. She then slid it between the door and the doorjamb, bending it back so that the side closest to her almost touched the doorknob and then in the opposite direction until the bolt pushed itself back into the door. Entering, she looked at the alarm box, which was on the wall to the left, and saw a green light. Thankfully, the police didn't activate it, probably because they didn't know the code and hadn't called the security company to reset it. If they had, she'd give herself two minutes inside at most. As it was, she still needed to be quick. There was no way of telling how long Moretti would be able to keep Cai Fu away or when the police might come back and check the premises.

She took a small flashlight from her jacket and searched the shop, looking in every drawer to verify that Ludewig hadn't lied about shipping the documents. Not finding Mao's diary, she walked to his office, grabbed a wheeled suitcase and backpack she found next to the couch, and placed his papers, Rolodex, and folders inside. Underneath the Rolodex, she found a small strip of paper, looked at it, and kept it in her hand. Several minutes later she left, wondering how Moretti was doing and if Cai Fu would save her the trouble of killing him.

He wanted to look back in the worst way and see if he was being followed, but Moretti feared that doing so might make Cai Fu suspicious. His back muscles were as tight as violin strings from the fast pace he was maintaining. That didn't bode well for the second phase of his plan, which was to jump the waist-high fence of the park just ahead, hide in the bushes, and ambush and kill Cai Fu with the knife Han Li had given him. He decided to risk a look. If he wasn't there, then he was on a fool's errand and needed to get back to the bar at the Hotel Bristol, where he was to rendezvous with Han Li.

When he passed under a streetlight, he slowly began to turn around. Halfway into that turn, his right ear felt as if it was being ripped off. The pain caused him to lose his balance and fall to the sidewalk. He could feel blood dripping down the side of his face and sliding under the collar of his shirt. When he realized what had happened, he dived flat on the ground. That saved his life because just as he did, the sash on the wooden door to his left exploded in a myriad of splinters. Looking behind him, he saw Cai Fu pointing a gun in his direction. He instinctively looked for cover, finding it when he rolled to his left behind a building planter just before a bullet hit the spot where his head had been a split second earlier. He looked frantically around for help, but there were no pedestrians in the area. Taxis and cars were on the Ringstrasse, which was fifty yards to his right, but he'd be an easy target if he tried to get there. Stadtpark was less than twenty feet ahead, and if he could get there, it offered his best chance to escape.

Crab-walking down the sidewalk while several bullets breezed past him, he reached the wrought-iron barrier surrounding the park and dived over headfirst. But when he tried to get up, his back had locked up, and he couldn't get off the ground. He heard the rapid staccato of footsteps approaching and getting louder by the second. It wouldn't be long until Cai Fu was standing over him. Then he'd be dead. With back spasms that were so painful it took his breath away, he crawled into a dense area of bushes ahead of him and wiggled his way as far back as he could into the dense brush. As soon as he lay flat, a bullet streaked over his head and hit the tree in front of him. He took the knife out of his pants pocket, unfolded the blade, and waited.

Cai Fu picked up the brown paper bag and looked at the newspaper inside. He was pissed for not taking a shot at Moretti sooner. But he thought he was leading him to hei guafu, and he so badly wanted to put a bullet in the center of her head that his emotions got the better of him and he didn't think things through. If he had, he'd have realized that they didn't have the documents. Otherwise, they'd be long gone from Vienna. Moretti was a decoy, leading him away from Ludewig's shop so that hei guafu could search it. That's when he took the shot. Only like his sister, he didn't stand still, and the bullet missed its mark. After that, he'd lost his cool and chased after him. When Moretti jumped the fence into the park, he took a few more shots but lost him in the darkness.

By the time he went to Ludewig's shop he saw that the police tape across the front door had been cut. The Black Widow had already been there. And if the documents had been inside, she had them now. Nevertheless, he wanted to search the shop on the off chance that she'd overlooked something. He believed that assumption was probably a fantasy, but nevertheless, it was the only straw he could grasp.

He took out his cell phone and touched the Mag Lite icon, which provided more than ample light for his search. Starting with the main viewing area, he looked in each of the document drawers before turning his attention to the bookshelves on the opposite wall. Coming up empty, he went into Ludewig's office. First searching the perimeter, he pulled back the red drapes. Behind the one to the left of the window he noticed that the wood paneling just above the floor had an almost imperceptible rectangular cut. Running his hand lightly over its surface, he pushed in and felt the section release. Behind the hinged piece of wood was an old floor safe. His heart began to beat faster, and he tried to control his breathing. Opening it wouldn't be fast, but it also wouldn't be difficult given his training. He shined his Maglite on the dial and noticed there was a small strip of paper taped to the top. It was the combination. His elation quickly faded and turned to anger when he realized who'd placed it there. Opening the safe, he saw that it contained several documents, but not the one he was looking for. He turned toward the desk, which was two arm lengths' away, and opened each drawer. Nothing was inside or on top of the desk except for a lamp. Believing it unlikely that the police did this, he asked himself why she'd taken its contents. The only answer that made sense was that she didn't find the documents and was hoping to find a clue to lead her to them. His elation returned.

Vienna wasn't a large city by Chinese standards, but it was big enough. He had a better chance of winning the lottery than finding hei guafu or Moretti within it. He shouldn't have killed Ludewig as quickly as he did. Originally, he intended to take his time and carefully question him. But then he'd seen a car with Italian license plates parked outside and knew who it belonged to. That's when his plans changed. When he entered the shop he was all business, no pleasantries or small talk. He drew his gun and asked Ludewig time and again where the documents were. He continually denied having them. He should have incapacitated him, locked the shop, and dealt with Moretti and hei guafu. If he had, he'd know the location of the documents. Instead, he let his temper get the better of him, frustrated with the old man's refusal. Stupid. *Somewhere you'll never find them.* He couldn't get those words out of his mind.

It is February 28, 1972. I am rapidly in decline. Before the American leader arrived in Beijing, I was in the hospital for nine days, regaining my strength and recovering from an old man's infirmities. My doctors and aides advised me to remain in bed and told me that any excesses could cause me to die. But I've faced death many times, and we're not strangers to each other. How could I stay in the hospital, lying flat on my back while the American president was in my country? I could not show such weakness, and I summoned all my remaining strength to be present and speak to the man I needed to meet.

For more than twenty years, the Americans and I have been at each other's throats, and now we are finally able to sit and speak about our differences. President Nixon was a guest of my nation for a week, staying at the Diaoyutai State Guesthouse in Beijing, not far from where I reside. I found him to be humbler than I expected, and his mannerisms and speech was respectful to both me and my people. These were pleasant surprises.

My country desperately needs trade with the United States. Once this happens, the rest of the world will follow, and my country will once again prosper. But this growth will require the Americans to protect us, something that's difficult for me to admit. The Soviets are strong and could invade my country at any time. Even though I've threatened to use our nuclear weapons in our defense, the Soviets disregard this threat and show no respect for our borders or sovereignty. They openly invite conflict and taunt me to fight them. Only a relationship with the United States can deter them from aggression and give me the leverage I need to negotiate a secure border.

When I first saw President Nixon, I noticed that he showed an energy and vigor that I did not have at that age. He also had a sense of humor, which I didn't expect. He said through his translator, "I believe our old friend Chiang Kai-shek would not approve of this." My heart soared with joy at his comment and the anguish Chiang must now feel knowing that his savior and protector has given my country the recognition it deserves. This sends a message to the world that Taiwan does not speak for the Chinese people.

My meeting with President Nixon touched on many subjects, and he seemed eager to hear my opinions. We spoke at length about America's support and recognition of Taiwan, and I told him that I desired a unified China with one land, one ruler, and one flag. I asked for his assistance in accomplishing this. To my astonishment, he did not avoid this topic. He told me that a strong and unified China would act as a stabilizing force in Asia. He offered his assistance in this endeavor, but in return, he wanted my help to end his country's conflict in Vietnam. If I would do that, then he would reciprocate the favor and arrange for a dialogue between me and Chiang with the goal of unifying China. I readily agreed, and we shook on it. Afterward, our staffs established procedures so that we could secretly communicate with each other by using my aide and one of his trusted assistants as go-betweens.

At the conclusion of his visit, we jointly issued what the world now calls the Shanghai Communique. In it we jointly expressed our foreign policy views, forging an era of cooperation that has been vacant for far too long. The American president stated, "This was the week that changed the world, as what we have said in that communique is not nearly as important as what we will do in the years ahead to build a bridge across sixteen thousand miles and twenty-two years of hostilities that have divided us in the past. And what we have said today is that we shall build that bridge."

The seed of a lifetime of struggle and pain has finally grown a tree from which we can now eat our fruit. We have been recognized by the United States as an equal. As a show of good faith and in what must have been a bitter pill for Chiang to swallow, Dr. Kissinger issued a statement that America intended to pull all of its forces out of Taiwan and work toward establishing a full diplomatic relationship with my country. I now anxiously wait to begin my dialogue with Chiang.

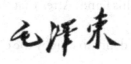

CHAPTER

18

MORETTI WAS LIMPING BADLY WHEN he tried to enter the Hotel Bristol. What should have been a fifteen-minute walk from Stadtpark was three times that. Hobbling to the front entrance, his back spasms were so severe that every step felt as if someone was twisting a knife in his back. He was looking forward to getting a drink, taking a hot shower, and then getting something to eat. But the doorman had other ideas and asked if he was staying in the five-star hotel. He couldn't blame him. His jacket was one mass of wrinkles, his pants scarred with dirt, and his white shirt was approaching brown in color with a touch of caked blood on the side of his face and collar, thanks to the bullet that had pierced his ear. His jacket, which was surprisingly intact, was as wrinkled as if he'd wadded in a ball and kept that way for years before he decided to wear it again. He was a stark contrast to the well-heeled clientele that passed him on their way into the hotel. Therefore, when he told the doorman that he was going to meet someone inside, he received a disbelieving look and was politely asked to leave. He knew he had no way of getting past the man, especially since there were now two security guards standing a few feet behind him. He was rescued from his quandary by Han Li, who apparently saw what was happening. Speaking to the doorman, she concluded their conversation by putting a large denomination euro in his hand. After that, he opened the door and gladly let them in.

Once inside, she told him to wait by the elevators, which were just ahead and to the left, while she registered. When she returned, they went to their second-floor room, where he went into the bathroom and examined his wound, seeing for the first time the ragged notch made by the bullet that had nearly found his skull.

"I'll be damned. He shot off part of my ear."

"It won't be fatal," Han Li responded from the bedroom, where she was emptying the contents of both bags onto the bed. "Think of it as a sign of Cai Fu's bad marksmanship. In China, it would be considered good luck."

He didn't respond. Instead he took off his shirt, placed it over the sink, and tried scrubbing the blood from it with soap and water. Although the blood didn't come completely off, enough of it did so that it wouldn't draw undo attention. He'd clean up in the shower. Bringing the shirt out of the bathroom, he hung it over the back of the desk chair to dry.

"These are all the papers I found in Ludewig's office," Han Li said, pointing to what she'd put on the bedspread. "Hopefully, somewhere in there, we'll find which transport company he used."

"This is written in German," he replied, picking up one of the pieces of paper arrayed before him.

"Which I can read. I'll go through these by myself."

With his ear and back in pain, he wasn't about to argue. He went to the minibar, took a highball glass from the shelf above, and emptied five miniatures of Chivas Regal into it. After taking a long swallow, he went into the bathroom for a hot shower. When he came out, Han Li had just put down the last piece of paper. The look on her face told him she had nothing. He took his empty glass back to the minibar, found several miniatures of Jack Daniels, and poured them into it.

"Do you really need that?" Han Li asked.

"My back is killing me."

"Is that why you drink so much?"

He thought about lying, but what was the point? He didn't care what she thought of him. He realized that same feeling applied to almost everyone he knew.

"I drink because my life is shit. Gina was the only one in my family I was close to, and now she's gone. My father and I get along, but we're not exactly best friends. My job doesn't excite me, and when I think I might be working there for the next fifteen years, I get depressed. Not to mention that I wake up every single morning of this fantasy life with back pains, sometimes so bad I can't stand, and I feel sorry for myself. You can point to any one of those pins of sunlight as to why I drink," he said before taking a swallow of Jack Daniels.

Han Li went back to what she was doing, and when she finished with the papers, she grabbed Ludewig's Rolodex, the only item she hadn't examined. She started going through the numerous cards contained within, cross-referencing the names to transportation and courier companies in the phone book. There was no match.

"It's late. I'm going to take a shower and then get some sleep," she said in a voice that seemed to reflect her frustration. "In the morning we can decide what to do next."

He was sitting on the couch and watching her, and when she walked into the bathroom, he pushed the Rolodex aside and stretched out on the bed. Trying to get comfortable, he leaned to the side and the metal box jabbed him in the side. As he pushed it away to give himself more room, he thought of something he should have considered before. Phoning the concierge, he asked a question, got his answer, and then picked up the phone book. He looked for logistics companies and cross-referenced those with names in the Rolodex. Eventually, he found one match. He pulled the index card, and barely able to contain himself, he went into the bathroom to tell Han Li, opening the door just as she stepped out of the shower and was reaching for a towel. The look in her eye told him that she was debating whether to level him with a kick to the head. Fortunately, she wrapped the towel around her instead.

"What?"

"Look at this," he responded, handing her the Rolodex card. "It's a match."

She took it from his hand. "Von Trapp. I already tried to cross-reference this, but I didn't find it listed in the phone book."

"Not under transportation, delivery, or courier companies. But you would have had you looked under logistics companies, which in German is spelled l-o-g-i-s-t-i-k."

"You figured that out on your own?"

"The concierge did give me the German spelling."

Han Li walked past him into the bedroom and sat down at the hotel computer on their desk. After agreeing to pay the fee indicated on screen, she logged onto the internet and looked up Von Trapp Logistics. Scrolling through the website, she saw that they operated an environmentally controlled document delivery service.

"We still don't know if this is the company."

"That's why we're going there in the morning—to find out."

Han Li agreed. "Let's get some sleep," she said, taking everything off the bed and putting it back into the two bags.

While she did this, he grabbed a pillow and comforter from the bed and settled in on the floor. Han Li hit the light switch next to the nightstand, and the room was cast into darkness. Immediately afterward, he heard her towel hit the floor followed by the rustling of the covers. He tried to get the vision of her in the shower out of his mind, but those images seemed to be on infinite rewind. It wasn't until early morning that he was finally able to fall asleep.

Mauro Bruno was getting nowhere. He had four dead bodies, five if he counted the American intelligence officer, a suspect who left the country, and the editors of the two local newspapers who were roasting him on a spit for not catching the murderer or murderers, depending on which newspaper one read. After Davidson's death, any uncertainty he had that Cai Fu was his killer was gone. The problem he faced was that there was no evidence linking him to any murder, only Moretti's eyewitness statement to his friend at the US Army Intelligence and Security Command, which could be easily debunked by any competent defense attorney who'd claim the American was also a suspect. He suspected his incineration at the hands of the press would continue for some time, and with the letter that Davidson promised almost certain to be forgotten, it'd take a minor miracle for him to keep his job and pension.

He lit a cigarette and took the smoke into his lungs, feeling its calming effect begin to take hold. The Americans requested that he meet with Davidson's replacement. He normally found American persistence irritating, but in this situation, he welcomed their help. If they were going to go after Cai Fu, he wanted to work closely with them. With resources he could only dream about, maybe they could get him the proof he needed to keep his job and perhaps even the letter that Davidson had mentioned.

Major Peter Cancelliere arrived promptly at ten o'clock, wearing a well-tailored gray suit, white shirt, and black wing tip shoes. He introduced himself in perfect Italian and accepted an offer of espresso. Inviting the major to take a seat on the couch across from his desk, he phoned one of his officers to get the drink for him.

"Thank you for seeing me on such short notice, Chief Inspector. My commander asked me to be the liaison between you and the Sixty-Sixth following the death of Captain Davidson. I have the specifics of your conversation with him, but what I'd like to know is whether there's something new you wish to add, given the circumstances."

He wondered how in the few minutes Davidson had before he boarded his flight, and the short amount of time he had before he died, he could provide any substantive information on their meeting. But considering American technology, he wouldn't be surprised if their conversation had been recorded and relayed by satellite to whoever was supposed to hear it. He took a puff of his cigarette, realized that he hadn't offered one to the major, and raised his pack. Cancelliere shook his head just as an officer knocked on the door and entered holding a cup of espresso.

He took a deep breath, at least as much as he could considering that he smoked between two and three packs a day, and began to give Cancelliere his thoughts. "I believe Matthew Moretti is caught in the middle between Cai Fu and Han Li and their search for the documents. He knows too much, and one or the other is going to kill him to keep their secret." He went on to tell him about the death of the FedEx clerk and the Asian, going into detail at what they found at the scenes of the crimes.

Cancelliere listened without comment, but his demeanor seemed to indicate that he agreed with everything that was said. When he finished, the major stood and asked if he could see where each of the victims were killed.

He'd been over the crime scenes numerous times and was weary of going once again. But he wanted the American's help, and therefore, he agreed. Grabbing a fresh pack of cigarettes from his desk drawer and stuffing it into his jacket pocket, he left his office for the Campo Santo Stefano.

Von Trapp Logistics was in the ninth district of Vienna, a few doors down from the former home of Sigmund Freud, and it was about half the size of Ludewig's shop. Moretti and Han Li entered shortly after it opened and approached the counter. Seeing no one, Moretti pressed a call button, and not long after, a wire-thin man in his early thirties opened the door behind the counter and approached him. He was five feet six inches in height, with unruly long brown hair and horn-rimmed glasses, wearing worn leather sandals and no socks. The plastic name tag, which he wore over the left breast pocket of his long-sleeved blue denim shirt, gave his name as Dieter. Looking like a holdover from the 1960s, he asked the tall stranger in front of him what he wanted, all the while not taking his eyes off Han Li.

Picking up on his interest in her, she walked up to the counter as Moretti, apparently seeing the clerk's infatuation, made himself unobtrusive and walked outside. In almost perfect German, she explained that her friend didn't speak German but that she needed to track a package but didn't have the shipping number. Dieter smiled at the attractive and athletic-looking brunette.

"Give me your name and address or that of the recipient, and I'll look it up," the impossibly thin man said with a smile.

"The name of the sender is Herr Ludewig, but I don't recall his exact address. I arranged for him to authenticate something for my client and then return it to him. Unfortunately, he hasn't received it. Since I know Herr Ludewig uses your company, I wanted to check on the whereabouts of the package."

"Didn't you hear? Herr Ludewig was killed yesterday."

"Killed? That's terrible," Han Li said, showing her distress. "He was like a grandfather to me. Do they know who did this awful thing?"

"Not that I've heard."

"Dieter," she continued in her sultry voice. "I came here because I couldn't get ahold of Herr Ludewig, and I was worried that he may have shipped the documents I'd given him to my client's old address and not the new one I gave him last week. Unfortunately, I was in a hurry when I left his office and forgot my backpack, which contained my computer. I was hoping to pick it up in case Herr Ludewig shipped it to my client since he knew I lived very close to where the documents were being sent. I desperately need my computer and for the shipment to go to the new address. Otherwise, I'd look twice as stupid. I hope you understand."

"Completely. I remember that shipment because I packed it myself and placed your backpack and computer in a separate holding container from the documents. I then put both in a larger environmentally sealed box. It left the day before yesterday and should arrive later today or tomorrow morning at the latest, depending on how many pickups our driver has. I don't schedule those."

"Can you check and see if it went to the correct address?"

"It would be my pleasure." He hit some keys on his computer and then swiveled the screen around.

"Is this the new address?"

Han Li looked at the recipient, displaying no outward sign of emotion.

"It is. I guess I'll have to retrieve the computer from my client. Thank you," Han Li said, kissing him on the cheek. "You've been very helpful."

Dieter kissed her hand and watched as she left the shop and joined Moretti on the street.

"Do you know where the documents are?" Moretti asked.

"Yes, and you're not going to believe it."

CHAPTER

19

"THEY'RE BACK AT THE MARCIANA!"

"If they're not now, they soon will be."

"Then why did my sister bother to send them to Vienna in the first place? It makes no sense."

"To protect them. My guess is that everything came to a head the night she died. She had the documents at her apartment, and somehow, Cai Fu found out or suspected they were there. We may never know how your sister discovered he was coming for them, but she did. Therefore, she needed to get them in the hands of someone she trusted. Sending them to Ludewig was the obvious choice since they had a working relationship. In the rush, she forgot that her computer was in the backpack along with one of the Marciana's prepaid FedEx airbills, which she had at home. This is the reason Ludewig sent them back without calling first because the address on the enclosed FedEx slip, which he assumed was for the prepaid return, was that of the Marciana. This would make sense to him since he probably returned everything she sent back to that address. The only difference in this situation was that she didn't use a climate controlled transport company, something Ludewig thought might have been due to budget constraints."

"Now you know where the documents are or will soon be."

"But I may still need your help to retrieve them," Han Li said.

"And Cai Fu, where is he now?"

"My guess is that he's on his way to Venice. Once he saw you this evening, he knew you wouldn't still be here if we had the documents. He'll go back to the Marciana, probably believing they were there the entire time."

"Any suggestions on how we get to Venice? I saw that we don't have a car."

"The person I work for will make the necessary arrangements. Once we get back to our room, I'll ask the concierge where I can buy a disposable phone and call him."

When they walked into the Hotel Bristol, Han Li went to the front desk to get their room key, while Moretti waited by the elevator.

"Mr. Moretti?" a police officer asked, approaching him from behind.

"Yes," he automatically responded before recalling that his passport was in a different name.

"Would you please come with us? We'd like to ask you a few questions," he said as another officer joined him.

A moment later he saw two officers escorting a handcuffed Han Li past him. One was holding their photos.

"Hands behind your back."

He complied and was handcuffed. Escorted out of the hotel, he was placed in the back seat of a police vehicle directly behind the one Han Li was in. He didn't know precisely what they were going to charge him with, but depending on what they knew, they could have quite a list to choose from. He needed to call the US embassy.

The ride to the police station, a five-story redbrick building that looked to be early-1960s construction, took less than ten minutes. Moretti saw the police car containing Han stop outside a door at the far-right end of the building, while his vehicle continued for another thirty yards farther to another entry portal. Taken inside by the two arresting officers, he was brought to a counter and his handcuffs removed. After emptying his pockets and taking off his belt, he signed an inventory of what was subsequently placed in a brown paper bag. Again handcuffed, the two officers brought him to a ten-by-fifteen-foot interrogation room containing a gray metal table with a matching chair on either side. All were bolted to a slate gray linoleum floor, and bordered by concrete block walls painted the same color as the furniture. A camera in the upper right corner completed the police department's idea of interior decorating. Moretti was placed in the chair facing the door, and his handcuffs were removed, after which the officers left the room without saying a word.

As he sat in his chair, he wondered why he hadn't been fingerprinted, had a mug shot taken, been given a full-body search, or gone through any of the other niceties of preincarceration. The only answer he could come up with was that he wasn't under arrest, which seemed curious given the number of illegalities he'd been a part of. After what seemed to be several hours, the door opened, and he was taken to a restroom. He told the officer escorting him that he wanted to speak with the US Embassy. There was no response. He didn't know whether the man didn't understand or was ignoring him. But since the officers who arrested him spoke English, he believed it was the latter.

When he returned to the interrogation room, he found a bottle of water on the table. Hours later he was again escorted to the restroom. This time when he returned, an army colonel whose nameplate read Pappas was sitting in his chair. He was six feet in height, and he had the athletic physique and tan of someone who frequently played tennis or golf. With dark brown hair in a regulation cut and piercing hazel eyes, anyone who saw him suspected that he was either employed by the military or law enforcement. His army service uniform, which didn't have a wrinkle, had five rows of service ribbons above the left pocket. The dour expression on his face indicated that he was not in a good mood. Moretti took a seat in the chair opposite him.

"You and your Asian friend have been leaving quite a trail of destruction, Mr. Moretti," Pappas said. "I suppose you have an entertaining story to explain all that."

"Colonel, with all due respect to your rank, the only person I want to speak with is someone from the US Embassy or an attorney. I don't answer to the military anymore."

"You're not going to be speaking to either. This is an issue of national security, and your rights are in the crapper. Either you talk to me, or you enjoy the fine hospitality of the Viennese police until we can arrange for a rendition to a country whose view of human rights is several centuries old. You'll go from strudel to goat meat if you don't get an attitude adjustment and cooperate."

Moretti took a deep breath and looked him in the eye to see if he was bluffing. He wasn't. He'd been in the military long enough to know that a full-bird colonel wouldn't be wasting his time sitting in an interrogation room with a civilian unless he wanted something important from that person. As the colonel suggested, he adjusted his attitude. For the next two hours, he told Pappas everything he knew from the moment Cai Fu entered his office to when he was arrested at the Hotel Bristol.

"Quite a story. The Chinese government and a not so patriotic general competing to get ahold of a set of documents that could unravel the Communist Party. And you're in the middle. You do realize that the second your friend down the hall finds them, you're dead. She gave you quite a bit of information so that you'd help her. Do you really think she'd let you just walk away, win or lose, with that knowledge? You're a liability."

"Meaning she intended to kill me all along."

"That's the long and short of it. And to make your life a little cheerier, Cai Fu will continue to try to kill you, even if he doesn't end up with the documents, because he believes Han Li told you too much and he wants to protect his boss. Or since he's an assassin, he may just do it to settle the score with someone who's given him so much trouble. That's the reason General Scharlau arranged to have you and Han Li arrested. He wanted to keep you alive."

"Thank him for me."

"His thoughts weren't altruistic. He wants you to find the documents for us because if the Chinese are worrying about them creating social instability and possibly a regime change, then we want them. Can you imagine the leverage we'd have if they were in our possession? We'd be in the catbird seat in trade negotiations, intellectual property disputes, and anything else you can name."

"And what happens to Han Li?"

"I saw her a few minutes before you, and unsurprisingly, she's refused to talk. She's a Chinese citizen, so there's only so much the police can do without formally charging her. But in the spirit of cooperation, they've agreed not to prosecute her for entering the country with a forged passport because it could get sticky with your involvement. I've asked them to keep her here until we've left. After that, they'll boot her out of the country."

"So I'm getting out of here."

"As long as you cooperate."

"As I told you, I'm only in this to kill Cai Fu. I don't give a flip about the documents or geopolitics. But once I find them and deliver them to you, he's gone. I won't get a chance to put a bullet in the brain of the man who murdered my sister."

"Find the documents. In return, I'll give you full access to the resources of the Sixty-Sixth so that you can track and kill Cai Fu, wherever he might be. You want him dead because he killed your sister. I want him dead because he murdered one of my agents who had a wife and two young children. I'd put a bullet into him myself if I could. But let's take one step at a time. First, we'll find the documents, and then I'll help you kill this bastard."

"On your oath as an officer?"

"When I drive to my office in the morning, I pass Captain Davidson's house. He has two girls, one and four years of age. The fact that Cai Fu has taken their father from them and brought years of anguish to this family, eats at my soul. So yes, you have my word."

Pappas stood and knocked on the interrogation room door. When the police officer opened the door, they left and went down the hall to one of the administrative offices, where a man in the suit was typing on his computer keyboard.

"Are we good to go, Detective?" Pappas asked.

"Your government has spoken to my government, and I've been asked to cooperate fully. I've erased everything on Mr. Moretti and the woman from our system."

"And she'll be released once we've gone."

"Just as we discussed. In two hours."

"That's very much appreciated."

"I'm happy to be of assistance. Mr. Moretti, I believe this belongs to you," the detective said, handing him the bag with his possessions in it. "I took the liberty of removing the Canadian passport for Matthew Grogan, which must have inadvertently been placed inside."

Moretti smiled, and then he turned and followed Pappas out the back door and into a waiting car.

It is June 1972. Thanks largely to the efforts of the Americans, yesterday my aide Cho Ling, while in the city buying supplies, was approached by one of Chiang's agents. I initially doubted that the letter that was handed to him was authentic. I am no stranger to treachery and deceit within my own government, and at first, I believed it was entirely possible that I was being tested by Premier Chou. But I also know Chiang's signature and recognized the strength and boldness of his hand.

In his letter Chiang told me that he believed it was our joint responsibility to unite China under one flag and one leader. He was emphatic that a divided people would only invite the unwanted intervention of foreigners, militarily or through outside economic aid. I never thought I would hear a call for unity from him or his thoughts paralleling mine. We were two aging leaders reaching the end of our lives, realizing that if we didn't agree to set aside our differences and unite China now, it would never happen.

This is not the first time the subject of reunification had been discussed. Decades ago, the United States and its allies wanted to use the United Nations to resolve our sovereignty issue. Both Chiang and I were against this because we didn't want China's governance and policies decided by a third party. In fact, at that time, I wrote three letters to the people of Taiwan agreeing with my archenemy on this issue. But it was Chiang who took the brunt of the criticism from the Americans for not letting the UN resolution proceed because it was generally believed that the world body would rule in favor of Taiwan, and in this manner, a unified and non-Communist China would be achieved. There was some truth to that, as the United States exercised great power within the United Nations. But he and I knew that for a lasting unity to succeed, the Chinese people would have to be ideologically united under a single leader. No foreign body could do that.

In the end, Chiang's position created a great deal of domestic turmoil. His people demanded an election, feeling that he was out of touch with the world. As a result, three candidates ran for the presidency of Taiwan—Chiang; Chen Ching, a general and assistant to Chiang; and Hu Si, a scholar. I supported Chiang by publicly acknowledging that I considered him the leader of Taiwan and by saying that he was the only person I would negotiate with. I did this because I understood how he thought. I did not want someone in power whose thinking I was not familiar with. I also wanted a strong leader who would be able to convince his people at the proper time to reunite. I knew he was the only person who could make that happen.

I asked my trusted adviser, Cho Ling, to be my intermediary with Chiang's contact, who was identified in his message. Later that same day, I gave my written response, requesting a face-to-face meeting with my longtime enemy.

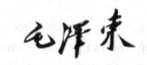

CHAPTER

20

HAN LI WAS RELEASED EXACTLY two hours after Moretti and Pappas left the building, and her personal items were returned then. Although the police now knew, thanks to the colonel, that the name on her passport was false, they wanted her out of the country as soon as possible so they could deny any involvement with what the Americans were up to. Therefore, they turned a blind eye to what normally would have sent them into a catatonic fit. A female police officer was summoned and instructed to drive the woman seated in the interrogation room to the airport and put her on any flight out of the country so long as it left today.

When Han Li and the officer entered the main terminal of the Vienna International Airport, the officer pointed to a departure screen and told Han Li to pick a flight to a foreign destination. Once she chose, they walked to the ticket counter, and the officer used a government credit card to purchase a ticket to Venice.

At the same time Han Li entered the airport terminal, Moretti was sitting aboard an Air Force C-20E, a stretched version of the Gulfstream III. His carry-on bag was beside his seat, his passport resting on top. In the seat facing him was an impeccably dressed man whom Pappas introduced as Major Peter Cancelliere. The colonel said that he'd be accompanying him and that he would drop them both off at Venice's Marco Polo Airport before returning to Germany. Moretti didn't know anything about the Cary Grant impersonator sitting across from him. Nor did he care. All he wanted was to find the documents and then use every speck of intelligence Pappas had at his disposal to search for Cai Fu. It'd been almost an entire day since he'd taken a drink, and he was on edge and irritable. He turned to Pappas, who was in the seat to his left, and asked if he had anything stronger than water onboard. The colonel didn't respond. Instead he opened a cabinet door next to his seat, exposing a dozen bottles of branded liquors. Moretti's eyes went wide at the size of the stash. Pappas laughed at his reaction, telling him that this aircraft was frequently used to transport members of Congress within Europe and that they invariably requested a drink when aboard. The army wanted to keep them inebriated and happy, so they always made sure the cabinet was stocked.

Handing Moretti and Cancelliere each an empty glass, Pappas poured them three fingers of an eighteen-year-old single-malt scotch, and then he did the same for himself. Touching glasses in a toast, all took a swallow of the golden liquid.

When their plane came to a stop in front of the Venice's General Aviation Terminal, Moretti and Cancelliere stood to disembark. The major was the first to leave the aircraft, but just as Moretti was about to follow him onto the tarmac, he felt Pappas's hand on his shoulder. "Find me the documents," he said, "then we'll go hunting."

As the Venice-bound Austrian Air flight picked up speed and lifted off, Cai Fu laid his head back into the thickly cushioned rest and closed his eyes. Trying to relax, he couldn't keep the images from that night at the Campo Santo Stefano from slowly creeping into his mind. He wished he'd handled things differently. He should have never tried to wound Gina Moretti. He merely wanted to stop her from fleeing and terrify her into telling him where the documents were. That was a mistake because instead of standing still for a split second longer, she turned enough so that the shot that should have gone through her arm went into her lung instead. And once she knew her wound was fatal, he no longer had any leverage over her.

What do you say to someone who's dying? "I'm going to kill you if you don't talk"? Ridiculous.

He was now more certain than ever that she'd sent Ludewig the documents by FedEx. Whether that was to have them authenticated or to keep them safe, he didn't know. But that didn't matter because the stubborn German had seen them. He was positive of that because except for denying that he currently had them, he wasn't confused about the subject of their discussion. This explained why Luca, as well as the heavyset woman at the library, couldn't find them. They were in Vienna. That being the case, what if he returned them after learning of Gina Moretti's death? In that context, his adamant denial made sense. It also explained why Moretti and hei guafu didn't have them. That's why he had to be at the Marciana when it opened.

It is March 14, 1973. I am nearly blind, a secret I have kept from all but a few. As my eyesight hinders my ability to write, I have decided to dictate my diary to Cho Ling, who now acts as my scribe, although I will continue to sign my name by placing my eyes close to the page in front of me.

I know I haven't much time left. My doctor tells me that I am in fair health and just afflicted by the infirmities of old age. But I know he is lying. Cho Ling overhead him speaking with Chou En-lai, telling him that I have an illness that will kill me within two years. He told the premier that this disease is called amyotrophic lateral sclerosis and is incurable. During this time my muscles will become paralyzed, and I will gradually lose my speech, eventually dying of respiratory failure. I believe Comrade Chou fears that if I discover I'm terminally ill, I'll make it known to the people. And once that occurs, I will no longer be the buffer protecting the party and the country's leadership from the ire of the masses who demand change and a path from their poverty. I'm sure Chou En-lai wants to use the time I have left to diffuse this anger and gradually announce to the people what he will say are my wishes. I have not been privy to what these are, although there are rumors. His greatest fear is that I will pursue an agenda with my people that he and the party have not endorsed. He is right in this regard, and I am working with all my remaining strength toward that end.

I fight daily to retain my privacy, and I have insisted that only my staff reside in my compound, resisting every attempt by Comrade Chou to send someone to stay with me. I do not trust the loyalty of outsiders. If I require a doctor, I will summon him to perform his services, but then he must leave. Strangely, even in my advanced years, my mind is clear. But my physical weaknesses cause me to fall often, and I have difficulty getting up without assistance. But I am determined to stay alive because I have much to accomplish in the next two years, and for the sake of my country, I cannot fail.

My correspondence with Chiang has been going on for almost nine months, but the process of exchanging letters has become increasingly difficult. Premier Chou has built a virtual cocoon of spies around my compound, making it nearly impossible for a vital meeting between Chiang and me to take place here and consummate what needs to be done. I wrote that I would come and see him. I am an old man, and if I'm discovered in Taiwan, there is little anyone can do. Therefore, I will make the journey. Chiang and I have devised a plan that takes advantage of my infirmities, and it will get me to Taiwan.

The start of this deception involved my personal pilot flying me to Shaoshan, which is not far from Changsha, and that's where I also retain a family home. I have gone there many times, and this trip will not appear out of the ordinary. Chou En-lai was not pleased with the timing of my trip, and he told me so. This was because we had a meeting scheduled, where I was to approve a slate of party members he wanted to appoint to positions of power. My acceptance was crucial because after my death, he wanted the people to believe they were my appointees. This would allow him to exercise more rigid control of the government. But I am in no hurry to give such approval, and I would have claimed illness to preclude attending.

Cho Ling and I left Beijing to change history. When my plane landed in Shaoshan, an imposter, one I've used in the past when Comrade Chou wanted me to look robust in public, was dressed as a technician and boarded my plane. Once inside, he changed into the clothes I gave him and assumed my identity. Comrade Chou's spies believed I left the aircraft and got into a car for the short ride to my ancestral home. Once there, my imposter was told to show himself several times a day and appear as infirmed as I would be to avoid suspicion. I have no doubt that Comrade Chou had his spies watching my compound and reporting back to him daily. I was counting on that.

Once the imposter was gone and the plane refueled, we took off for Taipei, which was less than a thousand kilometers away. For the first time, I thought about the short distance separating two enemies who had refused to work together to unite a country for too long.

I landed at night at a military airport in Taipei, where my pilot would be on the ground only long enough to take on fuel before returning to Beijing. This was one of the weaknesses in our plan. It was mathematical. If someone took the time to calculate how long it took my plane to fly from Shaoshan to Beijing, they would question why it was almost seven hours longer than it should have been. But I knew that my country's recordkeeping was so antiquated and inaccurate that there was every possibility this inconsistency would go unnoticed. Yet it was still a risk.

My pilot was directed to taxi to a remote part of the huge base, and it took some time to get there. During this journey I saw rows of new cargo and fighter planes parked in front of massive hangers. I had no idea that Chiang had amassed such a force or that it was this modern. In contrast, my military was antiquated. When we stopped, Cho Ling opened the aircraft's door and extended the metal stairs. Chiang was there waiting for me. At eighty-five, four years older than me, he had remarkably good stature, at least from what my limited vision perceived.

I cautiously walked down the stairs, holding tightly onto the rail as I descended and trying to not to look as feeble as I felt. Looking Chiang in the eye, I extended my hand, which he accepted by firmly grasping it with both of his. As we stepped apart, the vague outline of a figure standing behind him came forward. Even though my eyesight would not allow me to clearly see his face, there was no mistaking his silhouette. I realized he'd come to fulfill the promise he had made to me last February, and I immediately knew that Chiang and I would succeed.

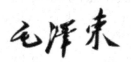

CHAPTER

21

THE WATER TAXI CAME ALONGSIDE the dock at the Hotel Bauer, where Moretti and Cancelliere disembarked. After showing their passports, filling out a single-page form, and Cancelliere giving him a government credit card, the clerk handed each a room key. As this was happening, Moretti looked at himself in the mirror and realized that his appearance had gotten steadily worse. He hadn't even shaved since he first arrived in Venice. Once they left the registration desk, he told Cancelliere that he needed to buy a change of clothes. Since he didn't speak the language, he asked the Carey Grant look-alike to come with him, and they both left the hotel. Fortunately, finding a clothing store in Venice was akin to falling off a log, and he was wearing his new attire, a clone of what he had on before, within thirty minutes. After picking up some personal items, they returned to the hotel. During this time Cancelliere carried a travel bag along with a metallic case, which Moretti surmised was a chic-looking briefcase carried by the fashion-conscious folks.

When they returned to the hotel, he told Cancelliere he'd join him in the restaurant once he showered and shaved. Less than half an hour later, he walked onto the deck of the De Pisis Restaurant looking like a new man. They sat at a canal-side table where a bottle of Collio Mueller Thurgau, a light white wine, was resting in an ice bucket. An epicurean dinner of roasted monkfish with leaf cabbage and candied lemon followed. Too tired for coffee and dessert, they decided to retire for the night and catch up on their sleep.

When he entered his room, his thoughts involuntarily went back to Han Li and the time they spent together. Although it had only been a couple of days, with all that had happened, it seemed like a month. He missed her company, although he couldn't exactly pinpoint why. Perhaps it was because they'd both come close to death so many times in such a short span of time and worked well together under adversity and pressure. Now all that didn't matter. Their partnership was now over, and he'd never see her again. He looked at the starlit sky outside his bedroom window and wondered what she was thinking on the long flight back to Beijing.

Han Li's flight was delayed because of a faulty aircraft door seal that couldn't be repaired at the gate. Alitalia promised that the plane would be fixed and that boarding would commence in no more than two hours. Three hours later the flight was canceled. The airline apologized for the inconvenience, although no one believed them, and they rebooked everyone on the 8:30 a.m. flight to Venice the following morning, which was scheduled to arrive at 10:00. Although meal vouchers and lodging at a local hotel were provided, Han Li was excluded from both. Instead she was escorted to a holding cell in the basement of the airport, where she remained until morning when a female officer unlocked the cell and bought her breakfast at a coffee shop in the main terminal. Han Li was the last to board and the officer remained on the Jetway until the aircraft door was closed and latched, at which time she walked onto the tarmac and got into her patrol car. She watched the aircraft taxi to the runway and kept it in sight as it took off and faded into the skyline.

The flight arrived in Venice early. Han Li's seat was in the back of the plane, and she was one of the last to leave the aircraft once they were at the gate. Thankfully, there was no issue with her passport, and she quickly cleared immigration. Five minutes later she was on a motorboat to Saint Mark's Square.

Following breakfast, Cancelliere and Moretti walked to Bruno's office, which was a little more than ten minutes from the hotel, for the nine-o'clock meeting Cancelliere had set earlier that morning. When they arrived, the chief inspector, who'd never formally met Moretti, introduced himself and extended his condolences on the death of his sister. He then motioned to the couch opposite his desk and offered refreshments. Cancelliere asked for a cup of espresso, while Moretti elected to have coffee with no cream or sugar. Once it arrived, they brought Bruno up to date on what had occurred in the last two days and answered his questions. On behalf of the US government, Cancelliere then requested Bruno's assistance in retrieving the documents from the Marciana Library. If this came as a surprise, the expression on the seasoned detective's face didn't show it. Putting his elbows on his desk and interlocking his fingers, he thought for a moment before responding.

"Notwithstanding that, without the approval of my government, I don't have the authority to give them to anyone. They are—at least for now—the property of the citizens of Italy, and I would have to arrest anyone who tried to steal them."

Cancelliere looked disappointed. "I understand, Chief Inspector. Perhaps we could work together to retrieve and protect them. Once they're safe, the diplomats can sort it out."

Bruno agreed, saying he welcomed their help, and at ten thirty, the three men left the police station for the Marciana.

Cai Fu entered the library at ten o'clock, exactly when it opened, and quickly made his way through the vestibule and into the anteroom. The heavyset woman was again working behind the counter, and she had a broad smile on her face as he approached. He'd rehearsed what he was going to say, but as it turned out, the story he'd concocted wasn't necessary.

"Signore. I've been hoping you'd return. The documents you were looking for arrived this weekend by courier. Someone forgot to enter into the computer that they'd been sent to Vienna for authentication. My apologies. Would you like me to get them and the certificate of authenticity for you?"

Cai Fu couldn't recall being at a loss for words many times in his life, but he stood speechless in front of the heavyset woman. "Si, if you would be so kind," he finally replied.

"For a friend of Signorina Moretti, it would be my pleasure. Please have a seat," she said, pointing to the same desk he sat at before. "I'll get them for you."

Cai Fu sat down, but he was restless and couldn't sit still. The thought of holding the documents in his hands made him euphoric.

He was thinking about the promotion and other benefits he'd receive from General Lin when the heavyset woman approached. "Here they are," she said, placing a rectangular leather box on the desk and handing him a pair of white gloves and an envelope. "This is the certificate verifying that the signatures are authentic. Please wear these gloves when you handle the documents. Although I'm sure I don't have to tell you that," she said before walking away.

He stared at the leather box, and with hands trembling, he opened it. Inside was a stack of weathered paper that was slightly yellowed and brittle around the edges. Gently removing them from the box, he examined each. There were eighteen documents in all, some more than one page in length. As he finished his count a wave of panic came over him, and it became difficult to breathe. It was as if someone was sitting on his chest. He willed himself to calm down, and gradually, his breathing returned to normal. He again counted the documents, using the signature at the end of each to determine their number. When he finished, he realized that one was missing. There were supposed to be nineteen.

"Were they what you were looking for?" the heavyset woman asked as she saw him approach.

"Yes, thank you. Can you tell me if these are all the documents that were returned? The reason I ask is that I translated nineteen, but there were only eighteen inside the box." It was hard for Cai Fu to speak without emotion. He wanted to pull the woman over the counter and start interrogating her as to why one document was missing. Instead he used every bit of self-control he possessed to keep his voice even and nonthreatening.

The heavyset woman looked surprised at what he'd said and went to her computer terminal. "Let me look," she said, typing on her keyboard and looking at her screen. "You're correct. There are supposed to be nineteen."

She came from behind the counter and walked to the desk on which the rectangular box was resting, put on the white gloves, and slowly counted the documents. The blood seemed to have drained from her face by the time she finished. "Let me ask if one has been removed," she said in a concerned voice. "I'll just be a moment."

Twenty minutes later she returned. "I'm sorry, but our records are a bit confusing. As I mentioned, they were sent for authentication, a fact I didn't know until they arrived early this morning by courier. I have no confirmed count as to how many were sent to Vienna, but the person who signed for the documents this morning showed me the paperwork from the courier, and eighteen were returned, one less than is listed in our inventory. She's already called the courier service, but they maintain they were only given eighteen. She's now trying to reach the person who authenticated the documents to verify how many he gave the shipper. But so far, she's been unable to reach him."

A man came through the door behind the information counter and called to the heavyset woman. "Please give me a moment," she said before following him through the open doorway.

When Cai Fu saw the heavyset woman leave, he decided to act. He'd never have another opportunity like this. Looking around the anteroom and seeing that no one was watching him, he placed his jacket around the box and tucked it under his arm so that its outline couldn't be seen. Quickly making his way through the vestibule and down two flights of stairs, he entered the crowd in Saint Mark's Square and was gone.

When the heavyset woman returned to the counter, she looked

at the desk and saw that not only was the tall Asian man missing, but so was the brown leather box containing the documents. Realizing what had happened, she began to run. Despite her large size, she showed surprising speed as she raced through the anteroom and into the vestibule. There she asked the guard if he'd seen a tall Asian man pass by, and she was told that he went down the stairs less than a minute ago. When she burst out the front entrance and looked at the wall-to-wall crowd within St. Mark's Square, she realized it was hopeless. The tall Asian was gone.

Bruno had been inside the Marciana Library many times, and he led Moretti and Cancelliere to the anteroom, whose information center handled all document requests. When they reached the counter, the chief inspector showed the heavyset woman his credentials and asked to see the Chang Hao documents. She immediately broke into tears. With her arms animating the story, she explained what had just happened. Moretti could speak and understand some basic Italian, but at the pace she was talking, he only comprehended about 10 percent of what she was saying. From the expression on his face, Cancelliere was at or near 100 percent. When the conversation ended, Moretti asked him why the lady was crying.

"Someone asked to see the documents just after the library opened. From her description, that person appears to be Cai Fu."

"He was just here?"

"Sitting at that table," Cancelliere said, pointing to his right. "The odd thing is that when he inspected them, he noticed there was only eighteen and told this lady that there should have been nineteen. She checked her computer and found he was correct. Just then she was interrupted and went into the back room to assist another employee. When she returned, Cai Fu and the documents were gone."

"There are very few ways to leave Venice, and my department is familiar with all of them," Bruno said, apparently overhearing their conversation. "We'll catch him. Let's go back to my office."

The three men turned and were on their way out of the anteroom when Moretti, the last of the group, heard the heavyset woman calling his name.

"Signor Moretti, I have something for you," she said, holding up her hand and indicating he should wait.

He told Cancelliere and Bruno to keep going and that he could find his way back to the station. When the heavyset lady returned, she handed him a backpack.

"This belonged to your sister. It was returned with the documents. I'm afraid one of our staff searched it and even unstitched the lining to make sure something from our library wasn't behind it. But the backpack only contained your sister's laptop. He apologizes for any damage he may have caused. And please accept my condolences. Gina and I were friends, and I will miss her very much."

Moretti could see tears beginning to run down her cheeks. "Thank you," he responded, giving her a hug and taking the backpack. He turned and ran out of the anteroom, hoping to catch up with Cancelliere and Bruno, but he slowed down when he saw them speaking to someone in the vestibule. He couldn't see that person because they were blocking his view, but as he got closer, he saw it was Han Li.

"I was about to tell Miss Li that it would be best if she returned to China," Bruno said as Moretti came beside him. "She's caused quite enough excitement in Venice."

Han Li looked at Moretti with an icy stare and then turned her attention back to Bruno.

"Cai Fu has the documents," Moretti said, "but only eighteen. That's all that were in the container."

Han Li showed both surprise and concern.

"We have to go," Bruno said, tapping the face of his watch. "I have calls to make."

"We're going after Cai Fu," Moretti yelled back as he was leaving.

"I can find him for you."

All three men quickly stopped and turned around upon hearing this.

> It is March 14, 1973, and I decided to make this a separate entry in my diary because of its importance, putting it on an equal plane alongside my shaking of Chiang's hand. Standing on the tarmac with my old enemy, I watched as the familiar figure approached and put his arms around us. We've all been adversaries at one time, but today we've set aside our differences to act in unison. If Chiang and I are to sew our nation back together, then the thread of that union will be this man—President Nixon.
>
> Cho Ling previously told me that the American president has endured much criticism this past year for spying on his political rivals. I cannot see what difference that makes in a world of deceit and danger. It is to be expected. Yet despite this turmoil, he has kept his promise to me. I doubted that he would come, as politicians are known to make promises of convenience only to ignore them after they get what they want. But President Nixon has given me another perspective on America. Today the three of us have come together to heal a fragmented country, achieve the greatness for which China was destined, and establish a union with the West that I did not previously believe was possible.

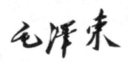

CHAPTER

22

ALTHOUGH THE SMALL RESTAURANT DIDN'T open for fifteen minutes, the twenty-euro note that Cai Fu handed the maître d' instantly overcame his objections and allowed him to select a table in the back. He was angry at not having the nineteenth document, and he didn't know how he was going to find it. To complicate matters, he believed the heavyset woman had called the police by now and given them his description. That was very bad news because even though they couldn't put him in jail for what he'd done, they could expel him from the country. Thankfully, earlier this morning he'd told two of his agents from the Florence consulate to take the next train to Venice, bringing with them his Beretta 92FS with suppressor and alternate passport and credit cards. The text he'd just received indicated that they'd arrive shortly. He'd give them the documents to place on the diplomatic courier flight that the general was sending to the Marco Polo Airport.

He ran his hands across his face and past his bloodshot eyes. He was exhausted. The last two days had been an emotional roller coaster. At this moment, the only joy he had was imagining the look on hei guafu's face when she discovered that he had eighteen of the documents. Was this the first time she'd failed? That's when it occurred to him. She could no more return to Beijing without the last document any more than he could. If he hadn't been so tired, he would have thought about this earlier. It also meant that she and Moretti were either in Venice or on their way. With every fiber of his being, he wanted to find and kill them. But giving into this base instinct would be stupid, even if it would be satisfying. He needed their unwitting help to find the nineteenth document. And he thought he had a plan to do just that.

Cancelliere, Bruno, and Moretti were standing outside the Marciana Library, waiting for Han Li to make good on her promise. While she was using Cancelliere's phone, Bruno was speaking to someone at the station, instructing them to circulate Cai Fu's photo to hotels, transportation hubs, and businesses throughout the city. When he finished, he walked to where Moretti and Cancelliere were standing.

"I wonder who she's speaking with," Bruno asked.

"Whoever it is, they'd better help us find Cai Fu quickly. Otherwise, they'll be on their way back to China and out of our reach," Cancelliere said. "Don't forget. This assassin is technically a diplomat, and once he puts them into a pouch, it's game over."

The three discussed this possibility but abruptly stopped when Han Li called to them.

"I have him."

"Where?" Bruno asked.

She pointed south across Saint Mark's Square and took off in that direction, eventually crossing the Accademia Bridge to the other side of the Grand Canal. Fifteen minutes later she stopped thirty yards from a small restaurant.

"He's in there," she said, the phone still held tightly against her ear.

"How do you know?" Moretti asked.

"General Lin installs a GPS chip on all his operative's cell phones so he can follow their movements. Each one has a unique code. Thanks to a bribe, my sponsor obtained the agent's identifiers years ago from the person who installs the modified China Mobile software. One of our technicians is tracking Cai Fu's GPS signal, as well as that of the two other agents who are with him."

"There are three Chinese operatives within the restaurant?" Bruno asked.

"Yes, that's what our tracker shows, and you can assume they're armed."

"Then we need to know much more before we go in—where they're seated, how many restaurant patrons are near them, and anything else that might prove helpful. Since Cai Fu knows all our faces, except for yours, Mr. Cancelliere, perhaps you can walk by the restaurant and get us this information?"

The army intelligence officer walked toward the single-story brown stucco building as if he was on a midday stroll. He stopped in front of the restaurant and looked at the menu displayed in a window to the side of the entrance, giving the impression that he was considering each of the numerous dishes offered. When he was through, he walked down the alley on the right side of the building and worked his way around back to the other side.

"Cai Fu's sitting with two Asian males," Cancelliere reported upon his return. "Their table is in the far left corner, which gives him an unobstructed view of the front door. It appears the three of them are just having coffee."

"Are there many people inside?" Bruno asked.

"Six customers, two at one table and four at the other plus a chef, bartender, and two servers."

"I believe we have to act now. Saying that, I wish I could get reinforcements here in the next few minutes, but that's not possible," Bruno said. "Consequently, we have two obvious options. We can arrest Cai Fu and the two men with him inside the restaurant or wait until they leave. The streets are relatively uncrowded since it's early for lunch. Therefore, even if he has a gun, arresting him outside would pose little risk of civilian causalities. However, he also has a better opportunity to escape. Alternatively, if we enter the restaurant we have the advantage of containment. The flip side is that there are customers and staff inside who could be wounded, killed, or taken as hostages."

"We can't let him outside. If he gets away, there's no telling who else he might kill," Moretti said.

"I agree," Cancelliere added. "Take them where they stand."

"Then it's settled. Mr. Moretti, go to the rear of the building and take this," Bruno said, handing him the gun from his ankle holster. "Stop anyone who tries to escape. Ms. Li, I don't have another weapon, but I suspect you don't need one. Please station yourself just around the corner and watch the far side of the alley. Likewise, if anyone gets past us and tries to escape, make sure they don't. Mr. Cancelliere, I believe I saw a shoulder holster under your jacket. Am I mistaken?"

"No, you aren't."

"Then you'll come through the front door with me. Everyone, please remember there are civilians inside. No one shoots unless someone's life is in danger." He then turned to Moretti and Han Li. "Mr. Cancelliere and I will be entering the restaurant on the count of twenty." And with that, he started counting. "One ..."

Moretti and Han Li headed to their assigned positions, silently counting to themselves as Bruno and Cancelliere drew their handguns.

"Eighteen, nineteen ..."

When he reached twenty, Cancelliere and Bruno burst into the small restaurant. Cai Fu, whose chair was facing the front door, saw them and recognized Bruno. In an instant he turned his table on its side and fired at Cancelliere and Bruno. Both bullets passed less than six inches over their heads, and they scrambled behind the bar for refuge. Cai Fu ordered one of the agents to leave and take the documents with him, while he and the other agent provided cover fire. That man grabbed a travel bag off the floor with his left hand and withdrew a Beretta from his shoulder holster with the other. He ran toward the back door as Cai Fu and the second agent let loose a volley of shots that pummeled the bar.

When the agent threw open the weathered wooden door, he slammed into Moretti, who was entering after hearing the second set of gunfire. The collision knocked both to the ground in a tangled heap. The travel bag along with Moretti's gun slid behind a large wooden planter to the right side of the door. Both men, who were approximately the same height and weight, rolled on the ground and tried to get an advantage over the other. Moretti had a good grip on the agent's gun hand, but the strain of maintaining that was clearly visible on his face. Once it loosened, the man could move his weapon three inches to the left and pump a round into him. Realizing this, he released his grip on the man's other hand and thrust his palm into his face, driving the nose bone into the brain. The agent's body immediately went limp.

Moretti pushed the dead man off, and he was about to get up when the other agent rushed out the back door. Both were startled to see the other, but Moretti reacted first, driving his right foot into the man's kneecap and throwing him face-first to the ground. He then got on the man's back, grabbed his chin with one hand and his temple with the other, planted his knee in his back, and arched it until the man's neck broke. He was still on top of the dead man when Cai Fu came out the back door. The assassin looked Moretti in the eyes and started to reach for the gun in the small of his back. Then he turned at the sound of rapidly approaching footsteps and saw Han Li. He appeared to be conflicted between killing Moretti and saving his own skin. Contorting his face in anger, he turned and ran. Not long after, Cancelliere and Bruno bolted through the back door with their guns raised, looking for someone to shoot just as Han Li arrived. By that time Cai Fu had turned the corner into the alleyway and was long gone.

They went back inside the restaurant, except for Moretti, who remained outside for another minute before he entered.

"I was just saying that Cai Fu couldn't have gone far," Bruno repeated as Moretti approached, carrying the gun that had been given to him along with a travel bag. "There are four bridges in this area across the Grand Canal. We'll keep him boxed in on this side and check all watercraft leaving the area." With that, he took his cell phone from his pocket and implemented those instructions.

The six customers who'd been privy to the gun battle were long gone. Moretti readjusted his sister's backpack, which had been on his shoulder this entire time, and then placed the travel bag on an empty table in front of him. Bruno ended his call and approached, as did Cancelliere. Everyone was silent as he unzipped the bag and gently removed a rectangular brown leather box and opened it. Han Li looked at the top document for a moment and then examined each of the others. Once she'd placed them back inside, Bruno stepped forward.

"Thank you for your assistance in getting these back for us, Ms. Li," Bruno said as he picked up the box. "The Italian people are most appreciative."

Cai Fu got into a motorboat taxi not far from the restaurant and asked to be taken to Burano, an island at the northern end of the Venetian Lagoon renowned for its lacework and brightly colored homes. The driver, undoubtedly wanting to get underway before the tall Asian changed his mind on the 130-euro trip, immediately cast off.

Once they entered the broader section of the Grand Canal, he looked back and saw that police patrol boats were starting to cordon off canals behind and to the side of him as he expected. He'd escaped just in time. He had no doubt that Han Li had the eighteen documents and that she'd send them to China at her first opportunity, which he believed was tomorrow since a plane from Beijing couldn't arrive before then. He'd bought himself an equal amount of time by going to Burano since the Italian police were unlikely to expand their search to the outer islands until tomorrow. That gave him around twelve hours to retrieve the documents. For that to happen, he'd somehow have to exert enough pressure on Moretti so that he'd hand them over to him before then. And he thought he knew how to make that happen.

He removed his cell phone from his pocket and called Lin Bogang, explaining that he'd lost the documents to Han Li. The general, understandably angry, was ripping him a new one until he calmed down enough for him to present his plan. Once he did, his attitude immediately changed, and they discussed how to implement the operation.

Bruno opened the top drawer of his desk, took two aspirin from a nearly empty bottle, and swallowed them without water. He hoped they would calm his raging headache. Looking at his watch, he saw that it was a little past eleven in the evening. Everyone had just returned from a late dinner after spending hours writing their accounts of what had happened at the restaurant. He attributed the pain he was experiencing not to the shootout with Cai Fu or the paperwork but to his nonstop arguing with Han Li. At dinner she'd spent the entire time contending that her country had a right to the documents because they'd been illegally conveyed to the library. His position was the opposite, indicating there was no proof that Mao's diary was illegally obtained by Chang Hao because they were never reported as stolen. And unless his government indicated otherwise, they were going back to the Marciana. He was about to chase everyone from his office and go home when his phone rang. The caller, Detective John Lester of the Anchorage Police Department, asked to speak with Moretti. Curious as to how someone would know that he was here this late at night, he placed the call on speaker phone.

The detective explained that the duty officer received an anonymous call informing him that Moretti's father had been kidnapped. Upon hearing this, Bruno looked at the former army ranger's face, which rapidly transitioned from an expression of disbelief to one of concern and then anger. It looked as if he wanted to interrupt the detective and ask a litany of questions; however, Lester continued speaking, and he listened instead.

The Anchorage detective provided an internet link that the

kidnappers had given him. The image, which appeared on the screen, showed the senior Moretti bound and gagged, and on a whiteboard beside him, there was a list of demands written under the heading "Conditions for Release." The first was that someone from the Anchorage PD call Chief Inspector Mauro Bruno in Venice, Italy, and inform Matthew Moretti that his father had been kidnapped. Bruno's phone number was given at the end of the first condition. The second was that the eighteen documents, left at the restaurant earlier that day, were to be brought to the Campo Santo Stefano at exactly midnight, Venice time. The third was that Matthew Moretti and the Chinese woman accompanying him deliver them and come unarmed. The fourth and final condition was that they carry the cell phone they'd find in the flower pot outside the front entrance to the police station. The caller went on to say that if he even suspected they were being followed, the senior Moretti would be killed.

He had no doubt that Cai Fu was the one who had orchestrated the kidnapping, the surveillance of his office, and the placing of the cell phone. The chief inspector lost a few words of what Lester was saying as he thought about this, but he mentally rejoined the conversation as the detective went on to explain that as soon as the caller hung up, the duty officer sent a squad car to the senior Moretti's residence and confirmed that he'd been kidnapped. They found, pinned to a kitchen cabinet with a steak knife, a piece of paper with the same four conditions written on it. Lester said they called the FBI but they couldn't help because the kidnappers had given Bruno an impossibly short amount of time to comply, not to mention the fact that the actions required for release were in Italy. Their efforts were, therefore, necessarily limited to investigating the Anchorage crime scene.

The clock on his desk indicated that it was 11:25, and therefore, time was running short. He thanked Lester, got his contact number, and ended the call. Briefly considering having the three officers currently on duty change into civilian clothes and stake out the area around the Campo Santo Stefano, he quickly decided against it when he realized that it was largely deserted at night, and therefore, their presence would stand out. With no other alternatives, he got up from his desk and went to the evidence room, returning a few minutes later with the leather box containing the documents.

"You realize you're dealing with Cai Fu and that he's going to kill the both of you as soon as he gets the documents," Cancelliere said to Moretti. "And after that, he'll order your father killed."

"Then what do you suggest?" Moretti asked.

"Tell him you want to verify that your father's safely in police hands before you hand over Mao's diary, no matter how much he objects or what he threatens to do."

"Why would he agree to that?"

"Because your father's not the end game. The documents are."

"What if he shoots us on sight?"

"He can't afford to until he verifies you have what he's after."

"So your plan is to have him set my father free, give him what he wants, and then let him kill us?" Moretti asked Cancelliere.

"Not exactly."

Moretti and Han Li walked down the narrow cobblestone streets of the business district. The city was asleep, and the only sounds people could hear were their shoes echoing off the cobblestones. They were nearly halfway to the Campo Santo Stefano when the cell phone Cai Fu left for them began to vibrate. Moretti took it out of his pocket and answered. He listened to the caller and then acknowledged that he understood.

"Change of plans," he said. "We're now going to the monument at the Campo Manin." He pressed the map icon on his phone, saw his new destination, and touched it to get the directions.

The Campo Manin was not far from Saint Mark's Square. In its center was a statue of Daniele Manin with a large winged lion at its base. The east side of the square opposite the waterway was dominated by the very modern Cassa di Risparimo di Venezia bank. This mid-1960s structure stood in stark contrast to the neo-Gothic buildings to the north and south. The area was moderately lit, but it lacked security personnel since none of the buildings in the square were particularly important.

They arrived a little after midnight, standing in silence for twenty minutes until they heard footsteps approaching from behind. When they turned around, they saw Cai Fu standing ten feet away, a suppressed pistol in his right hand and a small square box in the other.

"If you'd both could take off your coats and throw them toward me," he said without preamble.

Moretti and Han Li did what they were told. Putting the box in his pocket, he kept his gun trained on them as he bent down and picked up their coats. He searched each with one hand but found nothing inside.

"Mr. Moretti, lift your shirt to the middle of your chest and slowly turn around."

He did as he was told.

"Pull your pant legs above your knees, one at a time. That's it. Now turn your pockets inside out and let whatever's in them fall to the ground."

He complied, dropping the cell phone, his wallet, and some cash.

"The same for you," Cai Fu said to Han Li, who mimicked Moretti.

"Both of you, take five steps back."

When Moretti and Han Li did as they were told, he stepped forward, picked up what they'd dropped, and stuffed it all into his jacket pockets.

"Where are the documents?"

"You didn't seriously think I'd hand them over to you before I made sure my father was safe?"

Cai Fu could feel his temper starting to overcome logic. He wanted to kill them for the enormous amount of grief and loss of face they'd caused him. But without Mao's diary, they had to remain alive, at least for now.

"What do you propose?" he asked, his mind gaining control of his body.

"That you release my father unharmed. Once I receive a call from the police verifying that he's safe, I'll take you to the documents."

He questioned whether "I'll take you to the documents" meant that he'd be walking into a trap. For all he knew, they could be on their way to China. But with diplomatic immunity and the fact they knew he could kill them and there was nothing the Italian police could do about it, he felt he'd have the final say. He indicated his acceptance, took a cell phone out of his jacket pocket, hit a speed-dial number, and spoke to the person at the other end. He then told Moretti and Han Li to sit on the ground. Fifteen minutes later, his phone rang. He listened for a moment, placed it on the ground, and motioned for Moretti to pick it up.

He allowed the conversation between father and son to last for fifteen seconds, too short a time for anyone to accurately determine his position, before he grabbed his phone out of Moretti's hand and crushed it under the heel of his shoe. He then subjected the cell he'd left at Bruno's office to the same trauma.

"After our adventure at the restaurant, I decided to throw away my cell phone. I picked these up today," he said, looking at its crushed remains on the ground. "Mr. Moretti, where are the documents?"

"They're in the evidence room of the police station. Please feel free to ask Chief Inspector Bruno for them. He'd love to see you."

Cai Fu's finger was tightening on the trigger. "Are you naïve enough to believe I won't kill you?"

"I believe you always intended to kill us. It was just a matter of when."

"Then why did you come?"

"How do you know I came alone and that the police didn't track the cell phone you gave me?" Moretti asked.

"Even if they had the phone number, tracing it would take time, especially on such short notice and at this hour of the morning. Aren't you going to ask how I knew you weren't carrying an electronic homing signal? The answer is this little black box," he said, taking the small palm-sized square from his pocket. "It picks up transmitted signals. As you can see, there's no red light. No red light, no transmission."

"And you," he said, looking at Han Li. "Any last words before you join your ancestors?" When she didn't respond, he raised his gun and extended his arm toward her. "Pity."

At that instant an invisible hand shoved him to the ground, jarring the gun from his hand. Han Li ran and picked it up as he slowly turned over on his back and saw a red stain expanding down the shoulder of his white shirt.

"You two took your sweet time," Moretti said to Cancelliere and Bruno, who walked out of the shadows and came forward. They both had a gun in their hands, but only Cancelliere's had a suppressor attached to his.

"We had a small problem," Cancelliere replied. "More about that later." He walked to Han Li, who had Cai Fu's gun pointed at the assassin's face and looked ready to pull the trigger. "Not just yet, Ms. Li," he said, gently taking the gun from her and handing it to Moretti.

"I believe Colonel Pappas gave you an officer's oath, Mr. Moretti. He told me to tell you that he always keeps his promises. He also wants you to know that if you're tired of being a paper pusher, give him a call. He has a job waiting for you that just might prove more interesting than being an archivist."

"You intentionally didn't make your shot fatal, did you?"

Cancelliere merely smiled.

"Inspector, can I talk you into making me a cup of espresso back at your office? I believe we're done here."

"It would be my pleasure. I'll send some officers back later to clean the scum off the street."

As they walked away, they heard Moretti say, "Hasta la vista, baby," followed by a faint metallic sound.

Bruno turned to Cancelliere and repeated, "Hasta la vista, baby?"

"It's cultural. I'll explain on the way back."

It is March 15, 1973. Cho Ling informed me that he'd given Chiang my recommendations, and without hesitation, he's accepted them all. This came as a surprise as we've disagreed on almost everything during our lives. Looking back, the half century of hate between us now seems so meaningless. I should have found a way for us to work in unison much earlier. He should have found a way. But we became so absorbed in our own historical importance that we ignored what was good for our people and necessary for their future. Now we must accomplish in the abbreviated time we have left what we should have done decades ago.

It was midday when I decided to take a nap. When I awoke, Cho Ling informed me that the garden behind my residence was quite beautiful and that sitting under the sun would be good for my health. I agreed. He guided me there and found a bench near a stream, where we sat and listened to its soothing music. Shortly after, I saw the outline of a man approaching. Cho Ling whispered that it was Chiang and that he was alone. When I asked him to leave, he stood and bowed to me, walked briskly to Chiang, gave him the same sign of respect, and then continued out of the garden.

My former adversary took a seat next to me, and for a long moment, we did not speak. My eyesight is poor, but now that he was in the sunlight and so close, I saw that he looked emaciated. He is much too thin, and his face carries the same wariness that I have engraved on mine. I know that we both have a short time left in our lives and that tomorrow may be the last time we ever see each other. I cannot keep the charade of my being in Shaoshan for much longer, and neither can he indefinitely keep my presence here a secret. Consequently, Cho Ling has arranged for my pilot to arrive tomorrow afternoon after Chiang and I have concluded what needs to be done.

I don't know why, but I removed my lapel pin, a replica of my country's flag, and handed it to Chiang. This small gesture caught him off guard, and he looked at me in surprise. After a moment of thought, he bowed his head, looked down at his uniform jacket, and removed an emblem that I knew to be that of the office of the president. Bending toward me, he pinned it on my gray jacket before affixing my pin to the spot where his emblem had been. We both looked at each other and started to laugh. Afterward, we remained sitting by the stream until Chiang sensed that I was becoming fatigued. He then helped me to my feet, put his arm through mine, and walked me back to the guesthouse.

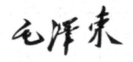

CHAPTER

23

MORETTI AND HAN LI ENTERED Bruno's office and found him sitting with Cancelliere on the couch across from his desk. They each had a cup of espresso in their hand.

"Ah, there you are. I'll be right back," Bruno said as he walked out of his office. A moment later he returned. "My men will clean up the area, and tomorrow I'll speak with the medical examiner and coroner. It's a shame that Cai Fu and the men at the restaurant were in a fatal car accident."

"Cai Fu has two bullets in him," Moretti said.

"That's not what the autopsy will say. I don't believe the Chinese government will want to delve into his, and a car accident seems the most diplomatic of solutions."

"You said you had a small problem in getting to us," Moretti said as he took a seat in the chair to the side of Bruno's desk while Han Li stood in the corner of the office facing him. "What did you mean?"

"The nano drone ran out of power," Cancelliere responded. "As I said before you left, because of its compact design, it only has a battery life of around twenty-five minutes. I had it hovering nicely thirty feet above your head and the feed it sent to my controller screen was crystal clear. But when your destination changed, it didn't have the juice to continue following you. After it crashed, Chief Inspector Bruno and I continued walking in the direction the drone was headed. Eventually, we ended up at the Campo Manin. We got there just before Cai Fu pointed his gun at Han Li. I took the shot."

Moretti said nothing, the expression on his face seeming to indicate that he understood how close he and Han Li came to being killed.

"It's been an adventure, Chief Inspector," Cancelliere said as he got off the couch and put his espresso cup down on the end table. "The colonel's plane should be here within the hour." Walking to Moretti, he bent forward and spoke in a low voice. "Think about what the colonel said. The man I saw today stared down the barrel of a killer's gun and didn't flinch. We need someone like that on our team. There are a lot of bad guys who would love to take away our freedom." Cancelliere patted him on the shoulder and picked up his metal briefcase, which contained the remains of the nano drone. He gave Han Li a quick nod and then handed Bruno an envelope.

"I believe Captain Davidson promised you a letter in return for your cooperation."

When he opened the envelope and unfolded the enclosed letter, his eyes were immediately drawn to the presidential seal at the top and the signature at the bottom. His mouth was slightly agape as he read it.

"Captain Davidson arranged for that before he left for Vienna. It arrived by courier just before I left to get Mr. Moretti."

Bruno tried to speak, but everything he wanted to say seemed inadequate given that Davidson had kept his word, even in death. The letter was a copy of one addressed to the prime minister of Italy. It expressed the US government's appreciation for assigning Chief Inspector Mauro Bruno to investigate the murder of US citizen Gina Moretti. It also praised the secrecy that the Italian government maintained in such a sensitive investigation that ultimately led to the discovery of Cai Fu as the killer of Gina Moretti, Pietro Luca, and the FedEx clerk. The president hoped that both countries would continue to work together on matters of mutual interest.

Although Bruno's superiors would be angry at not being consulted, there was little they could do since the prime minister seemed to have authorized his actions and the secrecy surrounding it. Davidson protected him just as he had promised. As he placed the letter back inside the envelope, a tear ran down his left cheek.

Cancelliere left Bruno's office and closed the door behind him.

"There's still the matter of the documents," Han Li said as she took a seat on the couch.

"I'm not going to discuss that issue without another espresso."

Moretti felt more alive today than he'd felt since his days in the army. For the first time in more than five years, he didn't think about his back problems or about drinking. It felt good. Maybe Pappas was right. A change in career would be good for him.

"I think you'd be good at that job," Han Li said as if reading his mind. "You should take it."

"You heard what he told me?"

"I have excellent hearing, and he has a deep voice. It wasn't difficult."

Goodbyes were awkward, and he knew that later that morning he'd go to the US consulate and complete the paperwork to take his sister's body back to the United States for burial. After that, he'd never see her again. That thought made him sad; however, when he tried to analyze why, he couldn't put his finger on any single reason. He just liked being around her. His uneasiness caused him to look down to where he'd laid Gina's backpack beside Bruno's desk. He knew there was nothing in it except for her laptop and a power cord. He, Bruno, Han Li, Cancelliere, and the person at the library had all searched it. There was no secret compartment or false lining. It contained only an old thirteen-inch Dell laptop and a power connection. Taking a seat on the couch next to Han Li, he pulled out the computer and plugged it into the wall socket beside him just as Bruno walked back into the office with his espresso.

"Do you have wireless internet in your office, Chief Inspector?" Moretti asked. "I want to check on flights back to the States."

Bruno told him they did and gave him the password.

He opened the lid to the laptop, and when he looked for the power button, saw a large rectangular plastic envelope lying over the keyboard. He knew immediately what was inside. Opening it, he gently removed the nineteenth document. He was about to tell Bruno and Han Li about his discovery, but he saw their eyes were transfixed on what he was holding.

"Is that what I think it is?" Bruno asked.

"There's only one person who can tell us." He looked at Han Li and handed it to her.

Handling it as if it was a wafer-thin piece of glass, she examined the two-page document. On the second page were two signatures, and under each there was an official looking foil seal. Han Li took her time reading it, and when she finished, she gently placed it back inside the plastic envelope.

"I take it that's what you've been searching for?" Moretti asked.

"It's the nineteenth document."

"And your government wants it and the other eighteen back, as you've told me, to prevent a revolution," Bruno said.

"A change in my country's leadership, which is why they must return with me to China, so that no one could use them to their advantage. President Liu doesn't want the sins of the past to determine the future of our nation."

Bruno put out his cigarette and looked at Han Li. "If I give you the documents, will you and Mr. Moretti promise to refrain from killing anyone else until you leave Venice?"

"Thank you," she said, bowing her head in his direction. "Shie, shie."

"It's a shame that the leather box and documents were consumed in the fire from the car and only their residue could be seen. Now no one will ever know what was written on the documents that were inside." He put on his jacket and turned the light off on his desk. "Would you both like to come to my house for breakfast? I make a fantastic frittata."

"I'm in," Moretti said.

"It would be my honor," Han Li replied.

The three of them left Bruno's office, went to the evidence room and retrieved the other documents, and then walked outside into the cool morning air.

> March 16, 1973. It is done. Sitting in the office of my former enemy and with my eyes nearly touching the paper in front of me, I sign my legacy. Also in the room with us is the president of the United States, offering his encouragement and support. My trusted assistant, Cho Ling, and Chiang's wife, Soong May-ling, stand in the back and look on.
>
> Today I am wearing the emblem that my newfound friend has given to me. He laughed when I walked into the room wearing it. And then when I stepped close to him and looked at his uniform, I saw my country's emblem pinned to his jacket pocket. I laughed like a schoolboy, and soon everyone in the room followed suit. The mood was joyful, hopeful, and resolute. On this day we were poised to again become one country.
>
> We were all in agreement that our first task was to simultaneously prepare the people and those within our government. Secrecy is extremely critical. We cannot afford for anyone to find out about what we've accomplished before we explain and endorse what we've signed. The changes we've agreed to will be hard for many in our governments to accept. But both Chiang and I know that without this transformation, we would continue to drift apart and lose forever the chance for historic greatness that this reuniting imbues upon us.

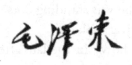

CHAPTER

24

GENERAL LIN PLACED THE PHONE back in its cradle and stared out his window for a few minutes, trying to get his thoughts together. An hour ago he received a call from President Liu's assistant notifying him that Cai Fu along with three staff members from the Florence consulate were found dead in a car accident just outside of Venice. He knew this wasn't true, but there was nothing he could do about it. The death of the agents didn't concern him. They were tools he used to accomplish an objective. What did bother him was their failure, allowing the Black Widow to obtain the documents. The call he just received, asking him to immediately come to Zhongnanhai, the American equivalent of the White House, all but confirmed that the president knew of his involvement.

He took a cigarette from the pack on his desk, lit it, and drew the smoke into his lungs before slowly exhaling. He took one more deep puff and then extinguished it in his ashtray. Walking in front of the mirror in the corner of his office, he straightened his tie, pulled at the bottom of his jacket to remove the creases, took his hat from the corner of his desk, and left.

Outside of the August 1st Building, a black Audi was waiting with its back door open. An athletic man dressed in a dark suit and wearing an earpiece stood beside it. The general got into the back seat, and the person who was standing outside followed him. Once the door closed, the driver took off.

Beijing traffic was heavy in the late afternoon, and it took an hour to get through the heaviest concentration, which was the area around the Forbidden City. The car passed Zhongnanhai, continued eastward through the Chaoyang District, and wound its way into the nearby mountains.

After receiving a call from Han Li telling him that she had all the documents, Cho Ling walked onto the back porch of his house and sat in a reclining chair facing the lake. He sent his nurse away for the remainder of the day despite her objections and looked out at the placid water. Closing his eyes, he thought back four decades to that fateful day when Mao asked Premier Chou En-lai for a private meeting. The chairman, who was in ill health, seldom wanted to have face-to-face discussions because he did not have the endurance for a prolonged conversation. Instead he relied on intermediaries. Therefore, when Chou learned that Mao wanted to meet, he canceled the remainder of his schedule for the day and flew from Beijing to Shaoshan. He was alone when he entered the residence that evening, and he told his staff to wait in the courtyard.

He greeted the premier and escorted him to the chairman's study, and once inside, he stationed himself in front of the door to ensure no one would disturb them. Not long after, he heard an angry and combative Chou yelling and expressing his displeasure with what the chairman had done. Fifteen minutes later he barged out of the study and came face-to-face with him, demanding to know the location of the document that Mao said he'd signed. Otherwise, Chou said he'd have Cho Ling summarily executed. Feigning ignorance, he told the premier that the chairman had signed many documents in the past and asked which of these he was referring to. In an uncharacteristic loss of control, the premier slapped him across the face and stormed out of the house.

After Chou's entourage left the courtyard, he went into the chairman's study and saw him on his hands and knees, lifting a brown leather box from a concealed space under the wooden flooring and placing it on his desk. He knew it contained a diary, as well as the document that Chou wanted.

Looking frail and defeated, the chairman sat down heavily on the thickly padded cushion of his chair and said that he was worried that Chou would send his people, possibly as soon as this evening, to search his residence. Believing that the agreement would never be safe if it remained in China, he wanted it and his diary out of the country. Reflecting on the conversation, he remembered being told to select someone he'd trust with his life, someone who would never know what he possessed, someone who would agree to return it at a moment's notice. He knew such a person.

That night he put a foil seal through the metal loops on the front of the leather box, using a tool that joined both ends together so that he'd know if someone looked inside, and then he wrapped the box in thick brown paper. Taking the package out of the compound in the back of a horse-drawn refuse cart, he handed it to the intermediary he'd used when communicating with Chiang and paid him to deliver it and a note to a trusted friend in Hong Kong. From there the package went to another intermediary, and it was eventually delivered to his nephew, Chang Hao, in Brazil.

Mao's instincts had been right. The following morning he became a virtual prisoner. Military personnel searched the compound for the document, and when they failed to find it, Chou restricted access so that no one could enter or leave without his permission. All phones along with the shortwave radio were removed, cutting off electronic communication with the outside world.

Eventually, the chairman and his staff were relocated to Beijing, the move explained under the pretext of him receiving medical treatment. During this time all communication with Chiang was lost, and Mao was never informed of his newfound friend's declining health but only of his death from cardiovascular disease on April 5, 1975, at the age of eighty-seven. Seventeen months later on September 9, at the age of eighty-two, the chairman died.

He put aside these thoughts and returned to the present. Han

Li would be on her way home as soon as the plane he'd sent arrived in Venice. When they last spoke, she recommended that she not kill Moretti, arguing that if she did, then the others who were involved in retrieving the documents would also have to be eliminated. She felt this number of deaths would initiate an investigation by authorities in both the United States and Italy. He agreed.

He sat back in his chair and let the warmth of the sun heat him. A feeling of serenity, a sensation he hadn't known in decades, enveloped his body. Perhaps one day the leadership in Beijing and Taiwan would once again decide to go down this path, using these documents as the foundation for reunification. In the hope that this would occur, President Liu informed him that the documents would be stored in a safe within his office that only he and his successors could access.

Looking at the swans taking flight before him, he followed their progress skyward and slowly drifted off in the serenity of the moment.

Moretti looked at his sister's coffin for a considerable period of time, and he was only brought back to the present when Chief Inspector Mauro Bruno put a hand on his shoulder.

"It's time to go."

He knew that he was right and that they needed to get his sister's remains on the plane. He nodded to Bruno, who then summoned two of his men to take the coffin to the waiting Delta flight, while he, Han Li, and Bruno followed in a police car.

A few minutes later they stopped beside the exterior boarding ramp of a Boeing 767, whose passengers and crew were already seated on the plane. Getting out of the car, they all stood in awkward silence.

"Let's stay in touch, Chief Inspector," Moretti said, extending his hand to Bruno, who shook his head in the negative.

"It's not chief inspector. It's Mauro. My friends call me Mauro," he said, taking Moretti's hand in both of his.

"And mine's Matt."

Bruno smiled, and with a trace of sadness in his eyes, he broke their handshake. He then looked at Han Li, who was standing next to him. "Whenever you're ready, Ms. Li. The plane your country sent is parked at another part of the airport." Bruno then got into the car and closed the door behind him.

"I see you have the documents safely in hand," Moretti said, looking at his sister's backpack, which Han Li held in her right hand.

"Yes, thanks to you. And thank you for the gift," she said, lifting the backpack slightly.

What happened next would keep him awake for most of his flight back to the United States. At that moment, Han Li walked forward and gave him a long, lingering kiss. Immediately, he grabbed the back of her head with his left hand, deepening their kiss, and he placed the other behind her back, drawing her closer. They continued their embrace to the cheers of passengers and crew who were watching from the aircraft.

CHAPTER

25

THE MERCEDES S550 PULLED INTO the entrance of Zhongnanhai, and it was immediately waved through the security gate of the high-walled government compound. It passed down several streets bordered on both sides with huge trees and lush landscaping, skirting a lake until it stopped in front of a building known as the Hall of Purple Light. A security guard, waiting for the car's arrival, opened the rear door, and Han Li exited, carrying a rectangular brown leather box.

President Liu met her as she entered the building. No one else was visible as he escorted her down a long central hall. Ornate crystal chandeliers hung from an arched gold leaf painted ceiling. The walls were covered in light blue silk that was interrupted at intervals by thick pieces of white lacquered wood extending from floor to ceiling. A thick red carpet ran down the length of the corridor. They stopped at the end of the hall, where the president opened an ornate hand-carved wooden door on the right.

The room they entered was square, fifteen feet on a side, with a crystal chandelier hanging in the center of the fourteen-foot ceiling. Below were two thickly padded white club chairs, and there was a small table between them. Resting on top was a steaming pot of tea and two cups. Nothing else was inside the room.

President Liu motioned for her to sit. "Are those the documents?" he asked once they were seated.

Han Li told him they were, and then she gave him the box.

She watched as he opened it, carefully removed the documents, and examined each one. When he reached the nineteenth, he read it very slowly.

"Have you read this?" the president asked once he'd finished reading the jointly signed letter and placed it back inside the box.

"I've read all the documents to ensure they contained the wording that my uncle asked me to look for."

"Then you know now is not the right time to release them. It will take years if not decades to prepare our politicians and people, as well as those in Taiwan. Nevertheless, I intend to secretly contact my counterpart in Taipei and start this process very soon.

"I summoned you here today because I wanted to tell you that you're now working directly for me. Your grandfather suggested this before he died, and I wholeheartedly agreed. Our country has many enemies, and fighting them cannot always be done with diplomacy or in the public eye. There will be no record of what you're doing or of what you've accomplished. If you're caught, I won't come to your assistance. For all practical purposes, you won't exist. You have only one goal—complete your assignment, no matter what, even at the cost of your life. Is this a responsibility you're willing to accept?"

"Yes, sir."

"Then I want to show you your new home, although I believe you're already familiar with it." With that, he walked to the back of the room and pulled a hidden lever. Immediately, a portion of the wall slid aside.

Han Li followed him into a well-lit area and then watched as he pushed a button that sent the wall back into place. He then guided her down a long flight of stairs and along a corridor that stretched for several hundred yards. Eventually, they reached an ascending staircase. At the top he pressed another button. The wall in front of them slid aside, and they entered a study. They passed through several rooms, eventually emerging onto a large patio overlooking a lake. Han Li knew exactly where she was. As a child she'd played here many times with her grandfather, and it felt as if she was home.

CHAPTER

26

A LETTER TO OUR PEOPLE

FOR MORE THAN FIVE THOUSAND years, China has been the foundation for civilization. Once we were the greatest nation on earth, feared by our enemies and admired by our friends. Our inventions advanced mankind. Our navy sailed the world with impunity, and our global merchant trade brought us immense wealth. We achieved this greatness because of our national unity. We were one people with a common goal, flag, and purpose. But these achievements also came because of great sacrifice. Our ancestors shed their blood and gave their lives in fighting foreign invaders who would do us harm.

Over time our greatness began to ebb with the onslaught of a new enemy. This wasn't a formidable foreign army who would claim our land and leave our people divided. Instead it was us. Our divisiveness and internal conflict ripped the country apart until we became two ideologically divided nations, allowing our internal political differences to obscure what was in the best interests of our people. And in the process, foreigners invaded our lands, killed those who would defend it, and attempted to change our culture and future.

Therefore, to protect our people and culture, we have decided to reunite our nations. No longer will we be known as either the Republic of China or the People's Republic of China. Those names now belong to history. Instead we are China. In recognition of this reunification, we have readopted our first national flag, initially used by our ancestors in the Qing Dynasty, as the symbol of a unified people.

One person will rule from our historic capital, Beijing, and that person will be given the title of emperor or empress. This position will not be inherited or determined by bloodline. Instead it will be conferred by a majority vote of the people. They will serve a single term of seven years and cannot be reelected or hold another political office. We have done this because our country will continually need new visions and a diversity of ideas to survive and prosper.

Each citizen over the age of eighteen will have the right to a single vote and to run for elective office. Once elected, the emperor or empress will have the power to make and enact laws, except those that would result in personal enrichment or benefit family or friends. We recognize there are many details still to be addressed. Therefore, the formulation and implementation of the multitude of tasks necessary for this unification will be made by the National Committee, to which each government will appoint fifty representatives. They will write a constitution, establish the administrative and judicial framework for our nation, and be given the absolute legal authority to implement these changes. And on the day of ascendance of the first emperor or empress, it will be dissolved.

There are many who will oppose our efforts and try to destroy any attempt at reunification. They do not welcome change because they fear the loss of power, national identity, wealth, or other selfish needs. But history will eventually prove them wrong. A unified China will achieve a greatness that neither country can attain on its own.

Our efforts are wholeheartedly supported by the United States, which has agreed to withdraw all American ground and naval forces from the area and provide us with the economic support necessary to make our unification a reality. In return, we will abrogate our relationships with the Soviet Union, and in its place, we will sign a treaty of mutual civil and military cooperation with the United States.

The first election will be held on March 14 the year after next. We rely on the collective wisdom of our people to wisely choose the person among them who would best govern our country.

We take these actions out of respect for our ancestors, on behalf of our citizens, and for the prosperity of future generations.

毛泽东　　　蒋中正

AUTHOR'S NOTE

ALTHOUGH THIS IS A WORK of fiction, a great many portions of *The Archivist* accurately relate historical events. The story line was inspired from a July 16, 1936, interview between Mao Zedong and American journalist Edgar Snow. During their conversation Chairman Mao, through his interpreter, indicated that he had no issue with allowing Taiwan to become independent once the Chinese Communist Party defeated the Japanese. However, he later changed his tune, stating there was an error in interpreting what he'd said. Nevertheless, the seed of the story was planted.

Mao's diary, the nineteenth document, and the eventual friendship between the Chairman and Chiang come from the imagination of the author. Mao and Chiang never had a friendship, and they carried their mutual dislike for each other to their graves. However, most of the information presented in the first eighteen documents is accurate, and the author tried to keep historical disparities to an absolute minimum. The nineteenth document, of course, is fictional.

The first entry in Mao's diary describes his arrival in Shaanxi and the end of the Long March, which lasted from October 1933 to October 1935. This was not one continuous march but a series of retreats by the Red Army, which later became the People's Liberation Army (PLA). They traveled six thousand miles while fleeing the army of the Chinese Nationalist Party, and only one-tenth of those who started survived. However, as strange as it sounds, this established

Mao's leadership position and became the impetus for his rise to power.

The second diary entry, which comes from the summer of 1936, showed Stalin's fear that Japan would attack the USSR. He wanted a unified Mao/Chiang army to confront the Japanese, believing that neither of them alone had the military strength to succeed. Therefore, on August 15, 1936, he sent a telegram advising Mao to cease military operations against Chiang. The chairman, however, ignored this directive. However, because he relied heavily on the USSR for his army's weapons and money, he knew he couldn't survive without Soviet aid. Therefore, he ultimately followed Stalin's dictates.

Chiang Kai-shek's son, Chiang Ching-kuo, was indeed held captive by Stalin as leverage against his father. In 1925, he went to Moscow to study, and he soon became an enthusiastic follower of the communist ideology. When his father purged communists from the central government and expelled Soviet advisers from the country, Chiang Ching-kuo became a *guest* of the Soviet Union. In 1935, he married a native Belarusian and had a son and a daughter. He eventually returned to China two years later at the urging of Stalin, accompanied by his wife and two children. He became president of the Republic of China on May 20, 1978.

Chiang Kai-shek was abducted at 5:00 a.m. on December 12, 1936, when two hundred troops attacked his residence in Xi'an. Hearing gunfire, he escaped through his bedroom window, barefoot and wearing only a robe over his nightshirt, leaving behind his false teeth. He was later discovered hiding in a crevice in a nearby hill, shivering so badly from the cold that he had difficulty speaking. The dissident army officers who kidnapped him did so because they felt he was not effectively using the army to fight the Japanese. Instead he was too focused on killing Chinese communists. After thirteen days in captivity, he agreed to focus on killing Japanese, and then he was released. This temporarily united both the nationalists and communists.

The famine in Henan occurred. It was not only the result of drought and warfare but because of the heavy taxation on grain. In their book *Thunder out of China*, Theodore H. White and Annalee Jacoby give a riveting account of what occurred. No one knows exactly how many people died of starvation in 1942, but estimates go as high as three million. As terrible as this number is, the Great Chinese Famine, which occurred between 1958 and 1961, is thought to have caused the death of between thirty and forty-five million people. The official estimate from the Chinese government is fifteen million deaths.

Chiang Kai-shek did make off with the entire gold reserve of mainland China. On December 2, 1948, his soldiers absconded with 3.75 million taels, which equates to 4.9 million ounces. Although the price of gold varies, at $1,261 per ounce, that's $61,789,000,000 USD. Some estimate that there was so much gold that it took twelve months to transport it to Taiwan by both sea and air. This newfound wealth enabled the Republic of China to recover from both the war and high inflation, and it also formed the basis for its economic success in the decades that followed.

Soviet prime minister Alexei Kosygin did come to China after attending Ho Chi Minh's funeral, and he was met at the airport and not given a formal reception as would have been customary for a person of his position. However, just to keep things straight, Kosygin was met not by Mao but by Premier Chou En-lai.

Hostilities between China and the USSR did increase in the post-Stalin era. China thought the Soviets were becoming too westernized and abandoning communist ideology. Distrust between them intensified and eventually led to border conflicts. Mao had a deep-seated paranoia that the Soviets would attack his country's nuclear facilities. However, many believe that this was not paranoia at all and that had he not threatened to use nuclear weapons in their defense, they may have done just that.

There were very few conversations between Mao and Kissinger, as well as between Nixon and Mao. Because of the Chairman's health, Dr. Kissinger and President Nixon's conversations were primarily with Premier Chou En-lai. Dr. Kissinger's trip to Beijing did take place under the guise of becoming sick in Pakistan while, in fact, he secretly traveled to Beijing. Pakistani president Yahya Khan was instrumental in helping to set this meeting and in fabricating and maintaining the deception. In his conversations with Chou En-lai between the ninth and eleventh of July 1971, Dr. Kissinger told him that the Republic of China would already be under Beijing's authority if it wasn't for the Korean War. Premier Chou replied that if that was the case, then the United States should publicly acknowledge that Taiwan was a part of the People's Republic of China and settle the issue of his country's right to the island once and for all. But Dr. Kissinger said he preferred not to discuss this issue. Instead he wanted it to be a topic of discussion during President Nixon's meeting with the Chinese leader. Dr. Kissinger's main thrust was to seek China's help in settling the Vietnam War. In working toward this end, he wanted to alleviate fears of US imperialistic tendencies in the region. Therefore, he told Premier Chou that the United States would not fight against communism in general. Instead it would deal with communist states individually. In diplomatic talk, this meant that Dr. Kissinger had left open a possible future relationship between the United States and the People's Republic of China by saying that the United States didn't condemn all communist countries.

In President Nixon's discussions with Premier Chou, he was asked to clarify his position on Taiwan. He did so by announcing that the United States would not support any movement toward Taiwan's independence and that he intended to withdraw American troops from their soil. He also said that the United States would not support and would discourage a Taiwanese invasion of Mainland China. Subsequently, the Chinese became more amenable toward the United States.

Mao did have a residence in Shaoshan, which is approximately sixty miles outside the city of Changsha in Hunan province. I've made his residence more opulent than it is. In reality, it's a brick farmhouse with curved wooden shingles and a barn attached. It's now a museum. There's no airstrip in Shaoshan. In fact, if you want to visit Mao's former home, you'll have to take a nearly two-hour bus ride from Changsha.

President Nixon never had a secret meeting in Taiwan with Mao and Chiang Kai-shek. Nor did the chairman ever make a secret trip there, although some sources reported that he wanted to. His doctors and Chou En-li both kept his illness, Lou Gehrig's disease, from him and his staff. Mao knew that he was sick, but he did not know the extent of his illness.

Chou En-lai's anger and animosity toward Mao is fictional. He was Mao's face to the world because, unlike the chairman, he had tremendous diplomatic skills and charm. All indications were that he followed Mao's instructions in directing China's political hierarchy. Mao was bigger than life to the average Chinese citizen, and Chou En-lai wanted to maintain this image and also continue his close relationship with the founder of his country. He died eight months before the chairman.

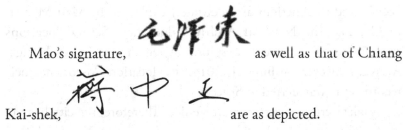

Mao's signature, as well as that of Chiang Kai-shek, are as depicted.

The Politburo Standing Committee is a seven-member committee comprised of the top leadership of the Communist Party of China. It's believed to meet weekly and arrive at its decisions by consensus. It is the most powerful decision-making body in China. Since the mandatory retirement age for the PSC is sixty-seven, the author gave Cho Ling substantial leeway in that regard.

The Chinese government's control of the country's internet is as depicted, monitoring all forms of electronic communication among its citizenry, as well as conducting extensive hacking operations outside the country. I've assigned both functions to Unit 61398 or Byzantine Candor, as it's referred to by US intelligence agencies. However, this highly secretive organization is thought to focus its sophisticated hacking techniques on both foreign businesses and governments. The author depicted its location as Beijing, for the sake of the story line. However, its headquarters is a twelve-story building in the Pudong area of Shanghai. Operationally, it's part of the Second Bureau of the PLA.

The US Army Intelligence and Security Command (INSCOM) is located at Fort Belvoir, Virginia. It is a component of the Central Security Command, and it is functionally integrated into the NSA. There are fifty-one thousand employees on the installation, twice as many as the Pentagon, and it is the home to sixteen military organizations. The Sixty-Sixth Military Intelligence Brigade, located in Wiesbaden, Germany, is part of INSCOM and provides intelligence support throughout Europe.

The National Archives and Records Administration is headquartered in Washington, DC. It serves as the nation's record keeper, and its functions are accurately explained by Matt Moretti to Cai Fu. The National Archives does have several locations throughout the United States, one of which was in Anchorage, Alaska. However, on June 21, 2014, that location closed, and their records were transferred to Seattle.

Violent crime is very rare in Venice. Therefore, the city has my apologies for strewing bodies throughout its streets. You won't find a safer and more charming city in Europe. Additionally, for the sake of the story line, the author located the business district between the residential and tourist areas. However, all three areas are so intermingled as to be indistinguishable.

There is no FedEx office in the Campo Santo Stefano. It's an elegant residential neighborhood, probably the most affluent in Venice, and its bars and restaurants are popular gathering places for locals. If you're there, try Paolin for amazing gelato. Anchoring the northern end of this elongated square is the beautiful Church of Santo Stefano, built between the fourteenth and fifteenth centuries.

The Marciana Library is spectacularly beautiful. Most people are so enamored with Saint Mark's Square, the Doge's Palace, and the general ambiance of Venice that they don't realize the library is there. The description of its entrance and ceilings are as portrayed, although the author took some liberties with its interior. The ceiling in the main room does have seven rows of paintings by Venetian artists, and Titian's painting of Wisdom in the anteroom is as described. However, the description of the information desk in the vestibule, the employee entrance, and the administrative hallway was crafted to fit the story line.

The Hotel Bauer Il Palazzo is one of the world's great hotels. Francesca Bortolotto Possati is the owner, and Pietro Rusconi is the resident manager. They're extremely gracious hosts and make their guests feel as if they're part of the family. When you're there, try the De Pisis restaurant. The author had Han Li and Moretti partake of some his favorite dishes from its menu, not to mention the wine from the owner's vineyard. The back deck has a spectacular view of the Grand Canal.

The Hotel Bristol in Vienna is located opposite the Vienna State Opera. Along with its sister hotel, the Imperial, it offers the romantic ambiance and top-notch service one associates with this city. The Ritz-Carlton Hotel is in the center of the city and contains Dstrikt, the author's favorite local restaurant.

The Schonbrunn Palace is magnificent, and in the author's opinion, it rivals Versailles in its dramatic beauty. It does not, however, have a detached multileveled parking garage. If you're there around the holiday season, visit the Christmas market in front of the palace. It's open from November through the first of the year, and it's a must-see.

Sources used by the author to obtain information on Mao Zedong include *Mao: The Unknown Story* by Jung Chang and Jon Halliday, *Red Star over China: The Classic Account of the Birth of*

Chinese Communism by Edgar Snow, and *Mao Zedong and China in the Twentieth-Century World* by Rebecca E. Karl. In addition, the Professor Chen Wen-Chen Memorial Foundation provided valuable insight material.

An author doesn't work in a vacuum. In my case, I've been blessed with amazing friends who unselfishly contributed their time, ideas, and comments.

To Kerry Refkin for her ideas, attention to detail, editing, and insights, I couldn't have done this without you. You're unbelievable.

To Scott Cray, Todd DeMatteo, Cindy and Dr. John Cancelliere, Aprille and Dr. Charles Pappas, Doug Ballinger, Dr. Meir Daller, Alexandra Parra, Nancy Molloy, Mark Iwinski, Mike Calbot, Blair McInnes, Ed Houck, Cheryl Rinell, and David Dodge for being my sounding boards. You all have perfect pitch!

To Zhang Jingjie for her extremely detailed research.

To Dr. Kevin Hunter and Rob Durst for their technical advice on all things relating to computer technology. You're both world-class.

To Clay Parker, Jim Bonaquist, John Thomas Cardillo, Steve Zhu, and Greg Urbancic, thank you for your extraordinary legal advice over the years.

To Corey Fischer, John Lucas, Bill Wiltshire, and Debbie Layport, thanks for your superb financial and accounting skills.

To our friends at Jane's Garden Café in Naples, Florida — Zoran Avramoski, Piotr Cretu, Aleksandar Toporovski, and Billy DeArmond. Thanks for your insights.

To Winnie and Doug Ballinger and Scott and Betty Cray, thanks for all you've done and continue to do for the countless people who are unable to help themselves.

ABOUT THE AUTHOR

ALAN REFKIN IS THE COAUTHOR of four previously published books. He received the iUniverse Editor's Choice Award for *The Wild Wild East*, and for *Piercing the Great Wall of Corporate China*. He lectures internationally on how to conduct business in Asia and lives in Florida with his wife Kerry. He is currently working on *The Abductions*, his next Matthew Moretti and Han Li novel. For more information on the author, including his blogs and newsletters, visit www.alanrefkin.com.

Printed in the United States
By Bookmasters